IT WILL LAST LONGER

It Will Last Longer

Tara Sanders Brooks

Book Cover Design & Typesetting by Barış Şehri
sehribookdesign.com

ISBN 979-8-218-58963-9

tarasanderesbrooks.com

To Emily—
When I told you I wanted to try writing long form prose,
you called it what it was:
a novel

PRIVATE DISCORD SERVER

LOS ANGELES FORUM FOR CRITICAL
THINKING CHANNEL: # DEADMANWALKING

Ted H. (he/him) 1/1/2025 1:05 AM
Of course, this ended up with someone "unintentionally"
dead. Yet again. Look, I'm not superstitious, but I
wouldn't mess with this kind of thing myself. She
was asking for it.

CONNOR B. (HE/HIM) 1/1/2025 1:10 AM
She was asking for it? You do know how that sounds,
right, my dude? The names were changed in the
article, by the way. To speak geek to you: It's pure
hypothesis that **she** was even involved. Don't get
mired down in conjecture based on one editorial.
You're so weirdly obsessive I'd say you had a crush
on her, but I can't imagine you as a sexual creature,
so I'll just stick with calling it a weird obsession.

TED H. (HE/HIM) 1/1/2025 1:11 AM
It was her. It has to be. And it wasn't just anyone who ended up dead—it was a journalist. This feels like a cover-up, and I'm telling you, the photographer is behind it. She always has been. She's the key into this whole world.

CONNOR B. (HE/HIM) 1/1/2025 1:20 AM
Dude, chill. It's, like, one in the morning and I've had a couple too many beers celebrating New Year's to put up with your amateur sleuthing. There's only one place I wanna put my key right now, and it ain't got anything to do with you or this freaky shit, if you know what I mean. Log off and get some sleep, man.

TED H. (HE/HIM) 1/1/2025 1:22 AM
Fine. Pretend you need to go have intercourse with your "girlfriend." But I'm telling you—it was Viv Klein. She was responsible, just like she was the first time around with Karen Elmes. Death follows her, and it will continue to do so unless someone puts an end to it. She obviously has the media on her side, even after what happened this last time. We funnel our tax money into this police state, but it's defunct. No one is seemingly able to curtail one photographer and her camera. It's reprehensible.

CONNOR B. (HE/HIM) 1/1/2025 1:30 AM
Sure, man. I'm going to get some sleep, even if you won't. And yes, that will be with my extremely hot girlfriend who you know very well does exist. So, suck it. Happy New Year, psycho.

TED H. (HE/HIM) 1/1/2025 1:32 AM
I'm just saying, I wouldn't be surprised if someone tried to put a stop to her. You should keep your eyes open for that.

A YEAR EARLIER
VIV

My problem, it seems, is a basic lack of integrity or any inkling of common sense. So, no, speaking with you is probably the last thing I should do.

No. Scrap that. Prolonged backspace.

Tuesday at 3 PST works great! See you there!

Send. Instant regret. Too many exclamation points. Any astute reporter can sense desperation, and it's just oozing from server to server in an instantaneous show of how repugnant every syllable is. The caged canary has no choice but to sing.

Viv slams the laptop shut. Her mind is in overdrive. She feels a momentary sense of discomfort. She wishes she understood how email works or what a server is. One of the great mysteries of the modern world. She shakes it off and takes a swig of her macchiato, her over-caffeinated hands already shaking. When she's nervous, she tends to spiral about how much is unknowable in the universe. In her own life.

The café is crowded, too crowded for a nervous system stretched so taut. It's one of those hipster places on the Eastside of LA that pop up in what was a derelict building up until a week ago. A fresh coat of pastel paint and a six-dollar coffee. The great march of gentrification goes on.

Viv hates it on one level but pulls out her credit card nevertheless.

A mustachioed man in an oversized T-shirt sits down diagonally from Viv at the farmer's table she's stationed at. He smiles, shaking his mullet out of his eyes in what she can only guess is supposed to be a winning greeting. She opens the laptop again, stares at the blank screen. Her eyes flick up. He's still looking.

He can't know who she is. What she did went as viral as a life-threatening infection, but not *her*. Well, her name did, too, but the only photo that was ever shared on actual news sources, as far as she knows, was *the* photo. She had immediately deleted everything off of her social media, posted the classic Notes app apology, a single, stark communication to the outside world. Even so, the Internet, of course, found her, dragged her name and face through the ringer, but still. It seemed improbable that he would know her face from her one day of Internet infamy.

She's just another midsize bottle blond with an intentionally roguish pixie cut that's supposed to denote to the world that she's artistic. A full, round, Nordic-looking face. Bland, European mutt. Muscles defined from carrying equipment, but never enough. An LA six at best. Maybe that's his type. With her bloodshot blue eyes and chapped lips from drinking nothing but coffee for the last week. No, he has to know who she is. Maybe he's one of the anonymous profiles sharing the detailed ways they'd like to kill her for what she did. The irony seems lost on them.

Viv downs the rest of the macchiato and gingerly sets the reclaimed ceramic mug on the table. She shoves the laptop in her messenger bag with one swift look at Mustache. He's staring down at his phone now. Probably posting about her. A small, horrifying part of her wishes he would just try and kill her and get it over with.

She's out the door and on the street. Another glaringly bright LA day, unpleasantly hot for September. Seasons are nothing but a mention in an action line here, and the writers are on strike. Days like this, she hates LA. It's a hard city to feel hidden in. So spread out, spread thin, spotlights shining into every corner. There's no mystery to LA. Just one big ring light aimed at her.

It didn't feel like this in the beginning. Or maybe it did and she just overlooked it. Five years ago and the SUV from Minnesota full of duct-taped cardboard boxes feels like a different lifetime. Connor curled up on her lap, panting, the AC full blast ruffling his whiskers. She was so worried the damned cat was going to suffer heatstroke in the shitty airflow of the 2012 Subaru. The first thing she did when they pulled into the apartment complex was hold him up, *Lion King*-style, in front of the one air vent in the studio apartment. Standing absurdly, hands over head, in the empty apartment, everything had felt so new and exciting.

Connor is full-grown now. Of course, that doesn't mean much for a cat. You blink and they are full-grown. But Viv is full-grown, too. Supposedly, her frontal lobe is finally fully developed. Closer to thirty than twenty. Part of those years swallowed by a pandemic that left time feeling ephemeral and separate from her. Viv existed. Time, she wasn't so sure.

The walk from the café back to the apartment complex, which she dubbed "the Blight" when she moved in, is mercifully short. Two blocks, one right turn, and there's the hulking, modern structure, replete with its garish color blocking. Stationed proudly between two gracefully aging Spanish-style apartment buildings, the Blight looms over St. Andrews Place like a beacon of the LA to come. A future of uninspired architecture.

Half a decade and it feels like home, begrudgingly. When asked, Viv never has a good reason for why she still lives in the ugly, overpriced building. It's too easy to stay in what's familiar, even if she can barely afford the lease. She hates moving, vowed not to do it again for as long as she could. That streak might be running out now.

She turns to check behind her, which she has been doing every ten feet. Still no mustachioed man. For better or for worse, her assassin has stayed behind in that café, drinking his latte. Viv buzzes in, forgoing the elevator in favor of the stairs. To get to them, she has to pass the besuited desk man beaming from amidst the pots of fresh orchids. He knows about the incident, and passing him causes the heat to rise in her cheeks. Mercifully, he seems to read her body language and doesn't try to speak to her. She needs to get this energy out somehow.

There has been nothing to do but sit around, wait, try to figure out next moves. She takes the stairs two at a time. It doesn't help, but rather elevates her heart rate in a way that feels too much like a panic attack. This little journey to the café is the first time she's stepped outside in a week. She doesn't like it.

Inside the safety of her studio apartment, Viv perches on the edge of the unmade queen bed. Connor sleeps, blissfully unaware of the toils of humanity, on a pile of pillows behind her. Sometimes, when things are really bad, looking after him is the only responsibility that can get her out of bed. Cow cat, she calls him, for his Holsteinesque spots. She loves him too much to want to switch places with him. But she does often wonder what it would be like to have no sense of anxiety or shame. A full sense of self-worth and a desire to do nothing but sleep. Maybe, if reincarnation is real, the good souls get to be house cats.

No one would call her a good soul. Instead, she has to figure out what to do about the reporter. Abby. Abby Katz, *LA Times* correspondent. Abby Katz, who wants to speak with her about her single biggest lapse in judgment. Who probably wants to skewer her alive for the masses, who will likely just read the article's one-line synopsis as they scroll through social media. Isn't that what she deserves, though? What's penance without punishment?

Viv has never been able to shake her belief in purgatory. Too many years bouncing between Evangelical youth group and Catholic school. One prevalent takeaway: Guilt is all-encompassing and inescapable. That is the human condition. And she's been fully feeling the human condition recently.

Viv takes out her laptop, Googles the reporter for the umpteenth time. Nothing new. She's young. Probably close to Viv in age, maybe slightly older. Journalism degree from Pepperdine. Until just last year, everything under her name seems to be city council reports for the *San Gabriel Valley Tribune*. Now she's a staff writer for the California section of the *LA Times*, listed in the directory under "Culture." Is Viv some sort of cultural interest story? Maybe a macabre spectacle. Or rather, that's what they think she created: a macabre spectacle.

There's no real purpose to repeatedly looking up the reporter. It doesn't explain why she wants to speak to Viv, what kind of story she's trying to paint. Maybe it's foolhardy to meet with her on Tuesday. Perhaps that's the kind of blunder someone with a PR team would never make. Except people with PR teams are always saying stupid things, and the hole has already been dug so deep, Viv isn't certain what else she has to lose.

Abby Katz isn't the only journalist who has reached out. But she is the most reputable. Or rather, the *LA Times* is. And despite the shame and regret, a fragment of Viv's ego remains intact. If she's going to speak, she's going to speak to the *LA Times*, not some gossip rag. There is still that small, searching sense of hope that her career isn't finished—that people have moved on from worse. Then, there's the self-hatred that she could even be thinking about her career right now. It's an ouroboros. No matter what, the self-preservation sets in.

What is this horrible prison of self, that everything has to be about *her*? This whole circumstance has arisen because she was only thinking of herself, her art, her unique and insufferable voice in this world. The constant flip-flop of hope and shame has caused physical repercussions. Bile rises in her throat yet again. She ran out of antacids yesterday—not that they were helping.

In times like these, there are two options: the healthy and unhealthy. Usually, Viv would take out her old beater camera, the Canon AE-1, and hit the streets with a cheap roll of film, firing off shots until the world settled back down into a recognizable landscape. Spend hours in her makeshift darkroom burning and bleaching and making something out of the endless, relentless grain of reality. The acid would settle and her heartbeat would reach a regular pitter-patter in her chest. The healthy option.

But she hasn't touched a camera since the incident. She opens the top shelf in her tiny corner kitchen and pulls down the rye whiskey. The unhealthy option. Sets two crystal glasses on the counter. Why drink if not with flare? She takes out her phone and hesitates before pressing the call button, but only for a second. The sun is getting dangerously close to the horizon, and the idea of another dim night alone in the studio, pacing and thinking and ignoring the Internet seems impossible. Her strength is worn dangerously thin, and she doesn't know what happens if it breaks.

As for whom to call, there aren't many options. During the great pandemic migration, her LA friends moved back to their hometowns, where they could afford houses and children. Either that or they went to New York. For a lot of people, the pandemic had been the litmus test of whether or not their specific LA dream was working out. For most people, as always, it wasn't.

Viv had felt on the edge herself, unsure whether to stay or leave. Photography wasn't an inherently Southern California profession the way the film business was. She enjoyed shooting behind-the-scenes photography for films, but it wasn't as compelling to her as portraiture or street photography, which could be done anywhere. But still, she wanted to stay. Maybe it was inertia. Maybe this was the first place she felt was really her own.

So she stayed and drew her smaller social circle in around her. A bubble of wayward twentysomethings pursuing a slew of different crafts, all discontented and antsy. Few that she would call for something truly substantial. Many only good for promoting unhealthy habits while talking about banalities. But at least one of them is good in a crisis.

David appears before she even has a chance to fully regret inviting him. But as he hunches through the doorway, impossibly tall and lean and well-groomed, the doubts fly away. This is what she needs. There's some false sense of being put together, composed, that comes with such beauty. It's hard to believe that someone who looks like that doesn't have the answers. It's as if some divine knowledge has been imparted between his Liz Taylor eyebrows, below the perfectly coiffed Afro. He moves through life with such apparent ease, hardly a wrinkle in his dark, luminous skin. Maybe that could rub off on her. At the very least, he's historically been very open to getting blackout drunk in the safety of Viv's apartment.

"Took you long enough to call me back. I've been worried you would do something stupid. Well, more stupid."

Viv ignores this, closing the door behind him as Connor rubs against his ankles. The only man Connor has ever liked. When David got kicked out of his rooming house for a vague *something* he did to another model, he crashed on the blow-up mattress in the kitchen for two weeks. Connor slept with him every night. It's been months since David's last visit, and Connor purrs loudly, tail raised. Viv wonders if the cat's affection makes David feel guilty for his absence.

"Hopefully I didn't drag you away from any desperate young men this evening."

"There will always be desperate young men and, even more appealing, desperate middle-aged men. Don't worry too much, babe, I have a couple of hookups lined up depending on how long I'm here tonight."

Viv laughs hollowly, pours them both drinks. In the end, she knows it isn't a joke. David always has one foot out the door. Friendship is a tertiary interest, when it aligns with his schedule. At least, that's how the last few years have been, since he got his agent and she started substitute teaching to get by. That's why she hardly calls him anymore. A pathetic game of chicken to see if he will ever reach out. It took the incident, but here he is. She hands him a drink.

"Only rule of the night is that we don't talk about it."

"Deal." His eyes narrow like he doesn't plan to stick to his word, but for the moment, glasses clink, and it's easy to slip back into conversation, light and shimmering over the surface of anything real. There are new men, as always. Heartbreaks and conquests and modeling gigs. It's easy to get swept up in David's life, in him. They both moved to LA at around the same time, knowing no one and nothing. But David made something of himself. Not everything he wanted, but something. He had always wanted to be a stand-up comedian. But his face, his arms, his serratus anterior muscles betrayed him. The man was born to model. Charm came easy; comedy, less so—but he never fully gave up on the dream of his sense of humor being broadcast into people's homes across America. So far, no progress has been made in that direction.

There was the national Gap campaign, though, the local green juice billboards, the extremely lucrative orthotics commercial. Enough money to help send his sister to private school, to move his mom out here into a one-bedroom in Culver City. Some of that came from older male patrons, true, but most of it came from his own work, even if it isn't his *art*. He is truly proficient as a model, running himself as a brand. His business acumen intimidates Viv, who lacks it completely. While she's floundered helplessly as a romantic idealist trying to run a freelance enterprise, he has thrived.

"Are you actually paying attention to me, or are you just staring into the middle distance somewhere in front of my face?"

Viv clears her throat, squints at David. It's been so easy to disassociate this week. "I was contemplating whether or not you got Botox."

"I did. But that isn't the point. Actually, it's the opposite. Were you even listening to me?"

"Of course. There was this guy who wrote for the *New Yorker*—" "He wrote one piece for the *New Yorker*. One."

"Okay. One piece. And he didn't think you read it?"

"He didn't think I *could* read it. Too complex for my mind."

"That sounds . . . racist."

David leans forward and smacks Viv with the pillow he's been resting on.

"Astute observation. I asked him whether it was racism, classism, or just because I'm a model that he didn't think I could understand his little think piece on growing up in New England with cystic acne."

David waits for Viv to respond. She winces at him. "I won't say anything about the fact that you're actually distinctly upper middle class now or that the rest of us are all just pretending to read the *New Yorker* so we seem literate. But all of that aside, what did he say?"

David leans back on the pillow. "He didn't. He just fucked me until I couldn't come up with any more retorts. Honestly, much preferable to him trying to debate me." He bursts into raucous laughter, waking Connor from where he was sleeping near David's feet. Connor jumps up onto David's lap, rewarded with head scratches. There's something about this that feels like home. Viv has missed it.

"For what it's worth, I haven't read the *New Yorker* since college, when I was trying to cosplay as a certain type of intellectual. We all know the real intellectuals are terribly depressed and do nothing but watch reality TV. He was probably just sad no one will ever actually read his work."

David lazily finishes his whiskey. "I actually do read the *New Yorker*. Sometimes."

They lapse into peaceable silence. David checks his phone. It's almost eleven. They've been talking about nothing much in particular for hours. The whiskey is reaching low levels. Viv can tell he wants to leave, to move on to the next, more exciting portion of his evening.

She embarks on a torturous, roundabout show of gratitude. "Thank you. For still coming here, despite everything. I hope you know that I know I made a terrible mistake. I appreciate that you came. I needed to not be alone tonight." It comes out stilted, awkward. She doesn't make eye contact. To articulate her weakness to him is something foreign, but she needs a friend. David looks up from his phone, contemplates her. He stands, stuffs his feet back into his loafers, chooses his words carefully.

"I don't know if you did make a mistake. No one knew who you were. Now they do. Notoriety is something, isn't it? I'm just saying, you could try and capitalize on it instead of being a hermit. I mean, do you still want to see your work exhibited some day? You have to market yourself, Viv. Don't just sit here and feel sorry for yourself. It's all about hustling if you really want to make people see your art. So hustle. This gave you a platform."

He pats her on the arm, heads for the door. He's already texting someone else. To him, he's done the right thing. He comforted her the best he could and now he's off. Brain already in someone else's bed. They had tried to sleep together once, had laughed about it after. Neither of them attracted to the other's gender, they were infatuated with each other's personalities. It wasn't enough. Viv had wondered at the time if she'd missed her one chance to have him take her seriously.

"You should really try and think about what I said, babes. For real. You know I want you to succeed. Now get some sleep. I'm definitely not going to."

Viv stiffens. She hates it when he lectures. Hates it more when he patronizes. Like he has any answers. His success is based on his good genes. "Of course I want people to actually see my work. But it's not that easy for me, especially now. I haven't exactly had the easiest time trying to make this career work, and now I've squandered whatever progress I made. You don't understand what it's been like for me. I've gotten death threats. Things haven't exactly been hard for you in the same way."

She hates how generic and whiny she sounds, but it's true. He doesn't understand what it's been like to pursue something for so long without any recognition, without any substantial income. To have a damned college degree in something you've never made a living wage from. She's such a textbook late-stage Millennial, she loathes it. Loathes herself.

David sighs, beleaguered. He puts his phone in his pocket. "You think it's been easy for me?"

"I know it has. I'm not trying to diminish your success, but at least you've had some. And it came so quick. You barely struggled."

"You have had all the same chances I've had, plus some, to make something of yourself, Viv. We came here at the same time. Went to the same shitty bars to whine about what we wanted from life. It's honestly sad that you haven't done anything with yours. I wanted more for you. I still do. You need to as well."

He's always good at hitting where it hurts. And he has always been so touchy about his success, wanting to feel like it's earned. But Viv can hit back, too, even if heavy-handedly.

"That's all you have to say? Thanks for the advice. Let me give you some: Try not to be so jaded. I'm still waiting for your stand-up special, but I'm afraid you aren't very funny anymore."

David's anger flips like a switch. Viv is intimately familiar. His eyes go dark, and she knows she won't hear from him for a while after this. "I didn't come here with any support, Viv. I didn't have any safety net back home. Maybe if that was the case for you, you would get off your ass and stop feeling sorry for yourself. I mean, wow, Viv, that's rich. Feeling sorry for yourself for capitalizing off of someone else's grief and pain."

He opens the door, turns back to her. Connor rubs at his ankles, unaware of any turbulence between his two favorite people. "Don't forget, what you did was take a photo of a dead body and post it on the Internet. Who does that? Only someone really, really sad and fucked-up."

The door slams. Connor stares for a second, then makes his way slowly back to the bed. A cow returning to pasture. Viv stands in the middle of her apartment, uncertain of what will happen if she moves at all. Her bones might all break at once. Or maybe she'll just continue on. She isn't sure which is worse.

That's the truth of it, stripped naked and standing there, cellulite, pock marks, and all. You can say what you want about the why, the circumstances, but in the end that's the ugly, bloated truth of it. Regret, motive, all the what-have-you-s aside, she took a photo of a dead body and posted it on the Internet.

A choice she made, though she couldn't articulate why. A choice she now has to pay for, in any case. Perhaps with her career, and perhaps that's warranted. It wasn't much of a career, anyway. A fine art photographer in name only. The occasional wedding photo shoot and behind-the-scenes snapshots of micro-budget independent films making up the bread and no butter of the workweek. Endless slogging interspersed with substitute-teaching high schoolers basic mathematics. God, they probably won't let her around children now.

Part of her still rebels, still wonders if the vitriol is fair, though. If it was *just* a photo of a dead body on the Internet. There had been something about the shadows, the light dappled across the akimbo legs. It had seemed to encapsulate the city, encapsulate something indefinable and bigger than the city.

There is a reason she clicked the shutter. There is a reason she didn't destroy the 120 film. Or any of the prints she made. Did she dream it? The indefinable *it*? Isn't there something about the photo that is starkly, terrifyingly beautiful? Or does she have it all wrong, a fun house mirror in her head turning horror to something else entirely?

ABBY

The photographer is late. Five minutes late, but still, Abby is impatient. She hauled herself to the Eastside for this, and traffic was bad. Traffic is always bad. A lifelong Angeleno and true Westsider, traveling to the Eastside is near the top of her list of the worst ways to spend a Tuesday afternoon.

Then, there will be the traffic *back* to the Westside right before dinnertime. It'll take an hour to get home. An even worse way to spend one's Tuesday afternoon. Abby doesn't know why she's so on edge, so irritable. It isn't the first time and it won't be the last time she has to speak with a subject she finds unpalatable. She reminds herself, yet again, that she should feel grateful to write anything for the *LA Times*.

On their dime, she sits here in this innocuous, corporate coffee shop eating a perfectly fine croissant and waiting to interview a subject who could lend a different perspective to her article addressing a local story that has been gaining national attention. The article is short, five hundred words. Mostly already written. Just needs a quote from the photographer. It's scheduled to go live online later this week. Address some of the Internet outrage. Get a decent amount of clicks before fading away for the next big scandal.

Abby takes another bite. The more she chews the more the croissant seems stale. It sticks to her mouth. The photographer is six minutes late.

Abby's mind wanders to the transcriptions she has to complete tonight. Two articles on the docket. Little progress made because she's been so spacey lately. It doesn't help that the damned AI software always messes up non-American accents and these interviews were with two native Oaxacans. She wonders vaguely what would happen if she were to use a Mexican software. Is AI across the board biased toward American whites, or just American AI? She mentally notes to look into Hispanic transcription software.

The door opens with a jingle, and the photographer walks in. Abby recognizes her immediately from the photos the Reddit trolls have been circulating alongside calls for her murder. She looks paler, more fragile in real life. That is to be expected. Most people don't fare well with death threats.

The photographer looks around warily. Abby puts on a friendly smile before raising her hand to wave her over, crossing her perfectly pressed chinos, one leg over the other. It's her journalist pose—the pose she knows she does when she wants to look put together and at the helm. It always feels slightly false. When Isaac saw her dressed up in her work clothes for her first job at the *San Gabriel Valley Tribune*, he laughed and said she looked like someone from one of Mom's films. No use in thinking now about how Gwen has only costumed fantasy films for the last twenty years.

They lock eyes. The photographer has startlingly blue ones. They remind Abby of an ice bath. Cold. Shocking. Not necessarily unrefreshing. Set in a moon-shaped visage dappled with a light freckling that isn't at all unattractive. She has a wholesome, 1940s, corn-fed beauty to her. If you don't look at the eyes. The eyes are something from time immemorial. Something cutting, decisive, outside the social contract. But maybe Abby is just editorializing.

The photographer is shabbily dressed in ripped jeans and a plain gray T-shirt, scuffed combat boots. Abby feels a vague sense of being overdressed, and then immediately admonishes herself for it. This is what always happens—her overactive imagination starts filling in the details of the person before they ever speak. A horrible tendency for a journalist. But it goes hand in hand with her obsessive attention to detail. A wonderful tendency for a journalist.

The photographer hurries across the room and sits haphazardly, half on top of her messenger bag. Abby watches her note the single coffee, the partially eaten croissant. She looks uncertain of the etiquette and like she might bolt.

"Please, get a coffee. It's on me. I'll keep this quick and relatively painless." Abby smiles as warmly as she can. The photographer's apparent anxiety has put her on edge.

"I'm good. If it's going to be quick, let's just do it." The photographer takes a deep breath, sticks out her hand. "I'm Viv Klein." Abby matches her firm grip.

"Abby Katz. Thank you for meeting with me today." Abby uncrosses the chinos, leans forward. Before she can say anything else, Viv is speaking again.

"As I said on the phone, if I am going to give any comments, I want to do it in person. I feel . . . there's less of a chance my words will be misconstrued." Viv lapses into silence, then seems to remember something else she wanted to say. "I understand that what I'm saying here today is on the record." She nods solemnly.

Abby holds back a smile. Viv is so serious. Of course, it *is* serious, what she did and the backlash against her. But Abby has never seen a subject so scared of *her*. In some ways, it's kind of nice being taken so seriously. Especially for a five-hundred-word cultural blurb about a viral photo already forgotten in the social news cycle. She assumes Viv has never spoken to a reporter before. Probably learned everything she knows about the profession from the movies, the kind of pulpy mysteries Abby's grandfather used to write.

"I'm not trying to pull anything out of you. Or to misconstrue what you say. To that point, I'd love to go ahead and record our conversation for my own transcription purposes later on. To make sure I get everything right. Is that okay?"

Viv nods. Abby takes out her phone, starts recording. She feels an odd sense of relief at Viv's American accent. Less work cleaning up the transcription later. Though there is still her own odd lilt, the bastardized accent of a half-Hispanic West LA Jew. But what she says doesn't matter as much. Always the quoter, never the quoted.

"I thought you would be using something . . . more high-tech?" Viv peers at the phone as if it's something more interesting than an Apple product two years out-of-date.

"Than my phone? This thing is a tape recorder and telegraph machine all in one. Plus, it's what the paper gave me."

A small smile flickers across Viv's face. As nice as it is to be feared, it's always best to have a rapport going. Abby notes that Viv looks nice when she smiles. Kind. Not like someone who would callously post something just for the reaction—but isn't that everyone nowadays? A bunch of modern Ted Bundys to greater or lesser degrees.

"So. Let's begin. Thank you for meeting with me today. I'd like to start by checking in.

How are you doing with the Internet backlash against you?" Abby tries to look compassionate. It isn't completely false. The photographer has been mercilessly dragged around the virtual town square, pelted by everything under the sun. Abby is no stranger to the poison people can spit from behind a screen.

Viv leans back from the table. "Are you asking out of politeness or because you want to put that in the article? Or both?"

"Both, I guess. I'm a reporter, not a monster. No one should be treated that way."

"Just like no one should do what I did." Viv stares for a little too long. Abby isn't sure if she's trying to unsettle her or trying not to cry. Maybe both.

Viv abruptly pulls a piece of paper out of her pocket and begins to read in a monotone, rushed and self-conscious. "I apologize for my callous actions—posting the photo without any trigger warning or regard to the psyches of strangers and, most importantly, the family members of the deceased. I acted out of a sense of misguided artistic license and deeply regret all the hurt I have caused." She puts the paper back in her pocket and looks at Abby expectantly.

"You came here to read something almost exactly like your social media apology? You do know I could just quote that in the article."

Viv shrugs. Abby changes tactics. She drove out to the damned Eastside for this. She's going to get a quote. She just has to get on Viv's side.

"Also, you really want me to quote you saying things like 'misguided artistic license'?

This is a chance for you to change the narrative and maybe lessen the vitriol aimed at you. Wouldn't you like that?"

"Why would you want to help me with that?" Viv looks at her like this is some sort of challenge. Abby feels her impatience rising. Why is Viv being so *difficult*? She was so easy to schedule with, had seemed nervous but willing. Now, here, with her wolf's eyes aimed at Abby, she is being infinitely obstinate.

"It's my job to impartially tell the news. You posted something sensitive. You really upset a lot of people. You received death threats for it. I'm not trying to stoke the flames of the stake they are trying to burn you at. Ethically, I want to report on this while also not inadvertently-causing your death. I'd feel bad about that." She meant it as a joke, but Abby can tell she sounds irritated. She's been too strung out recently. Is losing her touch. Be personable.

Viv narrows her eyes. "So you want to include an anti-bullying PSA. Okay. The death threats . . . have made me feel bad." She stands, shoulders her messenger bag. "I thought I could come here and say something to you that would make you understand, maybe, but I don't think the words are there. If you've seen the photo and you don't get it, what can I say other than I'm sorry, which is what I have been saying and what I truly mean." Viv is rambling, obviously upset. Abby feels the chance at a quote slipping away. The article can stand just fine without it, but still, it's disappointing.

Viv looks up one last time, twin blue spotlights aimed at Abby. She's about to walk out. Abby tries to keep her face neutral, but Viv *sees*. Damn it. How?

"You haven't seen the photo." It isn't a question. It's a statement. Abby is too surprised to deny it. Viv sinks back into her seat, laughs without humor. "You haven't seen the photo and you're writing an article about it? So much for the researching techniques of the *LA Times*.

Actually, it's pretty hard not to have seen the photo. How have you managed that?"

Abby wants to pick her words carefully, salvage this, but she's too tired, too irritated. On the wrong side of the interrogation.

"It isn't the type of photo I want to see. I can report on the aftermath of the post without seeing the photo. I know what it depicts."

Viv looks absolutely shocked. People don't usually find Abby to be particularly shocking. It's an odd feeling, but sort of nice. Like the fear. Like Viv sees her as someone

formidable and, in this case, infuriating. Very different from how Abby sees herself. It's not a bad feeling to have someone incredibly pissed at you. At least you're eliciting some kind of reaction.

"You don't know *how* it depicts what it depicts. I can't believe these are the journalistic standards of the *LA Times*. Wow." Viv looks like she is about to leave again. Abby can't find the words to make her stay, to fix the interview. Instead, she asks what she is thinking, what it seems is deep down beneath every "I'm sorry" that Viv has uttered.

"You're saying if I saw the photo I would understand why you posted it?"

It doesn't come out as a question. Viv looks at her like she's incredibly stupid. "I'm just saying you should have seen the photo if you are reporting on it. This is my life. Taking that photo has blown it up. And, look, I know it has affected other people as well. I'm not trying to disregard that. Hell, it's big enough that you're writing about it, right? So why don't you look at the instigator of this whole shit show?"

Viv waits expectantly. "Now."

Abby freezes. She doesn't know why, but she doesn't want to give in and do what Viv is asking. She understands, on one level, that she's been negligent in not looking at the photo, but there has been too much going on. Articles to write and family to disappoint. This impatient, rude photographer knows nothing about her, about her work ethic, about anything.

Abby waits too long to react, to respond. Something snaps between them, and Viv is out of her chair, through the door. Abby is left alone, cold coffee and half-eaten croissant. No quote. There's always the social media post. She has quotes from the deceased's sister and mother. It's not investigative journalism, just rehashing a blip on the cultural radar. Still, she's frustrated. Not at herself—of course not—but at the photographer.

She stands, throws away the detritus of the failed interview. Out back, behind the beige strip mall, precariously double-parked next to a dumpster and squeezed between two foreign sports cars, is her beat-up sedan. There's nothing to do but drive home, stalled on the 10 in mind-numbing traffic while her podcast joins the cacophony of blaring music and talk radio emanating from the rolled-down windows in the overbearing Southern California heat. Maybe when she gets home, she can find some transcription software that works on Mexican accents.

VIV

She was late. Not terribly late, but still, there was no excuse. The coffee shop she was supposed to meet Abby Katz at wasn't far by LA standards. A mile and a half, so only a twenty-minute drive through Sunset traffic into Silver Lake. The corporate chain had its own tiny parking lot, a hot commodity in an area populated by a minefield of confusing street parking signs and overzealous traffic cops.

Still, it had been difficult—overwhelming—to get out the door. She hadn't left home since fleeing the café two days ago. After the fight with David, she ordered in another bottle of whiskey and closed the shades over the floor-to-ceiling windows facing Hollywood Boulevard.

In pitch darkness, she sat there and contemplated calling her family, but that would include opening doors she had closed for a reason. Instead, she fell asleep on the floor without opening the new bottle, Connor at her feet. Then Monday passed in a miasma of dread. It was starting to feel like nothing would get better until the interview was over. Maybe that was the starting point to moving on.

By Tuesday morning, however, any hope that the interview would miraculously change her attitude was fading. Rejections always hit Viv hard, but now they seemed to hold more weight. More finality. It was a freelance industry and impossible to know why you got passed over for any one job. And yet, the gig at the Fonda had been almost set.

She had gone to college with the bastard, way before he started going by the single letter D or had a hit EP that all the teen girls were sampling online under their thirst traps. Viv had shot every single one of his LA shows, even as they got progressively bigger and bigger. As

insufferable as D had always been, the shows were always electric. They allowed a style of photography that was active, exciting, always new. The frenetic energy of the fans, sweat flying as Viv writhed in and through the crowd, the bone-rattling pulse of the bass. And then, onstage, moving like a tiger, stalking and turning and catching the intricacies of the performance. It was a dance, hypnotic. Even if she didn't get the music.

D finally texted late Monday afternoon, responding to Viv's contract question from a week and a half before. He claimed he had forgotten to send the contract and in the meantime, his manager had hired a new photographer without his knowledge. *2 late 4 this 1. Maybe nxt time.*

Viv had known Grieg, D's manager and college roommate, for as long as she had known D. He had bought her a bottle of vodka when *Pitchfork* mentioned her photo—the one chosen for the EP's cover—in their article on D. The EP cover photo was a grainy 35mm snapshot of D she had taken at dusk back when he was still Derek. He'd made a rare mention of his mom, bringing tears to his eyes. He was shirtless and scrawny on the edge of the drained pool in the backyard of the rented two-bedroom he was calling his studio. Mid-puff on a rancid herbal cigarette. To Viv, he had looked like a wounded, defiant bird. The photo wasn't flattering, but it was compelling. She was surprised he had chosen it for the cover of his EP. She had often underestimated him.

Viv can still hear Grieg's Southern drawl shouting to her backstage about the *Pitchfork* article: *They critique music, but they still felt like they had to say something about your picture. Nobody can ignore it.* Those words had rung through her mind for a while—*no one can ignore it.* It seemed like she was on the cusp of something. It was the only photo of note she had ever taken. Until now.

There's no way Grieg would have forgotten about Viv and hired someone else. Hiring her was bad optics. So bad, apparently, she didn't even warrant a phone call. It was hard enough when a rejection was about something logistical—her rate, her camera. But this was about her.

They were saying no to *her*.

Tuesday afternoon, she fell down a rabbit hole of researching D's recent shows on the East Coast. There were a few different photographers credited between New York and Boston, and each of them had lengthy websites and social media profiles to delve through. Viv was certain she had narrowed her replacement down to either of two very cool and competent skater dudes who owned a production company together and also seemed to know every white boy indie artist on the market.

Their work was good. Their work was good, and they probably got the music more than she did. But that wasn't why they got the job. She knew that. Grieg knew that. D knew that. More than the death threats, it was the possibility that she may never get paid to hold a camera again that bothered her. It wasn't the only rejection in the past week, but it was the one that meant the most. The one that seemed like an omen that this wasn't something that would pass by, leave her alone if she just let enough blood. She festered over this long enough that she didn't leave for the coffee shop in time.

Late and suicidal, she thought lightly, but that wasn't the case. She didn't want to die. She just cared more about the death of her career than the hypothetical, nebulous death promised to her by the computer screen. She would prefer to have both. Her life and career. A woman really can have it all, or so they say.

Viv's brain was still racing as she opened the door to the generic coffee shop, faintly hearing the bell ring. She tried to center herself, put on a smile. The reporter sat there, neatly dressed with minimal attempt cover her disdain. Even more frustrating, she was attractive. Thick, curly brown hair and tanned skin. Attractive people were always intimidating. Viv tried not to be intimidated. She failed.

The next five to seven minutes passed by so swiftly that Viv is now left with very few impressions as she careens back through the LA heat lamp to her car. One: The reporter has not seen the photo. Two: The reporter looked at her in a way she couldn't define but wasn't totally accusatory. Three: She bungled the whole thing entirely. Viv drives home in silence, the radio too much along with her thoughts. She's half-afraid Abby Katz will call her, demand something more from her. But Abby Katz only has her email, and the phone remains mercifully silent.

Back at the Blight, Viv is restless. She feels the urge to run away, get as far from LA as she can. She raises the floor-to-ceiling blinds, squints at the dot that is Griffith Observatory on the horizon. Somewhere, a mile up Mount Hollywood, someone is probably looking out a metal tourist telescope bolted to a railing, chucking in a quarter to get a view of the metropolitan sprawl. Viv must be smaller than an ant to them, a darkened window on a garish building jutting above the rest of the block.

Perhaps leaving isn't the most practical urge to act on, as income going forward seems uncertain at best. But the more she thinks about it, the more it seems like the only thing to do. An ant under a microscope. The sun is getting hotter. Mustn't evaporate in the unforgiving glare. The ozone layer seems thicker outside of LA.

The apartment feels stiflingly small around her, which it is, but normally she finds it homey. Now, she can't help but think of places with grand expanses of kitchens, living rooms where you can sense the earth's curvature. The type of huge spaces that sprawled across acres of land back in Minnesota. She can barely pace here, barely think. Not that she has any desire to return *there*. But God, if only she could have the space to actually stretch, to do something with all of this anxious energy.

In her mind's eye, she sees a secluded cabin or rustic tent, sweeping forests, somewhere to lick her wounds and maybe even figure out a new career. A week tops of no one but her and Connor, no Internet, just walking among the trees, thinking, formulating some kind of miraculous plan that will put her back on track, or at least on a track.

The older she's gotten, the more she has found herself subscribing to the idea that there's something mystical and head-clearing about the great outdoors. Maybe she could purge herself through a National Park pilgrimage. Growing up, she always found peace through people—the teachers she idolized, her few hometown friends. But people have only become more and more complicated. Nature is what it is, and no matter what, it doesn't give a shit about her. There's something comforting about the idea that you are your own responsibility outside of the electrical grid. The freedom of an unobserved life.

She doesn't have *Walden* aspirations, any delusions that she could be self-made or live off the land, or that the isolationist lifestyle is purer and better. Thoreau's mom did his laundry. But still—there's something so pervasive about the idea that things can be fixed by going out into the "wild" for a bit. Even something as unfixable as her current situation.

Better to think of it as rehabilitation than running away.

Through a thirty-minute Internet search in which she learns how popular national park campsites are, she discovers her "wild" is, in fact, a house rental in Joshua Tree. Available starting that very night. Very much still in the electrical grid. Trees? Yes, but strange, alien shrubs scattered across the void. But the price is right, no need to use up *all* of her savings, and the house allows pets up to twenty-five pounds. It's not quite the fantasy, but it is perhaps the best reality. She books it.

As she haphazardly throws things in a suitcase, she considers calling David, letting someone know she'll be out of town. Despite their fight, he's the only person in LA who might potentially care if she were to disappear. The truth is, though, that their relationship has been deteriorating for years. She has always found him pompous, vain, and self-obsessed. He's found her desperate, clingy, and judgmental. The truth lies somewhere in-between.

She doesn't call. She doesn't want too much time to think. There's a relief to leaving the Blight, to leaving Hollywood and the ever-searching eyes of strangers. She turns her phone off, grabs the suitcase and cat carrier, and disappears into the late afternoon LA traffic, headed east until the endless houses and strip malls fade away and there's nothing but giant billboards for casinos and weed dispensaries. On past windmills and In-N-Outs until the desert imperceptibly begins to morph into high desert. Maybe here she can find peace, or at the very least—whether she wants to call it this or not—an escape.

LOS ANGELES TIMES

SUSPECT ARRESTED IN WHAT HAD BEEN BELIEVED TO BE HOLLYWOOD SUICIDE

By Fred H. Johnson | Staff Writer Sept. 30, 2023
Updated 3:10 PM PT

Los Angeles police have arrested a suspect in the death of Karen Elmes, the Hollywood waitress assumed to have died by suicide on September 18, 2023. Elmes's death was catapulted into the national media when a picture of her deceased body by photographer Viv Klein went viral the day after her death.

Elmes's family and the Los Angeles Police Department vocally denounced Klein's decision to post the photograph online. Klein reportedly found Elmes's body in an alley shortly after 1 a.m. that Monday. She took a single 35mm photograph immediately after calling 911. Klein then vacated the alleyway, waiting for police nearby in her car. Police investigation corroborated Klein's account.

While the Los Angeles Medical Examiner initially ruled Elmes's death a suicide, police have now opened an investigation based on discrepancies between the crime scene as observed by police and as captured in

Klein's photo. Police arrested Caleb Schwartz, Elmes's ex-boyfriend, in connection with the case earlier this week.

Schwartz released a public statement Saturday morning confessing to the premeditated murder of Elmes. A trial date for the case has not yet been set.

REDDIT

R/NEWS EX-BOYFRIEND CONFESSES IN ELMES DEATH BY CRAIGLOVESSOLVINGMURDERS

Sort by: Best

Bigbootyafficiondo5000 7 hr. ago
Yo, maybe Viv Klein is actually some kind of vigilante justice, solving crime with her camera? Like a photographer Clark Kent?
11K upvotes 301 replies

Shortking98 7 hr. ago
We all thought the photo was artistic AF anyway, even if it was in poor taste. Maybe now she should join the cops?
9K upvotes 580 replies

Potatosocks15 6 hr. ago
Fuck the police. Long live Viv Klein! 5K upvotes 119 replies

Goodsoupfriend99 6 hr. ago
It's always the ex-boyfriend. Why aren't we talking about that, about Caleb Schwartz? Sure, Klein's photo is truly art, but don't let that distract from the conversation we should be having about partner violence.
4K upvotes, 99 replies

Platonicdonkey2 6 hr. ago
You need to look up the photographer Robert Wiles and his photo "The Most Beautiful Suicide." I posted this here before and it didn't see any love. Come on, people, this has been done before. It isn't the end of evolved civilization—it's just a photo. Leave the girl alone.
3K upvotes, 72 replies

Dinonuggets4life1985 6 hr. ago
What that photographer did is still nuts, y'all. I'm glad it helped the cops, but damn, you're actually on her side now? Why don't you go ahead and donate to Elmes's family and help them pay for all the therapy they are going to be in after seeing what crazy shit she posted.
2K upvotes, 229 replies

ABBY

Abby has always loved the Brentwood Farmers' Market. It's soothing to walk among the cheery blond children half-heartedly hiding their terrier mix in a burlap tote bag, the put-together women in straw hats and expensive grocery wagons full of organic produce. It's a haven of fresh food and fresh faces, the most dog-filled dog-free space in the city. Before her abuela died, they'd come here together weekly, and now Abby still makes it out whenever she can to practice her Spanish with her favorite tomato guy. It's odd now that no one speaks Spanish at home anymore. Despite the bourgeoise patina, the farmers' market feels homey. It was where her abuela bought poblano peppers and small-batch goat cheese, and Abby can still hear her lecturing her on how to pick the right grapefruit.

The Brentwood Farmers' Market is so typically LA. Bright, sunny, replete with beautiful people and the full cornucopia of California produce. Usually, it would cheer Abby up to be here. She's not necessarily upset this particular Sunday, just . . . troubled. She can't stop thinking about Viv Klein, wondering if the photographer is okay, wondering how she's taking the news of Caleb Schwartz's confession.

She isn't particularly bothered that the story got passed on to Fred. He *is* the crime beat, after all. In some ways, it would make things easier, if she were to reach out to Viv. Not that she intends to. But if she were to, the fact that Abby never actually published a piece about her would make it easier.

Easier for what? She doesn't know. Not fully. All she knows is that she wants to reach out, and that seems wrong on some level. So instead, she picks out the perfect bag of plum tomatoes and allows Gordita to sniff at the strawberry stems discarded on the concrete. The rotund, square-shaped pit bull mix is in heaven, a green leaf half up her smushed nose.

It's hard to put work aside when you don't have a normal nine-to-five. The world doesn't stop turning, fumbling, creating newsworthy narratives on Sundays. There's always work to do, if you're looking to do it. But Abby has found it necessary to strive for some kind of balance. Monthly Shabbat dinners with friends, early morning runs with Gordita, the farmers' market. If she doesn't take moments to reset, she'll short-circuit. Forever just one step ahead of the monster that can end whatever momentum she has—burnout.

Today, though, work is impossible to keep out of mind. The man hawking fresh pita bread and hummus has the same sandy hair as Caleb Schwartz. The woman smelling the peonies in the stall one over wears a vintage film camera around her neck. The same model Viv Klein used to take that photo? And what about the poor husky trotting down the way with the orange bandana around his neck? A breed that should never have made it to this desert landscape. But the bandana could be the same color as the one that was mysteriously missing from the crime scene.

Such a small detail, barely visible in the lower left corner of the photo. Then gone. Nabbed by Caleb Schwartz after he scrambled from his hiding spot behind the dumpster seconds after Viv Klein ran retching to her car. The damning evidence that proved a Suds Place employee had been present in that alleyway that evening. An unmistakable, loud orange print with bright-blue suds on the edges.

Abby didn't clock it the first time she saw the photo, the night of the failed interview. When she poured herself a glass of red wine to fortify herself and then Googled the one thing she hadn't when researching the article. She rebuked herself for taking so long. She couldn't afford such delicate sensibilities in a career like this, in a world like this.

Still, she remembered being ten and seeing the photo of the self-immolating monk in Saigon. She'd had nightmares for a month afterward.

She never learned how to face death head-on. Not in life, not on a screen, not printed on a page. She'd been close enough to it for her own liking. She didn't need to be reminded of the ever-looming presence of finality. It was distinctly non-Jewish of her but went in tandem with the Catholic guilt inherited from her abuela.

Viv Klein's photo was surprisingly devoid of anything gruesome, at least on the surface. It had rained that night and the alleyway, retreating black and grainy to the vanishing point, sparkled with little glints of reflected neon. Elmes, who lay in the middle of the frame, looked as if she were doing the backstroke through the large puddle she had landed in, legs mid-kick.

There was no blood. She looked as if she were sleeping, not as if she had just fallen, or been pushed, from a fifth-story window. In the foreground, the standing water was so still you could almost make out the words reflected, upside down, from the sign high above the Bank of Hollywood. Perfection Is Forever. Of course, it wasn't really that legible, but Abby knew the intersection, knew the neon that rose above Hollywood and Vine.

Abby tried to look at the scene with Viv Klein's eyes, taking a shortcut through the alleyway to hurry home after a night out alone. Just tipsy enough to feel emboldened to walk instead of calling a car. She must have thought Elmes was drunk, or houseless, at first. Someone resting in the dark, away from the tourists and the bar crowds. How long had it taken her to realize? Had she already noticed the reflection, Perfection Is Forever? Maybe she had already raised her camera, drawn to the neon and chiaroscuro figure.

But she knew when she took it. She'd said as much to the police. She knew, and she took the photo anyway. Abby tried to feel that pull to press the shutter, knowing that Elmes wasn't just sleeping. But it spooked her, even thinking about being in that alleyway, so she exited incognito mode on Google, poured herself another glass of pinot noir, and took Gordita on a walk.

Now, she fills tote bags with produce, her mind still stuck in the dark alleyway. There are lists to be checked off, chuck roast to buy. Isaac and Mom are coming to dinner. She moved into the little bungalow two months ago, but she's been too busy to host them formally. Isaac has, of course, stopped by several times to raid her pantry and feed Gordita trans fats.

Abby gives the rest of the stalls a cursory look and turns toward home. The tote bags swing heavily into her side with each step, Gordita pulling ahead on the leash. She picks up the pace, forcing herself to focus on navigating past the slower shoppers. She jaywalks the wide lanes of San Vicente Boulevard. From there, home is unbelievably close, a couple quiet blocks of literal white picket fences and Teslas. So many slate-gray and whitewashed mini-mansions.

Gordita huffs around the corner and there it is: a two bedroom in a walkable neighborhood in LA. Abby's dream for so long. She still feels like she's playing pretend. She can't truly be a homeowner. In some ways, it doesn't feel like she really is. The home was her father's. Once he divorced her mom, moved back to Mexico, Abuela Maria lived there until her death. After that, it was rented out, staying in his name. Abby never would have asked for the house; it was too big an ask, and she loathed the idea of owing *him* anything. But he was tired of managing a property a country away and wanted to sell it. Abby was pretty sure he just didn't want anything tying him to LA or her mother any longer.

He sold it to her for an egregiously low price and she let him. The house is dandelion yellow, set back far on the property. Little mosaic stepping stones lead to the rounded oak door. There is no garage, just a covered carport on the side, where Isaac and Abby pressed their tiny handprints in the wet concrete as children.

Gordita doesn't feel any qualms about the ownership of the house. As soon as she hits the patchy grass in the front yard, she squats. Abby waits impatiently. The tote bags are getting heavy. Gordita kicks up dirt, overzealously burying the wet grass. Abby pulls her to the oak door, clumsily takes out her keys while Gordita investigates the potted plants Abby has already let die on the front stoop.

Inside, Abby lets Gordita off-leash, then follows her into the kitchen, saddled with the tote bags. It's strange, living alone for the first time. She can hear every click of Gordita's nails on the reclaimed wood, almost every tick of the clock. She turns on the record player. Too much silence isn't good for anyone.

As Amy Winehouse croons, she starts to chop. The renters wanted to renovate the kitchen, get new appliances, take out the old tile counter. Telling them no was one of the best decisions her father ever made. This is the kitchen in which she learned to cook, with Maria at her side. This oven baked countless birthday cakes, and as far as Abby is concerned, it still has countless more to go. Her father would call her sentimental, but the realtor would praise her for preserving the original terra-cotta backsplash.

Six p.m. comes quickly, as it always does when there is a lot to do and only two hands to do it. Abby misses, momentarily, cohabitation. Living in a house alone seems ridiculous, unethical even. Maybe Isaac will finally agree to move in with her. They would both hate it, but it might bring them closer together. She could cook for him, and he could keep the silence at bay with his raucous laughter.

When the doorbell rings it's shrill tremolo, she is still chopping the romaine for the salad. She neatly sliced off the top layers of her thumb skin, her blood swelling bright, oxygenated red all over the cutting board. She wrapped it summarily in a Band-Aid a shade lighter than her skin tone and went back to her whacking.

She hopes that it's Isaac at the door, not Gwen, with her shrewd gaze and tight lips. As she hurries down the hall, however, she can tell that it's her mother at the door. Gordita manically paws at the doorjamb, whining in a high-pitched way that sounds like she's being murdered. She absolutely adores Gwen—would probably prefer living with Gwen than Abby.

Gwen always has little treats in her purse. Human treats, pretzels and salt-and-caramel-covered nuts, but Gordita always manages to snag one or two. Abby opens the door to her mother pulling the dead succulents from the pots on the porch, her curls escaping the loose bun atop her head.

"These are dead," she says, thrusting the dirt-covered, shriveled roots at Abby, who takes the dead cacti silently, then throws them in the compost bin as Gwen gives Gordita her first round of pretzel twists. She looks in vain at the street. Isaac is, as always, fashionably late.

Inside, Gwen silently watches Abby finish the salad and take the roast out of the oven to rest. She wraps her olive-green pashmina around herself, foot tapping restlessly in her kitten heels. Always the most polished person in the room. Gwen looks around the sparsely decorated dining nook, mouth taut, no doubt noticing the lack of panache, of finish. Abby inherited her mother's attention to detail, but not toward the aesthetic. Abby felt helpless trying to create a feng shui in her home.

"How's the *Times*?" Her mother's question is punctuated by a kitchen timer going off, making Abby jump a little, which she immediately regrets. Gwen always calls the paper the *Times*, which makes Abby think of the old art deco Times Building downtown where the *Los Angeles Times* used to reside. Maybe if she went to work every day in a building with that kind of gravitas, her mother would take her job seriously. Gwen loves to remind Abby that she does not, in fact, work for the *New York Times*—the only newspaper to which Gwen has ever subscribed—but is, in fact, a mostly unappreciated staff writer at the less glamorous West Coast *Times*. The *LA Times* misspelled Gwen's name back when she won her Oscar, proving their incompetence.

The doorbell screeches again before Abby can answer the question. Gordita bounds to the entryway, albeit this time with less enthusiasm. Abby opens the door to a long-haired, bearded version of her brother. He looks like he has just returned to civilization—which he probably has. He's always catching a Greyhound to some obscure state, disappearing for a couple months for seasonal jobs in the Far North or Deep South. He's always fancied himself an itinerant adventurer and writer in the vein of Jack Kerouac by way of Jon Krakauer. A wanderer of the American frontier. Their mother calls him a romantic vagabond. His restless mouth lurches into a smile, and he pulls Abby into a large, fragrant hug. Patchouli and sweat.

Dinner goes relatively smoothly. Abby is reminded how much she enjoys laughing with people who share her lopsided grin. Gwen always mellows with Isaac, and they fit together in a comfortable way. As long as Abby's career or Isaac's lack of one aren't topics of discussion, things remain pleasant. Therefore, their relationship flourishes most when Gwen is deep in research for an upcoming production. The more she is consumed by something outside of her hopes for her children, the better. Abby and Isaac both agree that it's best for everyone when their mother's overactive intellect is aimed at recreating eighteenth-century fashion with a steampunk flare or creating the uniforms of a galactic dictatorship light-years away.

It isn't until the pavlova is sliced that Gwen returns to the question: "How is the *Times*?"

"Good," Abby replies, filling her mouth with meringue, taking her time to chew, even though the air-like substance melts immediately. Gwen regards her expectantly. Isaac is too absorbed in his second slice of dessert to clock the look of desperation Abby throws at him.

"I had lunch with Caroline the other day and she says you're fitting in quite nicely," Gwen says. Of course she's been lunching with one of

Abby's editors. "She actually mentioned you're a bit of a workaholic. I told her that runs in the family." Gwen pauses for Abby to say something, but Abby takes another hulking bite of pavlova. "Anyway, I just wanted to check in and see if you're still enjoying the job?"

Isaac has demolished his second slice of pavlova and leans back in his seat, lazily patting Gordita and sneaking her strawberries. He looks between Gwen and Abby, watches Abby bristle imperceptibly.

"Yes, I am. I feel incredibly lucky to be there, working with such a talented staff."

"It isn't luck." Gwen pauses long enough that Abby wonders if she's about to come out and say that it's because of her. She knows Gwen believes her personal status is what got Abby the job. "You're talented as well. I just worry that it's a very grinding profession. Have you given any more thought to meeting with that TV journalist I met in New York?"

Isaac snorts. Gwen looks at him questioningly. "Isn't television journalism also grinding?" Isaac bounces his foot heavily on the floor. Gordita barks once at his renegade boot, and Isaac quiets his fidgeting.

"Yes, but it's a more economically viable option. I'm just looking at things that Abby would be equipped for with her education," Gwen counters. The same well-worn argument.

"I'm not equipped for television journalism. I have no background in it, no interest in it .I've been working in print since the junior high bulletin I started at Harvard-Westlake."

Abby starts to clear the table. Isaac silently helps, picking strawberries off the top of the pavlova and popping them in his mouth as he carries it into the kitchen.

"You have a journalism background, which is a lot more than some of those pundits have," Gwen continues, unfazed. Abby puts the plates in the sink a little too forcefully and winces at the crash of ceramic on ceramic. She never wants her mother to know that her constant dissatisfaction with her career *gets* to her.

"I definitely could see Abby at Fox News. They'd love to land a biracial Jewess mouthpiece," Isaac deadpans. Gwen ignores him, as usual.

"I don't know why you always get so defensive. I just want to see you successful, happy. I just want you to consider your options." Gwen's nails tap sharply on the counter.

Abby opens the dishwasher, not looking at her mother. Her answer is quiet, barely audible, and not very convincing. "I told you I'm happy."

Isaac boosts himself up on the counter. "Meanwhile, I'm not at all happy. I'm in the midst of an everlasting existential crisis that hasn't abated since I turned eighteen."

Gwen sighs, beleaguered. She has never known how to actually communicate with her son.

"Alas, I know I reside in a trap of my own making and that I could escape, if I could only get myself to apply to law school. My hope remains on the horizon, only an application away."

"I don't know why you have to make a joke out of it, Isaac. You're restless. You really don't think you could benefit from settling down, focusing all that energy on something productive? You care so much about environmental rights. Why not make that into a career?"

Gwen rounds on her son, shifting focus. Abby knows what he's doing, deflecting and redirecting. His one protective, brotherly instinct kicking in. He's always been better about letting Gwen's expectations roll off of him. In some ways, Abby thinks it almost fuels his desire to eschew any conventional life goals. But then again, that is something so innately Isaac: He's never given a fuck.

Abby knows her brother judges her somewhat for her inability, or refusal, to stop caring what other people think. But she isn't him, and making her blood proud has always felt like part of the burden of being born into a family that expects things from you. Abby rises above expectations. She has to. She's never been Jewish enough. Mexican enough. Loveable enough to keep her father interested in the family. Confident enough to act like she fits in when she doesn't. She doesn't even know if she's enough of a writer, or if that was handed to her, like so many things have been, because of the privilege from which she hails.

Isaac can throw those expectations away because he doesn't want anything from society, but Abby does. Very badly. She wants people to listen to her voice, her thoughts. She wants to be visible. She knows that isn't a very altruistic goal, but it's why she started shouting into the void, writing her editor's notes for the *HV Weekly*. To have incisive opinions, perspectives, ideas on important events and be respected for them, to have others regurgitate those ideas themselves. That is what it means to be "enough."

And right now, one thing has been consuming her thoughts. One story she wants to throw into the ether, with perspective and questioning insight.

The story of Viv Klein. Abby turns to her mother, who has procured a brush from her purse and is running it roughly through Isaac's tangled hair as he sits, stoic, on the counter. She clears her throat, and they both look up at her.

"Actually, I'm working on a longer piece. I don't know what it's going to be yet, fully, but I'm in the research phase. It's a bit more of an opinion piece than I usually write."

VIV

Joshua Tree National Park has a diverse appeal, drawing everyone from white cowboy hat–wearing, fringe-covered influencers straight from Coachella to dirtbag climbers who haven't slept in a bed other than their Toyota Corolla in two years. The town outside the park isn't officially a town, just an unincorporated upspring of shops and liquor stores and oh so many new construction homes built as Airbnbs. For the most part, it's quiet, other than the live music that echoes out across the desert from the bars once the sun goes down. There's a distinctly American charm to the area's cultivated, yet real, rustic, Southwestern aesthetic. In truth, it's a bit of everything: hippie, lawless, corporate, commercial. Viv could fit in here, because there isn't much to fit in to. The place runs the gamut.

Viv loves Joshua Tree and always has, even before ever setting foot in California. Back in high school in Kimball, her favorite teacher, Mr. Smith, had a postcard of the eponymous tree on his desk. When she ate lunch with him in the photography lab, which was most days, he would talk about his adventures shooting nature photography across the country. He sparked her interest in seeing the world in a way no history class ever had. He was also the only man she has ever been a little in love with. Of course, he was a flagrant and flaming homosexual. And so was she—

she just didn't know it yet. That's part of what she loved about him—how he owned his otherness in such a small, monotonous place. He was himself truly, and he also had a great eye for framing.

She hopes some of his confidence and vision rubbed off on her over those years of sad lunches. Nevertheless, she can't go to Joshua Tree without thinking of him. Sometimes she fantasizes about her life if she'd stayed in the Midwest—going to school functions as his beard. Living a quiet, unexamined life as a general manager or a secretary. Something where shecould make reliable money, surrounded by a golden patina of security, of safety. Of course, general managers have their own trials, but at least they can mark out a discernible five-year plan based on more than just aspirations. It's a nice thought, but even so, in that other, hypothetical life, she's still always alone. Even so, to be alone and certain sounds more palatable than being alone and uncertain.

She hates to think of what Mr. Smith must think of her now, after the photo. For the first time in many years, she doesn't want to think about photography at all. It's hard in Joshua Tree. In so many ways, it's a photographer's dream. There's no dearth of interesting material. Viv has done a lot of both nature and street photography in Joshua Tree over the years. Observing the tourists and locals at Pappy and Harriet's Pioneertown Palace. Setting up long exposure shots of the scraggly trees in the inky black of the dark sky park. Of course, she hasn't done any of that this time. She brought her rangefinder, shoved at the bottom of her duffel, but hasn't even unpacked it.

Instead, she spends her evenings on the hammock out back of the overly air-conditioned one-bedroom rental, swigging from a bottle of cheap whiskey and reading mind-numbing historical fiction. The more banal the book, the more meditative the state she can enter, flipping the pages in an almost trance-like rhythm. During the days, she visits different coffee shops, then rambles among the boulders and Joshua trees until she is sunburned or tired or both. Afternoons are for slasher films and reruns of classic American sitcoms on the pleather couch with Connor. This exacting schedule has pulled her through five days. The house is booked for two more.

Viv isn't sure what she'll do when the rental is up. She hasn't let herself think much about LA or what comes next. Only one thing is certain: She'll never go back to Minnesota, no matter how much she daydreams about her alternate life there. There is no real security or safety back in Kimball. There never has been. Where she can go, what she can do, remains unknown. She much prefers to wonder whether Sam and Diane end up together—a question she vaguely recalls she once knew the answer to, but *Cheers* was before her time and the satellite channel on the TV isn't playing the episodes in any discernible order. Sure, she could Google it, but she still hasn't turned her phone on. It's sitting in the bottom of her duffel, along with her camera.

This morning, she finds herself at a trendy coffee shop, once again paying for an overpriced latte with an extra shot of espresso. She can't help it—their espresso is top-notch and the caffeine makes her feel momentarily less depressed. There's something romantic about flagrantly burning through her money on coffee and whiskey, no care for the future past this one week in Joshua Tree. Finishing the sweating drink in a couple large gulps, Viv leans back against the metal of her chair. There's a tanned hipster couple at the counter, an older couple with a young girl across the patio. Other than that, it's empty. The rush usually comes a little later. Viv has never been a morning person, but recently, she hasn't been able to sleep much at all. It's better to sit in a café and eavesdrop on the other early morning patrons than lie in bed, listening to her thoughts.

She tunes in to the older couple across the patio. The girl with them, barely more than a toddler, looks asleep at the table. The two adults lean over her, speaking German in hushed tones. It surprises her at first. Of course, she finds the high desert landscape beautiful, but she can't imagine traveling from Germany to see it. Then, she admonishes herself for having such an insular perspective on the value of America's national parks. She vows to appreciate the nature that she came here for. In repentance, she focuses her attention on a spiky cactus battling the concrete wall that encloses the coffee shop patio. Here she is, not enjoying her surroundings, drifting about, consuming caffeine like a depressed zombie. She bandies about the thought of doing a slightly longer hike today, trekking to see an old abandoned mine back in the park. It's as good a day as any. Maybe this will be what she needs to pull her out of her moping.

Viv lets herself dally, watches the tanned hipsters leave with their lattes. The German couple wakes the little girl, and the man carries her back to the car. A few more patrons come and go. The tiny cactus remains the same. Eventually, Viv manages to get herself up and heads back to her car. She's still in her flip-flops and socks, a stylish combination no good for serious hiking. The rental house is on the way to the park, so she stops quickly, grabbing her trail runners and giving Connor the requisite pets. Impulsively, she grabs the range finder out of her bag, as well as her phone. It seems like the responsible choice to have a way to call for help if something goes awry—if she even gets service that far back in the park. As for grabbing the camera, she chalks it up to habit. A little extra weight will only add to the workout, anyway. She doesn't have to use it, or the phone. But maybe something will spark her interest and she can fire off a snapshot. The first of her new life as a hobbyist photographer.

She still can't imagine putting the camera down for good, even if looking at it now makes her stomach drop. It's how she's always made sense of the world, through images. If she stops, the world just won't make sense—of that she's sure. She can't see another way. If she thinks too hard about it, her head reels. Some people love many things, relate to the world in many ways. Not her. She has always been stingy with her affection; you give what you get.

The trailhead's narrow parking lot is mostly full, but there aren't any other hikers within view. For the most part, Viv has avoided human interaction here in Joshua Tree. It's been easy, and she's enjoyed it immensely. The trail starts out uphill. Not extremely strenuous, but more so than her aimless wanderings of the previous days. Viv's heart starts beating faster pretty quickly, reminding her of the physical warning signs of an anxiety attack. Of course, since it's exercise, supposedly there should be an endorphin rush at some point, some kind of reward for this. Perhaps even a reprieve from the heavy fog in her brain. She pushes on. It's been years since she has truly trekked out into the world in search of anything other than a photo.

The path continues steadily upward, opening out as it goes up, with views over the creosote bush–smattered desert, the occasional cholla popping up along the trail that winds around the hills. Viv begins to warm up to the hike. Small lizards dash across the path in front of her. Quail warble in the brush. There's something comforting about the presence of so much wildlife. Underneath the occasional buzz of an insect or call of a bird, there is a deep silence—the kind that feels substantial, like you can almost hear it. Viv finds herself trying to step more lightly, lest she interrupt the quiet. When she rounds a corner and sees a couple of hikers coming toward her, she almost shudders. She flashes a bashful smile and steps aside to let them pass.

The hike reminds her of the "adventure walks" she would go on as a kid with her first point-and-shoot camera. Rambling about behind her house and in her neighborhood, trying to be as quiet as possible, an observer, not a part of the world around her. She would pretend that if she were quiet enough, she would become invisible, able to sneak up on grasshoppers and pigeons with impunity. Of course, back then, she would document the world she found underneath bushes and in the sidewalk cracks in grainy digital for her eyes alone. Countless photos tacked to the walls of her room, memories of blessed moments of invisibility. An invisibility that never lasted long enough.

Now, she pretends that if she is silent enough, she can become invisible, not to shoot anything, but simply to observe. To no longer have to act, and instead just watch the action, stepping softly past. She doesn't pass another group of hikers until she is almost at the mine—a stout building of dark wood surrounded by a chain-link fence. Less than one hundred years ago, gold and silver were pumped from the ground here. This was the California dream, before the miners hit a fault line and the luck ran out.

Lacking a foundation, the whole place has nearly sunk into the ground. Nothing but abandoned tunnels, a hollow trap of dirt and rock beneath an unassuming surface. A crumbling relic of a blip in time when men sought their fortunes with their hands, and if they were unscrupulous enough, or hardheaded enough, they might find it. Today, it looks like a good place for a snack. Despite the occasional cool breeze, the weather is upsettingly hot for this late in the year.

A trio of red-faced men in moisture-wicking clothing and wide-brimmed hats huff past, leaning heavily on hiking poles. Viv nods at their breathy greetings as they continue on, back toward the parking lot. She makes her way up the hill to the metal fence keeping visitors from trying their luck in the mine. From here, she can see out over the valley, toward the purple mountains rimming the horizon.

In the distance, an ant-sized hiker heads in Viv's direction. She watches idly as the three men powerwalk past. The hiker continues on, ever so slowly, toward Viv. Sweat slowly trickles down her brow. She takes a drink, unwraps the PowerBar in her pocket, leans against the fence.

The unrelenting sun bears down. She decides she'll continue on once the hiker makes it to her bend in the trail. Standing still in the heat isn't much of a rest, and if she wants to catch today's *Cheers* reruns, she'll need to keep a decent pace.

As Viv waits for the hiker, though, it becomes evident that they are not doing well. The dot takes an incredibly long time to come near enough for Viv to make out the form of a middle-aged person—short, graying hair visible in tufts around the ball cap drawn low over their eyes. As the person finally approaches the turnout where Viv made her way up to the mine, the hiker stops, leaning strangely forward over their toes, a spot-on impression of Michael Jackson. For a moment, Viv wonders how they can balance like that. Then, they topple forward. With a thud, the person is prone on the ground, face in the dirt. As she closes in, she can make out more specifics: middle-aged, male, overweight.

By the time Viv skids down the hill back to the trail, the hiker has managed to get into a half-squatting position, tottering back and forth as he attempts to stand. He thinks better of it and leans forward heavily again on his hands. Viv bends down, uncertain at first whether she should help the hiker up or to the ground. The ball cap falls forward off the graying head. Underneath, bright-red cheeks are working, contorting the face as he tries to move his weight back to his feet. She makes the decision—down, not up.

"I think you need to sit down. Here, let me help you." Viv grabs the back of the hiker's sweaty cotton shirt and helps him fully to the ground. She looks around, notices a plastic water bottle that has rolled off to the side of the trail. She grabs it. Empty. She kneels back down, handing the hiker her own water bottle instead. "I'm Viv. Here—drink some of my water."

The hiker shakes his head, breathing heavily. "Breathe first," he splutters.

After a few moments, the hiker grabs hungrily at the water bottle. Viv has already downed about half of it, and the hiker makes short work of the rest. She takes the empty bottle back nervously. No one else is visible on the trail, the only sound the incessant buzzing of insects in the nearby bushes. Viv takes out her phone, turns it on for the first time in days. Of course, no service.

She runs through the very little she knows about wilderness preparedness. It's bad to run out of water. It's worse to run out of water when you're in the state the panting hiker is in. The path is exposed, no real shade at this time of day. Nowhere to escape the sun's unforgiving rays. No trees, not even any tall bushes. Nothing. For the first time in days, Viv misses civilization, or at least Wi-Fi. Something tickles at the back of her mind, wanting to burble over, but she ignores it. Not now.

"What's your name?" The question comes out terse, clipped. Viv swallows, forces her voice to sound calmer, repeats the question.

The hiker seems to take a while to process and then, with a gargantuan effort, answers, "Cole." A small rivulet of blood runs down his beard from his lip, which he seems to have bitten open. His eyes look foggily past Viv.

"Okay, Cole. I really hate to leave you alone here, but I'm going to have to go find some help. There isn't any cell service here." Cole doesn't respond, eyes roaming over the path. Viv leans down, puts herself in his eyeline.

"If any other hikers come along, tell them you need help. And water. Try and get some more water from people." Cole's expression remains blank, but then he slowly nods. Viv stands up. "Okay. I'm going to go now. I promise I am going to get some help. People are going to come help you." No response from Cole. Viv turns back to the parking lot and sets off at a run.

The hike to the mine hadn't felt particularly long, but now, on the way back, it seems to elongate, each bend excruciatingly leading to another, no sign of the parking lot. Viv can barely breathe, never sucking in enough to fill her lungs, scared to pause or slow down. She keeps seeing Cole drop, face-first, into the dirt. Over and over, a single domino flicked on its side. That second he lay there, prone, not moving. She tries to keep her mind on just that, on just Cole, but there are flashes, uncontrollable, of another prone figure. Gliding on a neon sky.

Viv stumbles over a rock, almost topples to the ground. Her ankle throbs, but she continues on. Tries to clear her mind. After what seems like half an hour, but can't be more than ten minutes, she comes across four hikers trekking from the direction of the parking lot. She slams to an abrupt halt in front of them, waving her arms jerkily across their path, though they have already stopped.

"A man collapsed up by the mine. I think he has heatstroke. I'm trying to get somewhere I can call 911, or find a ranger, or something. Can you help him? Do you have water?" Viv barely waits for an affirmative before taking a big gulp of air and continuing her dash to the parking lot. It almost feels like she's running *from* something, like there is some horrible luck or fate that follows her without rest, Cole the latest victim. If she can go fast enough, the domino will cease to topple, over and over, into the dirt.

What seems like eons later, she arrives, staggering, at her car. The parking lot has cleared out in the unseasonable heat of the afternoon. Cole goes down. Red, meaty hands splayed in the dirt, face working into intricate, impossible contortions. Still no service. She has no idea how far she has to drive to *get* service. Cole goes down. Pale hands on concrete, legs akimbo. Why was there no blood? Where was the blood? Viv turns on the engine and accelerates down the dirt road back to the main park loop. Cole goes down. Baseball hat falling in the dirt with a soft, wet sound. Viv slams on the brakes, turning from the middle of the narrow lane to the side, letting a motorcyclist pass, one finger upturned as they rev their engine down the road.

There was a park service phone, yesterday, in a parking lot she had pulled into looking for a bathroom. She remembered a huge jumble of boulders, like some giant's pile of marbles. Of course, that's what much of the park looks like. The rocks were bespeckled with climbers, their shiny racks of hardware glinting in the sun. The area seemed to be more populated than others, and it was right off the main road. Maybe she can identify it again. Didn't she pass it this morning, someone jammed into a crack queasily high off the ground?

Viv turns on to the paved road and speeds back toward the park entrance. Everything looks both the same and unfamiliar. Still no service. The road stretches on in front of her toward the horizon, unbroken by other cars. She almost misses the turnout for Hidden ValleyCampground, halfway past before she yanks the car into a hard right turn. Giant's marbles. This is it.

The phone is attached to the bathrooms. Viv shoots out of the car, panting, and pounds in 911, taking deep breaths of the sour air around the glorified waste holes.

"911, what's your emergency?"

"I'm in Joshua Tree National Park. There's a man experiencing heatstroke at the Lost Horse Mine. He's a couple miles, I guess, into the trail? He's at the mine. He didn't seem to be doing well. Cole. I saw Cole collapse. I gave him some water, but I didn't have much left.

I should have brought more. Anyway, I ran back to my car, but it took a while to get to a phone. I'm sorry. I'm so sorry." Viv surprises herself by bursting into tears.

The rest of the conversation goes quickly, and by the time the operator hangs up, Viv can't remember what all was said. It seemed like fluff, placations that accomplished nothing. Viv did the right thing by hurrying to a phone and calling 911. Medical help would be sent as soon as possible. Viv knows it's irrational to expect the operator to be able to tell her that Cole will be all right, but she's still unsettled that she didn't.

Now, with everything done that she could do, Viv feels untethered. A little woozy. She walks shakily back to her car. Her legs feel brittle. Water, maybe that's it. If she drinks, she'll feel better. She scrounges under her back seats, finds an old plastic water bottle a quarter-full of warm water. She takes a sip, then another. She has to fight the urge for the water to come back up and out. She sinks into the back seat, awkwardly sitting sideways with her legs splayed out on the concrete.

Across the parking lot, high above her, a woman repels down from the top of the giant's marbles. Viv tries to focus on her descent, timing her breaths to the woman's slow steps down the rock face. Eventually, her breathing slows, and the world around her seems to expand again. Other sounds filter in from the periphery. A dog barks, a truck blaring pop music rumbles to a stop a couple of parking spaces away. She sits like that for a while, listening to the world continuing on around her. So many people on Reddit said that she must be a sadist, but they were wrong. She'd worried they were right, but they weren't. She wanted to help Cole. It horrifies her how relieved she is. She tries to think of nothing, steady her breathing.

Her heart rate gradually returns to normal. Viv slowly pushes herself up out of the car, closes the door. Without really thinking, she finds herself back in the driver's seat, headed to Lost Horse Mine. By the time she pulls onto the dirt side road, she can see the lights of an ambulance blinking in the distance. Partway to the parking lot, she has to pull halfway up the dirt embankment to let the medical vehicle by. Viv peers at the driver, trying to read his expression. Does he seem particularly grim, or is that just the set of his jaw?

Viv watches the ambulance grow smaller and smaller in her rearview and then slowly continues to the Lost Horse parking lot. She isn't sure what she's looking for but heads back to the mine, hoping for some clarity that Cole is okay. If anything, the afternoon has worn on to an even more unpleasant temperature. Viv moves glacially, passing no one. The silence weighs heavy around her in the thick, hot air.

At first, it seems as if there is no evidence that Cole ever collapsed at the mine. As Viv trudges the last couple of steps to where she thinks the hiker fell, the trail looks untouched. There aren't even scuffs in the dirt from Cole's legs flailing as he tried to get up, let alone any sign that multiple paramedics were recently here, lifting him and—what? Carrying him? Something to get him back to the parking lot.

But then, as Viv glances up the trail, she realizes she was wrong about where Cole fell. Ahead, off to the side, his ball cap lies in the dust. There's something else in the dirt in the middle of the trail. A smattering of dried blood, like a gob of spit.

Still without really thinking, Viv pulls her bag off her shoulders and grabs her range finder from inside. She pockets the lens cap and looks through the viewfinder at the tableau in front of her. She bends down on the side of the path, framing the dried blood in focus in the foreground. The ball cap lies askew in the midground, slightly out of focus, a long shadow extending from its bill. In the background, the mine rises, menacing above its metal fence, its shadowy surfaces fading into black against the hot, bright sky. A single bird wheels above. Viv clicks the shutter. Once. Again. Slightly reframing, a third and final time.

It's an odd, incongruous, unsettling photo. Not the most beautiful or even the most interesting. But for a moment, Viv finds herself at peace. Part of her thought she may never press the shutter again. She stands, caps the camera, and grabs the hat from the side of the trail. Placing both gingerly in her bag, she heads back toward the parking lot.

Z107.7 FM LOCAL NEWS

Hello, listeners in the Morongo Basin and around the world online at Z1077 dot com. I hope you're staying cool and dry inside, with temperatures in the low nineties today in parts of Yucca Valley. Here's today's local news. The Joshua Tree hiker hospitalized on Saturday for heatstroke has been released to recover at home. An unknown good Samaritan found fifty-five-year-old Cole Martin of Yucca Valley on the Lost Horse Mine trail near midday Saturday. This marks the second near-fatal incident sustained within the park during this unprecedented October heat wave after last week's rescue of seventy-one-year-old climber Patrick Gold from the Trashcan Rock area. Park rangers urge visitors to refrain from exercising during the hottest parts of the day, if possible, and to always turn around when your water supply is half-gone.

Cole Martin's family is asking for any information regarding the hiker responsible for saving Martin, as well as support for his medical bills. If you would like to help Martin through his recovery, or have any information, you can click the link on our homepage, which will take you to his GoFundMe. We've gotten several calls asking how to help Patrick Gold with his recovery, but Gold has asked for privacy at this time.

In other news, the Twentynine Palms Historical Society has released the names of the winners of this year's Weed Show. With a whopping three hundred entries this year, the competition was tight. The winners in each category can be viewed on our website. There was also a special award given to Carol Boon, ten-time previous Weed Show winner, for her lifelong dedication to crafting with recycled glass bottles. The winners of the Weed Show will be on display throughout the week, so get on down to Twentynine Palms before it's too late.

That's it for our news of the day. Stay safe out there, and don't forget to hydrate.

VIV

A meeting at Ruen Pair. It used to be commonplace. A Tuesday outing to bitch about deferred payments and client's notes and all the painful accoutrements of a freelance lifestyle over green curry and pad kee mao, downing endless Thai iced teas in a vinyl, window-side booth. That was back when the place was cash-only, though. Nowadays, Viv gets her noodles to go and pays with her phone. She doesn't know the last time David came here. Those Tuesdays are a thing of the past.

So Viv was surprised when David called. After the blowup fight, she'd expected to be the one to reach out, eventually. That's how their relationship always operated. He seemed excited on the phone, albeit cryptic. She had to look up what the hell he was talking about. Apparently, her photo had helped supply vital evidence to the police and, unbeknownst to her, while she was in a *Cheers*-induced vegetative state, a man had been arrested for murder. Viv was relieved, in a way. She'd harbored a small, irrational fear that the death wasn't suicide and worried the killer might come after her because she had been at the crime scene. In her nightmares, a shadowy figure watched as she snapped the photo.

She had built this fictional murderer up in her head as some larger-than-life, brilliant serial killer. The truth was much sadder and smaller—

another disgruntled, rejected man who felt he had the right to take the life of the woman he supposedly cared for. Even more surprising than her photo being useful to the detectives was the fact that the Internet had done a complete 180. The same Reddit threads calling for her demise now lauded her as a vigilante. Now, sipping her Thai tea, Viv assumes this is why David is so keen to rush back into her life. He always could smell the tides turning, and he'd be damned before he let anyone else beat him to a lucrative opportunity. What that opportunity may be, Viv has ideas. He must want to collaborate on some inane photo shoot, tag her on social media, something to boost his brand.

Part of her hopes he also wants to check up on her. Maybe this is both an opportunistic clout grab and an olive branch. Even thinking that makes Viv hate herself. She hates feeling desperate for friendship, and David has always left her feeling like she has to reach a little bit farther, give a little more of herself if she is ever going to win his affection. Well, not always. There were the early days of their relationship. But it became toxic and self-serving long ago. Giving up on friendships is one of the hardest things Viv has ever tried to do, and she's never been successful.

She watches out the window for David's Prius to pull into the parking lot. The place is busy, and the server keeps asking if she's ready to order yet. Feeling guilty for taking up the prime real estate of a booth by herself, Viv orders for the both of them. A couple minutes later, the black Prius pulls into the lot. Viv sits up straighter. She can't help but feel a little apprehensive. She never fights with people. After cutting her blood family out of her life, she opted to run from conflict with anyone else. She couldn't handle any more yelling, being left behind again. She let things with David go too far, and now she's stuck in a situation that is more than uncomfortable, it's unacceptable. She cares too much that they fought, that he doesn't seem to need her in the same way anymore. She knows it and doesn't know what to do about it. So, she smiles and waves at him through the window.

David takes his time exiting his car, walking languidly to the front door of the restaurant. Even when he's late, he never hurries. The bell jingles over the door as he enters, hunched a little, gaze roaming over the packed restaurant before settling on Viv. His face erupts into a huge smile, and he makes his way through the cramped space to her booth.

As he slides in across from her, he claps his hands slowly.

"Congratulations, Detective Klein! You're quite the talk of the town."

Viv shrugs off the compliment, uncomfortable. "I didn't do anything."

David waves over a server with aggravating ease. Everyone is always aware when David is in a room. He naturally exudes a confidence and presence like he owns the place. "Thai iced tea, please." He turns his high-wattage pearly whites back to Viv. "Please. You did. And you would look great in a uniform. You should consider it."

"I have a few too many abolitionist tendencies to be a cop." The Thai iced tea arrives, and David takes a sip. They lapse into silence, not particularly affable. Viv opens her mouth to speak at the same time as David. He waves her on.

"We didn't leave things very pleasantly the last time we saw each other. I was surprised that you wanted to meet up. A little dubious, actually." Viv leans back, can't quite make eye contact.

"You think this is some scheme to revitalize your image and boost my own. I'm ever the opportunist, and here's another opportunity." None of it is a question.

"Yes. I do think that's why you're here." Viv tries to think of more to say, but that's it.

"But you met up with me anyway. Interesting." David takes another sip of his tea. He looks at her expectantly, but she doesn't answer. "Despite your lack of faith in me, I am actually here completely altruistically. I have a job offer for you that has nothing to do with me. As for everything that was said last time we saw each other . . . water under the bridge, my dear. It's a tall, long bridge we've built. There are many more interesting things to discuss than any she said, he said. Wouldn't you agree?"

One thing Viv knows she will never get from David is an apology. She takes a second to ponder if she's all right with that. She's too tired to do much besides relent. "If you're good, I'm good. I'm sorry for being harsh the other night. Obviously, there's a lot going on.

That's no excuse, but it is the context. I don't fight with people. That's not me. I'm sorry." David waves her words away. The server returns with their food. Green curry for David. Larb for Viv.

"You remembered my order."

"I've only ordered it for you a hundred times before when you were late."

David takes a dramatic breath in, wafting the curry toward him.

He sits back, studying her. "Larb always makes you ill. You can't handle the spice. Tsk, tsk, Klein. You need to take better care of yourself."

"We haven't come here together in ages. Maybe my stomach has changed."

"Has it?" His smile is infuriatingly smug.

"No."

He seems to clock the tension in the air, pauses. His lips purse, then slowly curl into a smile again. He laughs his effervescent laugh. "Your body, your choice, girl. It's a shame we don't do this anymore. I've missed our Thai nights."

"Me too." They lapse into a lighter silence. David knows to take it easy on her, that her nerves are fried. He seems willing to oblige, for now. Her curiosity gets the better of her, though, and before she can stop herself she leans over the table— "So, you mentioned a job offer?"

David chews his curry slowly, trying to build anticipation. "I thought you'd never ask. All right, I'll start with this. The pay is good. Very good. I don't know exactly how good, but he said he would pay a premium. The client is one of the executive producers of that superhero franchise I always forget the name of. I met him a month or two ago at his house party in Hollywood Hills. We've been having some fun, but like I said, this has nothing to do with me. I just told him I could recommend a photographer. The project is time sensitive, so really, I need to know tonight if you're in."

Viv can already feel the larb rumbling in her stomach. She downs the rest of her tea. It doesn't help much. David looks at her expectantly, but there's something else behind his eyes, too. "So, what's the catch? All of that sounds great. Easy. Like my career hasn't imploded completely."

"Your career hasn't imploded completely. You may just need to pivot a little. Hustle.Rebrand yourself. You're at a place where you really need to keep your options open, babes."

He tries to look at her casually, almost bored, but there's something off.

"Rebrand myself as what? You're freaking me out. What does he want me to do? Photograph some *Eyes Wide Shut* sex party?"

"I've been to his sex parties, those people do *not* want to be photographed. Anonymity is key." David puts down his silverware. "Look, what do you know about death masks?"

Viv pushes her larb to the side so she can lean forward on the table. "What the hell are you talking about?"

David sighs with feigned patience. "I know you're aware of King Tut, yes?" "Please don't give me a history lesson right now."

"I'll keep it short. When you think of King Tut, you think of his golden funeral mask. Right? Right. Okay. So. People evolved, masks became more accurate; casts of people's likenesses were made out of plaster or something. Peter the Great, Stalin, James Dean. The Victorians got all creepy about it when photography became more affordable, and they would take death portraits of their children staged with their families. Disturbing, I know. This producer thinks the natural evolution from there is more of a death . . . candid? A depiction on film of the person as they looked at death, staged doing something they love."

David puts both hands flat on the table. He looks a little nervous, despite the winning smile he flashes. Viv stares at him in horror. Whatever she expected, it wasn't this.

"What do you mean, staged doing something they love? Actually, I don't want to know. Find me a sex party to shoot or something else, David. This is . . . I don't know what this is. What does he want me to do? Rob a grave or something?"

"You're making this into some huge, nefarious thing, Viv. His mother just died. He's sitting shiva for her this week at his house, where she lived with him the last couple of months as she declined. He has a little at-home studio set up in his garage. He just wants someone to help him commemorate her life. You'd be helping him grieve. It's basically community service, but you'll be paid for it."

David waves over the server, asks for to-go boxes and the check. He checks his watch. Always thinking of the next thing. He already seems more relaxed, now that he has said his piece.

"So, he thinks I'm some kind of creep, because of the photo. And what, you do, too? Why would you come to me with this offer, David? What you're talking about is so infinitely messed up. You're actually telling me to lean into this whole shit show? You do know I want to salvage my career, right? Not tank it even more."

The server returns with the check and boxes. David puts his card down and hands it back immediately. "This one is on me." He waits for the server to leave. "His mother was his favorite person on the planet. Weirdly so. It was unattractive, how much of a mama's boy he was. Anyway, he wouldn't let someone he thought was a creep anywhere near her body.

He could see the beauty in the photo you took. He wants you to do the same thing with her portrait. Capture the beauty in death. And he's willing to pay well for that beauty, believe me."

"You said you don't know how much he's offering."

David boxes up both of their leftovers, avoiding her gaze. "I lied. I wanted you to hear me out without the numbers hindering anything. I thought it would freak you out a bit too much. You have to understand, he's also buying your silence. No one can know about this. It's a very fair price, I think, to help someone through their grief."

David checks his watch again and stands up. "Look, I have to go. This has been really lovely. I know you love your pondering, but I need to know tonight what you want to do. Otherwise, I have a couple other photographers I can call up. There's a short window here, with the shiva. He has a permit to bring the body back for the last day of the week, to do an at-home funeral. He wants to keep this as aboveboard and legal as possible. I'd love to help you out, if you'll let me. I'd rather this job go to a friend. Also, I think you'd be great at it."

He starts for the door, leaving Viv alone at the booth, then calls over his shoulder, as if as an afterthought, "I feel like fifteen grand can make quite a difference, even in this economy. Don't you?" He turns on his heels and is gone, the door left jingling behind him. Viv watches his slow, smooth walk back to his car. She doesn't stand until the black Prius has turned left out of the parking lot and disappeared from view. She picks up her larb and starts the walk home, her mind whirling in a way she knows David would call her "pondering." For her, it feels more like free-falling.

ABBY

The hallway is impractically dim. It doesn't make any sense. It must be for some kind of ill-conceived ambiance, but Abby finds herself mildly annoyed as she squints at the numbers next to each apartment door. It's an ugly building: New, soulless construction meant to look modern but without any thought to functionality or comfort. At least the lighting is so low that you can barely make out the garish color-block carpeting. Maybe that's the reason.

Abby squints at yet another plaque next to yet another door. This is it. Her stomach tightens. She could leave now, and no one would ever know she was here. She could go home, work on transcribing her interview with the founder of the Echo Park Film Festival. Basically a promotional piece for yet another small film festival in LA that no one except the filmmakers will attend. But still, the founder seemed so earnest, so excited. Maybe the piece will help with attendance. Maybe.

Abby rings the doorbell. Fuck it. Too late now. After the chime stops, there is silence. Abby always finds homes without dogs to be disconcertingly quiet. No barking, no pawing at the other side of the door. Well, maybe those are just homes with disobedient dogs. Maybe Viv Klein has a super disciplined German shepherd just sitting there on the other side of the door, ears cocked, silent, ready to protect their home.

But there is no sound of any dog or human. Abby is about to ring the doorbell once more when she halts, hand raised in the air. She has the distinct feeling she is being watched. She squints at the peephole. She doesn't know what possesses her, but she waves. There's a thump, and then the lock scratches in the strike plate hole. The door opens and Abby comes face-to-face with a confused-looking Viv Klein. She's wearing a stained, oversized T-shir tand bike shorts. Rubbing at her ankles is a Holstein-patterned cat, who looks up at Abby with partially closed eyes.

"How did you get my address?" Viv closes the door halfway. Abby tries to give her an apologetic smile, inviting, understanding—not working. To show that she isn't a threat, she takes half a step back. The cat takes this as a cue to dart into the hall and rub against her chinos. Viv's eyes flick from the cat back up to Abby. She looks even more upset.

"It's public record. In some ways, maybe that's comforting? All those people sending you death threats could have found you pretty easily if they wanted to."

Viv looks at her incredulously, then laughs one sharp, single, hiccuping laugh. Maybe joking is the right tactic to get her to put her guard down.

"Thank you, that really puts me at ease. I'm so glad it's simple to stalk me." She waits for Abby to explain herself. Abby shifts, the cat circling her legs.

"I would like to speak with you some more, follow up now that more information has come to light. If you'd like me to leave, I will. I just wanted to give you a chance to share your thoughts on this turning into a criminal case. Public opinion has really done a one eighty on what you did. Surely you have thoughts on that?"

"You could have called me."

"I did. You didn't answer. So, here I am. Again, if you want me to leave, I will. I just wanted to give you the chance to speak."

Viv doesn't address the missed phone calls. "You're not the one who wrote the article about what happened. Why?" Viv bends down and the cat comes running. She picks him up and stands, returning to her position half behind the door.

"I'm not a crime reporter. Fred Johnson is. I think he did a very good job reporting on what happened. I'm sorry you didn't end up being interviewed at all. The article came together very quickly."

"So, what is this article you're working on, if it isn't a crime piece?" Viv's gaze flicks up and down the hall, like she doesn't want to be spotted conversing with a journalist.

Abby hesitates. She knew this question would come up, but it's difficult to answer, when there isn't really an article. None that has been assigned, at least, or even pitched as a possibility to her editor. Abby isn't even certain what an opinion piece on Viv Klein would look like. But there's something interesting to be gleaned from this subject—something there. Talking to Viv would reveal it, she is sure.

"It's an opinion piece about the nature and ethics of art as it pertains to . . . what happened."

Klein looks at her, hard. She still doesn't close the door. That's promising. But then, something switches in her face and her eyes narrow.

"That sounds a bit tedious and philosophical. I'm not sure anyone would be interested in reading that. Especially from a reporter who doesn't do her research. Though, maybe that makes it more interesting—the blind leading the blind. Thanks for stopping by. Feel free to lose my address."

Viv starts to close the door. She's all timidity and then flashes of anger. Abby can't seem to get footing. She inches forward, hands raised.

"I went to the alleyway. After I looked at the photo. I went to the alleyway to try and see it how you saw it. But I couldn't." The door pauses, swings back open slightly. Viv looks surprised for a moment, before frowning.

"Yeah, you really miss out on a certain *je ne sais quoi* when there isn't an active crime scene there."

Abby leans awkwardly to the side, trying to make eye contact around the door. "That isn't what I mean. Your eye is really unique. I . . . I see how you made it art. And it disturbs me. Please. Can we just talk?"

Viv taps the doorframe, considering. The cat takes advantage of her distraction to wriggle out of her arms and prance back to Abby's legs, weaving between them. Mentioning her art seems to have done the trick.

"I guess Connor has already decided. Come in." Viv flings open the door and turns on her heels, striding back into the apartment. Abby hurries after her, almost tripping over the cat, closing the door behind her.

The apartment is colder, more impersonal than Abby expected. The furniture is sparse, modern, upholstered in cool tones. The apartment is hot, warmed to a crisp by the strong western sunlight filtering in through the huge, floor-to-ceiling windows that look out over Hollywood Boulevard.

Other than a couple of wobbly kitchen stools, the only places to sit are on the bed shoved against the windows and a low-to-the-ground, midcentury modern, mint-blue velvet loveseat. Connor, the cat, immediately runs to the bed and jumps up, purring so loud that Abby can hear him from the kitchen. Not that the kitchen is that far from the bed. The studio isn't exactly spacious.

Viv disappears into what Abby presumes is the bathroom. There's some banging around, and then Viv reappears, shutting the door behind her.

"Can I get you something to drink? Since you're here, you might as well make yourself comfortable." Viv joins her in the kitchen, opening the fridge and taking out a mason jar of some kind of green, viscous substance. She notices Abby's expression. "It's my green juice. Don't worry. I also have water, coffee, black tea."

Abby notes the dark circles under Viv's eyes. It looks like she hasn't slept much since their last meeting a week ago. Her face is wan, hair pulled back in a greasy ponytail. The green juice seems like a patch on the hull of a sinking ship.

"It's really not necessary." Abby awkwardly shifts her weight between her kitten heels. Per usual, she feels overdressed. Faking it. In this case, though, isn't she? She should be home, working on the Echo Park Film Festival piece. She overeagerly told her editor she could have it in by end of day tomorrow, a full two days before the deadline. What kind of weird flex was that?

"Suit yourself." Viv slumps down onto one of the rickety kitchen stools, opening her mason jar. Abby takes the other stool. Viv looks at her expectantly, a slight nervousness showing itself again. "Aren't you going to record this?"

Abby jolts. She needs to stay focused. "Yes. If that's okay with you? It's only for my own transcription purposes." She pulls out her phone, waits for Viv's go-ahead.

"I remember the spiel from last time. Go ahead."

Abby starts recording. Her mind goes blank. She needs to ask something. Honestly, she never really expected to get past the door. She's never shown up at a source's house unannounced before. That's for hardcore investigative journalists and the movies. Not for culture writers.

Now, she's floundering.

"Let's start with what all has changed in the last week. Where were you when you found out your photo had been used to help find a lead on the Karen Elmes case?"

"I didn't find out until October 2, when I came back from Joshua Tree. I had my phone off for a few days. A friend called and told me the news." Viv is stiff in her chair, icy eyes fixed on Abby. All the fire leaves her as soon as the questions start.

"How did you feel?"

"Relieved, I guess. And then sad for her. For Karen Elmes. I was relieved because part of me had been worried the whole time it wasn't suicide, and that there was some killer who would want to tie up loose ends. It was neurotic, stupid. I wish it had been suicide." Viv pauses for a moment. "Can I retroactively ask for that to be off the record? I can see the headline now—Photographer Wishes Death Was Suicide." Viv's wan face is somehow even whiter.

"Don't worry. I won't print that. I'm really not here to try and villainize you. I understand what you mean; what happened to her was awful."

Viv looks at her with uncertainty. Her hands are shaking a little.

Abby pauses the recording. She's worried that if she stops now, Viv will never give her access again. But still, she isn't trying to traumatize the woman. Abby usually has no issue keeping a positive rapport with interviewees. But Viv seems to be living on an emotional tightrope.

"We can also continue this at a later time, if you want."

"You showed up unannounced at my doorstep. Now you want to continue this later?" Viv crosses her arms petulantly.

"You don't seem okay. I want to make sure that you're all right. Also, you let me in. You seem to want to talk. But I think you may be scared to. I want to alleviate that."

"I haven't been okay since any of this started. I'm not built for this much scrutiny—from other people or from myself. There's no alleviating that." Viv stands stiffly and goes to put her green juice back in the fridge. As she swings the door open, a yellow and purple magnet catches Abby's eye.

"You're a fan of the Oceanbrook Three series?" She keeps her voice light. Viv puts the green juice back and returns to her seat, looking absentmindedly at the magnet.

"Yeah, I grew up on the movies."

"Same." Abby looks up to see Viv staring at her.

"Don't do that."

"Do what?"

"Omit information like that. I looked you up, you know. I know your mom won an Oscar for those films. There's no need for false humility—it's not like it's your Oscar." Viv rubs her temples, leaving two red dots on the sides of her face. "I'm sorry, that was rude."

She reminds Abby of a turtle, coming out of her shell for quick swipes at her before retreating behind her impenetrable barrier. Abby decides to lean into the frankness of Viv's speech. Maybe that will make her less wary.

"It was rude, but I don't mind. Honestly, it's kind of nice when someone doesn't care who my mom is."

"I didn't say I didn't care. If I thought you could get me an autograph, I'd be working my ass off for it."

"Okay, people don't usually go *that* far for a costume designer. No need to flatter me by proxy." Perhaps this interview will get back on track somehow.

"I wouldn't be caught dead flattering you." Viv sits back on her stool. She gives Abby an awkward smile after the dig. "All right, if you're fine holding off on your questions for a bit, there is one thing that would make me feel more comfortable talking to you. Tell me some more about yourself. I don't like talking to strangers."

"I thought you already did your research on me?"

Viv glances at a kitschy rooster clock on the wall near her oven, an odd addition that doesn't fit with the rest of the modern apartment.

"Am I keeping you?" Abby asks, a little disappointed. She isn't ready to leave.

Viv's eyes flit back to her. "No. I have a job tonight, but I have plenty of time before that. So, tell me about yourself. And don't lie—I did my research."

Abby is amazed at the sudden mettle in her eyes. "How do you have so much confidence? I'm a journalist for the *LA Times*, sitting here trying to interview you, and you're roasting me about my mother and interrogating me about myself."

"I would hardly call this an interrogation." Viv raises an eyebrow, then shrugs. "I guess I stopped being intimidated by you when I realized you hadn't seen the picture. From then on, I've just been . . . intrigued. I'm nervous speaking with the press, but I'm open to it. I don't have many friends. I'm lacking in stimulating conversation. Don't overthink it. I'm sure you still scare many people. Maybe the ones you do research on beforehand."

Abby takes a deep breath. Keep it professional. "I'm sorry I didn't look at the photo sooner. That was a lapse in due diligence. I try not to judge my subjects, but I have to say I did. Death hits close to home for me, as it does for most everybody, I guess. I felt like you were trivializing it and it felt . . . crude. I don't believe that anymore. And my personal feelings were no excuse for not researching properly."

Viv nods, looking her over for a second. "Right, well, none of that was information about you." Abby chuckles nervously and decides to open up a little, just enough to show she's well-intentioned.

"I want you to know that you can trust me, and my journalistic integrity, moving forward. I could give the stats. I've written for one paper or another since I was fifteen. Graduated journalism school at Pepperdine." It all sounds like a resume, a dull one at that. Viv does not look impressed. Fine, maybe the photographer would relate to something about her constant dissatisfaction. Don't artists love being dissatisfied?

"From there, I just moved around the greater Southern California area, writing little of impact. I'm a culture writer, but I don't write about either of my own cultures, as a Jewish Latina who went to Hebrew school but can barely read it and never has been more than conversational in Spanish. One day, I'd like to think I'll write something that does speak to at least part of that experience. But mostly, I just want to write something that actually resonates with people." Abby stops, but Viv still watches her expectantly.

"Even saying that out loud sounds so trite. I've never known how to not sound like a self-righteous prick on my Bernstein and Woodward bullshit, while at the same time I write nothing that could be considered investigation and rarely even feels like journalism. But—that's the goal. And why I'm here. I think you have a story to tell."

Abby finishes, letting out a breath. Immediately, her cheeks flame red. She risks a glance at Viv, who is staring at her, just as she feared. She overshared, which was inappropriate, highly unprofessional, and also just so typical of her. She sets her jaw and lifts her gaze to Viv's, feigns ease.

"Thank you. For being so honest." Viv thinks for a second. "For what it's worth, I've read a decent amount of your work. You have a clear, concise voice. Truly, you don't need me. This was the story of the week—and that was last week. I don't have much of interest to add. I was at the wrong place, wrong time. I did something without thinking, posted without thinking, and now I'm glad some good came with the bad."

"I don't think that's the end of the story."

"I don't know what else you want." Viv shrinks into herself again.

Abby searches, but she has no answer. "I don't know. But I came here because of your photo. Maybe you could give me some insight into how you pick what you shoot. Would you be interested in that, explaining your work to me?"

Viv looks at her in a way that makes her wriggle in her rickety seat. Nervous, but determined. She doesn't seem able to say no when asked about her work. "All right. You told me some about you, it's only fair I do the same. What's interesting or true about me isn't really the stats, as you call them. What I have is my photography." She jumps off her seat and heads toward the bathroom, opening the door and stepping inside. Abby stays put, but Viv's head reappears, and she gestures for Abby to follow.

As Abby steps inside the room, Viv closes the door behind her. For a moment, there is complete darkness. Then Viv hits the lights. The room comes into focus in bright, fire-engine red.

"Inconvenient when I have guests, but luckily that isn't too often."

The bathroom has been turned into a full-on darkroom, with the enlarger perched haphazardly on the small counter next to the sink. Clotheslines run back and forth across the space, jammed full of clothespins and hanging photos. A couple of wooden planks have been set across the tub, creating a space for a slew of pungent-smelling bins, chemical baths Abby vaguely remembers from high school. She wonders for a second how Viv bathes. Then her attention is caught by a picture hanging in front of her. It's a copy of the photo of Karen Elmes, but not exactly. It's more contrasty, the reds popping garishly. Viv follows her eyeline.

"I made a lot of iterations before I found what I liked, saturation-wise, contrast-wise.

There's even this bleach bypassed version somewhere in here that's truly horrendous." Viv shifts from foot to foot in the red light, energized. "I don't know why I left them all up in here. I just couldn't bring myself to touch them. I haven't shot much since then."

Something catches Abby's eye: another image drying on the line directly above the tub.

"What's that?"

Viv leans forward, snatches the picture down. She looks at it for a second, frowns, turns it toward Abby dismissively. "Just something I shot in Joshua Tree."

Abby takes the photo gingerly, trying to only touch the edges. "There's blood."

"Yes. This hiker cut his lip." Abby studies the image. It's bleak, interesting enough, but it doesn't grab attention the way the photo of Karen Elmes does. There are disparate elements that don't seem to come together in any cohesive way. Viv leans against the sink, seeming to sense Abby's thoughts. "It isn't anything." She says it as a fact.

"It's not the most visually arresting, but the composition is . . . I don't know. I'm sorry. I'm not really the most articulate when it comes to this kind of art."

"It's okay. Most photos aren't *that* photo." Viv throws a rueful glance around the darkroom née bathroom. "I'm just relieved I wanted to shoot again. I was afraid I wouldn't, potentially ever. Maybe that's selfish."

Abby isn't sure what to say, but then Viv gestures at the clothesline. "So, if you want to see my work, this is it. A lot of trial and error and a couple good images."

"But you have a job tonight, yes?"

"Yes. I guess I'm back at it." Viv laughs with no humor. "You said the photo disturbed you. But you're here?" Viv stops. It seems like she's trying to find the words, the question.

"I don't mean it disturbed me in a bad way, per se. I'm not used to seeing beauty in something so brutal. I admire it. That's what disturbs me." Abby internally winces at how stupid she sounds. It's like she's a college student back in Art Appreciation class, making things up to impress the professor.

Viv looks particularly pale in the red glow. Abby hesitates, then blurts out, "Forget the impartial third-party thing for a minute. You're a journalist but also a person. A person who talked to the Elmes family and also saw something in the photo. What do you think of me?" She doesn't wait for an answer, but immediately pulls herself off the counter, turning off the lights.

"Excuse me?" Abby tenses. Viv shuffles around in the dark, opens the door to the bathroom, ushers Abby out. She's bashful again.

"What do you think of me—the person who created this . . . disturbing image? Now that you've seen it, now that you admire something about it, what do you think of me? Be honest. I've heard it all on Reddit."

"I think I see why you took it." This is a first for Abby—being asked what she thinks of a subject *by* the subject. It feels like a minefield. "I don't know what you want me to say. I'm not horrified by you. Do you want me to be?"

Viv walks absentmindedly to her bed, scratches Connor behind the ears. "No. I need to get ready for my job." This whole conversation feels like whiplash. Viv turns back to Abby. "Let's do this again sometime?" Viv's mind already seems far away from the apartment, probably thinking about whatever shoot she has to get ready for.

"Sure." Abby doesn't really know what this is or what a next time would entail, but she finds herself wanting to agree. Viv opens the door for her, watches her walk down the dark hall to the elevator. As the heavy doors thud closed and the elevator descends, Abby takes a deep breath. She still doesn't have a story, but her interest in the enigmatic photographer has only been heightened. Viv let her take a glimpse into her darkroom, her world, for some reason. Maybe simply because no one else is asking. No matter what, it bodes well for Abby's opinion piece. What that piece will ultimately entail still seems cloudy. All Abby knows is that she has to get Viv Klein talking again.

VIV

The road winding up into the hills starts wide enough for two cars, but quickly narrows to barely enough room for one. Viv doesn't know what she'll do if a car comes from the other direction. There are no streetlights up here, the houses eerily illuminated only by her headlights. Viv thinks the same thing she always thinks whenever she visits a house in the hills: She would never want to live here, even if she could afford it.

For one thing, any time she comes to the hills she thinks of Charles Manson. Being up here alone at night, with no ambient light other than the moon, the whole area feels so secluded and ominous, even though the lights of Hollywood do sporadically twinkle below between casitas and hedges. Any call for help must be like a call into the void. Viv can't imagine an ambulance trying to gun its way up this winding, one-lane road. Of course, Charles Manson is dead, and it's too late for an ambulance where she's going. This isn't as comforting a thought as she hoped.

Her mind wanders to this evening's conversation with the journalist. Her chest tightens. She can't explain why she let Abby Katz into her darkroom. She doesn't regret it, per se, but she feels panic just thinking about the *LA Times* journalist appraising at her work. It was terrifying, opening up to her a little, but also nice in its way. She seldom has the chance to really talk with people about her art. Abby Katz didn't seem judgmental. Maybe it would be good, letting her in, letting her write about what happened.

For now, though, she works to push Charles Manson and Abby Katz out of her head. To say she feels misgivings about taking the job David offered her would be an understatement, but her curiosity and desire to work won out. She won't have to worry about substitute teaching for quite a while after this. It is by far the most she has ever been offered for her photography work. Plus, this client saw some promise in her. Yes, disturbing promise. But promise, nevertheless. It's hard to resist.

Viv turns left at a fork and dips down a small incline in the road. At the end, a dark wooden gate is illuminated by uplights. This is it. She pulls to a stop at the keypad and presses the call button. She clears her throat, but no voice comes through the other side. After a few seconds, she is buzzed through. She nods at the small security camera above the call box. The gate rolls back slowly, revealing a boxy white house, thin and tall. Around the side, Viv makes out the aquamarine glow of a large pool. She pulls to a stop behind a couple of sports cars in the circular driveway. Still no sign of anyone.

She steps out of the car, leaving her equipment in the trunk for now. Hesitantly, she walks up the granite steps to the front door—a huge, black, sliding contraption with lines of decorative, metallic bolts. Half behind a ficus, a small, unassuming black button is set into the wall. Viv presses it. Almost instantaneously, the door slides open with some effort. A short Black man in a black velvet suit stands there. His dreads are pulled back into a tasteful ponytail. His aesthetic looks somewhere between funeral and red carpet. He looks at Viv solemnly. Behind him, steel-gray walls and heavy metal furniture fill what almost feels like a waiting room, dimly lit by candles.

"I'm Viv Klein, the photographer." Viv sticks her hand out uncertainly. The man grasps it in a warm, firm shake.

"I'm Andre, Jeremiah's assistant. Please, follow me. I'll take you to Jeremiah's study. There are still a couple of mourners here, so if you could be quiet as we pass the main room, that would be appreciated."

Viv nods and follows Andre silently through the foyer. On one side is a tightly wound spiral staircase; on the other, a doorway into the rest of the house blends with the gray of the walls. Andre slips through the door– Viv close behind.

On the other side, the house spreads out into a spacious, open floor plan completely unlike the entryway. The rest of the first floor seems to be the "main room." The steel-gray-and-metal motif continues. A couple of people in black sit on stools near the fireplace in the middle of the room. There is a casket against the far wall, in shadow.

Andre steps swiftly but softly across the concrete floor. At the far end of the room, he opens a glass door and ushers Viv into a tiny elevator, flashing her an apologetic smile. The elevator shudders to life and ever so slowly ascends to the second floor. Andre slides open the metal safety door. He opens a dark paneled door into another dimly lit space and Viv follows him out, eyes adjusting to the light.

"Sorry about that. Let me turn on some lights in here." He hits a switch and a couple of Edison bulbs hanging from the ceiling flicker on. This must be the study. The walls are lined with metal bookshelves, full of what must be first editions and other costly tomes, based on the antique spines. The room isn't small, but it feels claustrophobic. The only window is a small square high on the wall behind what looks like a drafting table.

"Please have a seat and we can start going through the paperwork." Andre gestures to the high-backed metal chairs pushed against the table. They sit, and Andre starts entering information on a tablet. Viv notices some brightly colored bobbleheads high on an opposite shelf. Maybe the superheroes from the latest film. She hasn't seen it. Hopefully, no one expects to have that conversation with her.

Andre passes the tablet over to Viv. "Feel free to look through it. Basically, it's just an extension of the NDA you signed before we gave you the address. Jeremiah didn't want to hit you with the whole thing until you actually showed up. It can be a bit overwhelming." Viv flips quickly through the endless pages of legalese. "Really, it's just your basics. Pretty boilerplate. Now that you're here, there's a lot of sensitive information about Jeremiah's work and personal life you may be exposed to."

Viv did a cursory Internet search into the legality of what they were planning, with mixed results available online. She decided she would rely on that ambiguity if anything went south. The fact that there is so much paperwork to be signed comforts her, like it's all more aboveboard than it feels. She turns back to the first page and starts signing.

"Is there a contract here as well? I brought my standard deal memo with me." Suddenly, the one-page contract that Viv found online for free years ago feels pretty paltry. But if Andre thinks she's out of her league, he doesn't show it.

"We had our lawyers draw up a contract, but give me your deal memo and I'll have them look it over. I'm sure we can get that signed as well."

Viv nods, trying to act like it's normal to have lawyers on call at 10 p.m.

Within minutes, everything is signed, excluding Viv's deal memo, which she decided to forgo after looking over the much more comprehensive contract presented to her on the tablet. Andre escorts her back downstairs, where the main room has emptied. He points her to the side of the house, where a four-car garage sits separate from the main building. She moves her car over and starts to unload her photography equipment. David didn't know exactly what the at-home studio included, so Viv brought everything. Lights, backdrops, her entire collection of portraiture accessories. But when Andre opens the garage door, Viv is reminded yet again that she is out of her depth.

The at-home studio is beautiful. What must be a fifteen-foot backdrop covers one entire wall. In the corner, on shelf after shelf, are neatly rolled backdrop paper options. Lights on stands line the back wall. Continuous, strobe, all well-known brands and latest editions. There is even a grid on the ceiling for overhead lighting, a ladder leaned in the corner for that purpose. Above a closed door is a lit sign: Darkroom in Use. Of course he has his own darkroom. He could hardly have her taking film rolls off the property. The garage smells like paint. She wonders if he created this whole studio just for this purpose.

The only item that seems out of place is a water tank sitting in the middle of the space. It looks sinister, with steel reinforcements, barely six feet tall and three across. Like something a magician would own. In fact, it could be a prop from one of the superhero movies. Viv can almost remember a sequence in which one of the heroes gets caught in the tank, has to escape before drowning. That's one of Jeremiah's films, right? Does he store props in here, too?

Faintly, she can hear the front door to the main house open and close. Voices echo around the corner. Soon, Andre appears, walking quickly to keep up with a tall, lanky white man in wire-rimmed glasses. He is also dressed in black—dress pants and a turtleneck that would give him a Steve Jobs look if he were clean-shaven. Instead, he sports an unkempt, hippie-style beard. He stops in front of Viv, gives her an appraising look. His eyes are a cloudy gray, not unkind, but also slightly birdlike. Despite his lankiness, there is something meaty about him. He's probably sixty-something, though it's hard to tell. He's had work done and done well, but there should be more lines on his taut face.

"I'm Jeremiah. You must be Viv. David had nothing but wonderful things to share about you and your photography. I'm sure you know as well as I do what a great eye he has—and how he doesn't give a compliment unless it's due. I'd say I'm excited to work with you, but the circumstances preclude that a bit. Still, I'm grateful you're here. Welcome." Jeremiah grabs Viv's hand, his large, cool palm enveloping hers. His voice is deeper than she expected. She knows his last name—Fink—from the credits of his movies, but he doesn't mention it.

"I'm sorry for your loss." Viv pulls her hand back.

Jeremiah looks past her to the studio. "I'd prefer everything to be done by morning. The shooting as well as the printing. It's easier that way, for me. I don't know if you've had a chance to look around yet, but I had David make a list of everything you have in your darkroom at home. Plus a 35mm to digital scanner, 7200 DPI. Light-wise, he said you prefer continuous lighting, but I had Andre bring in a smattering of different options. Whatever had the best reviews." He turns back to Viv.

"I want to give you creative latitude to make this portrait how you see fit; that is, within a couple of parameters. I'm sure you noticed the tank in the middle of the room?" Jeremiah leads her to it. "If it looks like a film prop, that's because it is. I bought it off an act I saw at the Magic Castle years ago, because the look was perfect for the film I was working on at the time. It's one of those odds and ends I've kept with me over the years, never knowing why. But now I have another use for it. Here, I want you to look at something."

Jeremiah pulls a phone out of his pocket and brings up a photo.

In it, an older woman swims in what is most likely the pool on the other side of the property. The background is out of focus, but the building is blindingly bright in the sun. She wears a bright-red swim cap and goggles, mid-butterfly stroke. "My mother was an avid swimmer until the day she died. This photo is from two weeks ago, during her daily swim. I took it to send to the doctor, to show how well she was doing. It's just a phone snapshot." Jeremiah pauses, looking at the photo. He sighs and swipes to a picture of a picture pasted in what looks like an old scrap-book. A younger woman, maybe midtwenties, stands on a beach in a polka-dot one-piece, beaming from a halo of soft brown curls. "See, here she is back in the fifties. Look at that swimsuit. Iconic. She could have been a model in a different life. Instead, she stayed at home and raised my brother and I."

Jeremiah pats the side of the water tank. "She loved the water, and that's how I want to remember her. I think that's how she would have liked to be remembered, as well. At ease in her favorite place."

Whatever Viv expected, it wasn't this. She had looked at some nineteenth-century photos for inspiration—thought beauty lighting, maybe laying the body down on a bed of flowers, thought maybe Jeremiah would want to sit with her in the photo. "I'm sorry, but I don't think I understand the logistics of what you want?"

Jeremiah turns to Andre, gesturing toward the house. "Go ahead and get the guys, Andre." He smiles bashfully at Viv. "Sorry. I jumped the gun a little on that part. Obviously, I know you're here without any assistance. I have a couple of men from my team who are here to help you however you need. I also took the liberty of hiring a makeup artist. She's getting mom in the outfit right now."

Viv tries to keep her face neutral, but Jeremiah seems to sense her mounting unease. "I know this is pretty unconventional. I want you to be able to relax. Look, why don't I get out of here and leave you to it? Connect to the speaker system, play some music. There's a minifridge behind the lights. Have a sparkling water—or a beer. Seriously, I want you to feel like you can get into your creative process. If it makes you feel better, Mom and I talked about this before she passed. She knew she was going up over the fireplace in the main room. She loved the idea."

With that, Jeremiah takes one last look at the water tank and then shoves his hands in his pockets, striding back to the house. For a minute, Viv is alone. She pulls out her phone, types in a message to David: *What the hell did you get me into???* Then, she deletes it. It's absolutely against her NDA to say even that much. She didn't read the paperwork fully, but she's pretty sure she can't even mention ever meeting Jeremiah without getting sued. She busies herself looking through the backdrop rolls. She picks a muted seafoam color, pulls it out.

There's a rumble from the house. It takes her a second to comprehend that it's the sound of something being rolled across the driveway. She looks up, bracing herself for whatever is coming her way. Four men in black are rolling what looks like a hospital bed, covered in a sheet, toward the garage. Viv wonders if it's another repurposed movie prop.

Unlike Andre and Jeremiah, the men's attire isn't formal. Black jeans and T-shirts. They look ready to walk on to a film set. Hell, maybe that's where they came from. Walking next to them is a woman with a large makeup case jostling against her hip. She's in head-to-toe

black as well, her pink hair poking out underneath a wide-brimmed black hat. They come to a stop next to the tank. The woman, all business, looks around the studio. "Hi. Anywhere in particular that's best for me to set up? I want to make sure I'm out of your way."

Viv gestures to the wall by the lights. "I'll be facing the backdrop the whole time.

Wherever is most convenient for you on that side works great." Viv looks at the men, trying to emulate the makeup artist and keep her gaze from lingering on the sheet. This is business as usual. "For now, I'm going to start setting up some lights. If you wouldn't mind, I picked out a backdrop. Could you hang it while I'm working on lighting the tank?"

The men don't even respond, just head to the backdrop and start setting it up. Viv closes the garage doors and turns to the tank. She tries to clear her head, to think solely of how to illuminate the water. The makeup artist procures a small stool and a ring light and gets quietly to work, bending over the hospital bed. Viv studiously avoids looking in that direction.

Thirty minutes later, the backdrop is set and the lighting is roughed in as much as it can be without a subject. Viv's Leica M is set on a side table, a neat row of Kodak Portra 400 cartridges lined up and ready to go. There's nothing left to set up. The men gather around the hospital bed expectantly, and the makeup artist looks up.

"If you're ready, I can show you how the harness works," she says.

"The harness," Viv repeats, faintly. She forces her feet forward, toward the makeup artist. The first look at the body on the hospital bed is the hardest. Then, it becomes easier to glance at the form again. The woman almost looks like she's sleeping, but there's a rigidity to her form that belies this. The makeup artist has her in a one-piece bathing suit with a decorative belt, the red swimming cap pulled down over her head, letting a few gray curls hang loose around the edges. Her eyes are closed, thankfully. Something about the idea of her vacant eyes makes Viv uncomfortable. It doesn't seem like the makeup artist intends to stage her in goggles. Somehow, her lips seem curled into a smile, though that could be a trick of the lipstick. Her skin looks vaguely like tissue paper. Viv fights off the thought of it tearing.

Viv listens to the explanation of the harness. Jeremiah has thought of everything. The men are already setting up two lines of thick, clear fishing wire from the grid on the ceiling. Each is rated for over one hundred pounds—unnecessary, given the small form on the hospital bed. The harness is almost imperceptible under the swimsuit, especially with the thick belt around the middle. Once the fishing wire is set, the harness will be attached, and the body can be lowered into the tank with a pulley system. All Viv has to do is let them know how far to lower the body.

It doesn't take long to get the entire system working. The body is so light, it only takes two men to heft it up the ladder and attach the fishing wire. While the body is lowered into the tank, Viv checks her camera. An excuse to try and get her shaking hands under control. When she turns back, the body is submerged. If anything, it looks even more unnatural now. Whatever read as a sleeping form on the hospital bed has gone away, and the sight is mortifying. Viv has the irrational thought that she has just come across a drowned person.

The body is stiff, bobbing a little.

"What do you want to do?" The makeup artist frowns, leaning close to the tank. "This looks like shit."

Viv joins her, mind blank. "Well, it's a dead body. I don't know if it's going to look like she's swimming." By the makeup artist's expression, this is not a sufficient answer. The body bobs stiffly.

"Okay. What if we have her floating in the water? What if I change the lighting, make it like the sun is filtering in from above and she's lying on the bottom of a pool or something? What if she doesn't *have* to look like she's swimming, basically?" This seems to please the makeup artist. The four men stand mutely by, and Viv starts altering the light. Slowly, the tank starts to look less like the site of a drowning and more like a sun-drenched pool. Viv grabs her camera and steadies her hands. She clicks the shutter. Then again. Surprisingly, the setup is working. Even the makeup artist looks pleased.

The shoot itself goes quickly. There are only so many angles she can get, and really just one pose. Viv leaves the men to clean up and wrap the lighting. She doesn't really want to know what the makeup artist has to do now before the morning's funeral. Viv shuts herself into the darkroom and starts developing the film. Neither the men, nor the makeup artist, nor Andre, nor Jeremiah himself come by for hours. Finally, around 2 a.m., there's a knock on the door.

Jeremiah enters. "I assume you've made some selects by now. Let me see. I want everything scanned digitally, and I'll keep the negatives of them all, but I was hoping you could focus your efforts on making one larger print for me. I'd love to have the portrait up in time for the funeral. Feel free to take a break while I look."

It's more of a command than an offer. Clients often want to speak a bit more, get her input. Jeremiah, however, seems to prefer to make his decisions alone. Viv steps back into the garage, surrendering the darkroom to Jeremiah. Surprisingly, the tank has been removed. The four men quietly load the lights and C-stands into a white truck that has been backed up into the garage. She wonders if the lights all belong to one of Jeremiah's sets, to be used tomorrow on some film. Andre stands by, typing on his phone. Viv makes her way to him. "Is there a restroom I can use?"

By the time Andre leads her back to the main house and to a small powder room with a covered mirror and pungent potpourri on every surface, Viv is shaking again. She splashes cold water on her face, glad she can't catch a glimpse of her reflection. The deceased body kept bringing to mind Karen Elmes. Flashes of that dim alleyway keep coming unbidden to her mind even now that the shoot is over.

Back in the garage, she knocks on the darkroom door, but there is no answer. She enters—and Jeremiah is gone. He's left one negative on the table. His select. Usually, Viv wouldn't let a client see every iteration of a print as she figures out the look she wants. Usually, there are quite a few photos that never make it in front of the client in the first place. But this is hardly a usual photo shoot, and so she lines up all her prints, puts every negative in the binders waiting for her, and digitally scans even the blurry outtakes in order to be safe. The best print, the final one, she leaves drying in the middle of the rest.

Impulsively, she signs a small *VK* in the corner. If Jeremiah doesn't like it, there are several almost identical prints drying on either side.

He doesn't intimidate her enough to curtail her pride in her workmanship. She feels revulsion and horror about the night, but also satisfaction. The photo is good. She knows it.

Finally, she grabs a tiny print, a 5 x 7, the first she made, from where it's drying in the corner, and stuffs it hurriedly into her photography bag. She doesn't even hide it well. If anyone tries to search her on her way out, they'll find it immediately. But she's too tired to be more careful, or to delve into why she even wants the photo. As usual, she prefers her decisions unexamined.

As she opens the door to the darkroom and hurries through the now vacant garage, she sees no one. Outside, the predawn air is sharp and chilly, and the house is dark. She thinks about ringing the doorbell, then thinks better of it. She packs as quickly as she can and forces herself to drive slowly to the gate. It opens automatically for her. Relief floods her as she starts to descend the one-lane road.

The sun flirts with the horizon as Viv makes her way down and out of the hills. She's almost at the bottom, about to turn back onto a real road, when her phone dings. She stops and checks it. Fifteen thousand dollars have just been transferred into her bank account. It doesn't feel real. Her stomach churns. She feels weirdly elated and nauseated. As she continues, the feeling veers more solidly into nausea. She ignores it all the way to Barham and the morning traffic. Finally, the feeling swells in a way she can't ignore, and she jerks the wheel, swerving across a lane of traffic into a neighborhood. Halfway down the block, she throws the car into park, jumps out, and promptly pukes into the flower bed of a sprawling Spanish-style mansion.

Z107.7 FM ONLINE

Yucca Valley resident Cole Martin is recovering at home after his Sept. 30 hospitalization for heatstroke. Martin is one of three hikers and climbers who have recently been hospitalized due to medical emergencies arising from the heat wave still hitting the Morongo Basin. Joshua Tree National Park rangers are calling this the most dangerous autumn in the last decade in the high desert for heat-related injuries, urging residents to stay home in a bulletin released earlier this week.

Martin's family organized a GoFundMe page for his medical bills following his hospitalization last Saturday. With the help of friends, family, and 107.7 FM listeners, the donation goal was reached in just two days. Cole Martin sent a statement to those who donated, republished here:

I want to thank everyone who has helped my family during this time. I'm profoundly grateful that so many strangers and well-wishers have stepped up, especially from our desert community. I also want to send special thanks to

Viv Klein, the woman who saved me. Without her, I wouldn't be here today. I was afraid I wouldn't ever find out the name of my good Samaritan, but luckily, I have, and I want to shout it from the hilltops. Thank you, Viv Klein! I was able to contact Viv, and it turns out on top of saving my life, she also saved my lucky Cardinals baseball cap. Let's hope that bodes well for the playoffs.

Turns out my savior is also a photographer. She took a photo of the place I collapsed by Lost Horse Mine. I want to share that with you over on my GoFundMe page, as a reminder of what can happen if you don't treat nature with the respect and caution she deserves. Stay safe out there.

The heat advisory in Twentynine Palms remains in place. For more information about the heat wave and what you can do to stay safe, visit our homepage.

ABBY

Abby stands in the kitchen barefoot, letting the early morning chill soak into her soles as she fills the French press. Isaac had lit the yahrzeit candle last night at sundown, evidently, because it is sitting in the middle of the counter, burning away. Abby hadn't even stopped in the kitchen when she had finally made it home past eleven last night. It embarrassed her to say it, but she hadn't even remembered to pick up a candle. It had been vaguely in the back of her mind that the anniversary of Abuela's death was imminent, but she kept pushing that thought away. He must have done that as well—buy the candle. He must have gone to the store for that express purpose. He definitely wouldn't ever go to help restock the kitchen. Despite how little he cared about convention or tradition, lighting the yahrzeit was one thing he would never miss.

A wave of appreciation for her brother washes over her. Abby watches the candle's warm yellow flickering over the countertops. Soon, it is overwhelmed by the sunrise, the harsh white light of morning gleaming off the stainless-steel appliances. Another Wednesday. This one just feels a little heavier. She stretches as the water heats, her morning routine, one ear always listening to make sure she grabs the pot off the stove before it starts to boil. The ritual is ingrained so deeply she hardly has to think.

At first, she felt odd in the house, like she was too small for all this echoing space. Now, it finally feels like it fits—almost.

A door slams, and Abby can hear Isaac humming to himself, endearingly out of tune, as the shower turns on. She pours two mugs of coffee, leaving one on the counter as she exits the kitchen. In a moment of generosity, she puts a chocolate croissant in the toaster oven as she leaves. Since Isaac moved in a week and a half ago, she's barely seen him. Still, he makes his presence known through his endless singing and clothes left on random pieces of furniture. It's not bad, having him here. Not this time of year. It's worth a pair of dirty boxers on the couch to feel like the house is inhabited by more than ghosts, Abby shuffling among the memories. It makes sense that the house feels particularly full of ghosts today.

As Abby heads outside to check her email on the back porch, she clocks yet another shirt draped on the dining room table. Maybe she could get used to this lifestyle and they could just keep going like this, living together like when they were little kids. Of course, they weren't the only people in the house at that time. But still, maybe they could become that strange, eccentric adult brother and sister who live together and everyone whispers about.

Decades could go by and they could grow old in the house. People would certainly talk: Were they incestuous? Why couldn't they fly the coop and make lives of their own? She and Isaac could laugh about it over a bottle of wine—laugh at the idiocy of all those people who don't understand how hard it is to find a person who can sit with you in your silence. Isaac would call them dumb people who can never shut up long enough to get scared of themselves.

Abby sighs and opens her laptop. The little, circular ceramic table that takes up most of the back porch is cool to the touch in the early morning. This is what she needs, a bit of fresh air to clear out the pipe dreams. Isaac will move on. He always finds his feet again and sets off on some new, shiny, idealistic plan to hitchhike the country or sail to Alaska. She wants him to keep chasing the sun. If anyone understands that he has to do what he can to stay sane, it's her. The clinginess she is feeling isn't fully about him, anyway; it's about holding on to what she can of the past. Isaac has always been rock-solid and real, dirty boxers and all.

Nothing to ground oneself in the present like fifty new emails to parse through. A few dreadfully tedious reply all-s later, Abby finds her coffee mug empty and her schedule filling up. With the film festival piece in for edits, everything in her inbox seems to be about the next small-scale arts event that needs coverage: a stand-up comedy festival in the San Fernando Valley. Abby gets up, shakes out her stiffened limbs, and heads back inside for more coffee.

Isaac sits at the kitchen counter, holding the remnants of the chocolate croissant in one hand. Abby tries not to focus on the crumbs she knows are covering the floor. Gordita is doing her part to make quick work of them. He turns his tousled head toward her, raising the croissant in acknowledgment. "Thanks for the sustenance," he says through a mouthful of pastry. Abby shakes her head, fills up her coffee mug.

"Thank you for getting the yahrzeit candle. I completely forgot last night, I got in so late."

"Of course. Abuela would be super pissed if we didn't light a candle. She always said that was the best part of her son marrying a Jew—twice the holidays."

"This isn't exactly a holiday." Abby turns to leave the kitchen.

"No, but it's a day to remember and honor her. She would have been obsessed that she gets this as well as Dia de los Muertos. Damn, that woman loved to be the center of attention." Isaac smiles wryly at Abby, pats the stool next to him. "Sit down for a second before you go back to all your important Lois Lane work."

Abby joins him, and they both look at the candle in silence. Isaac, croissant gone, picks up Gordita. He always has to do something with his hands. The dog immediately tries to drink from his coffee mug, something that he only stops when Abby glares at him. "No, no, mi perrito." Gordita obeys him, licking his face instead.

"I haven't seen much of you since I started crashing here. Busy with whatever vague 'important story' you were telling Mom about?"

Abby frowns, starts to speak, but he lifts one hand.

"I'm not saying you shouldn't have made something up to get her off your back. But you should've made up a few more details than you did. You didn't really provide anything for her to sink her teeth into."

"I *am* working on something, and I was telling the truth that I don't have many details I can share right now. Not everything is an elaborate ruse to placate Mom."

"Nothing everything, just most things. Okay. Well, tell me more about this 'thing' you're working on, then. If you do, I'll tell you where I'm planning on going next, and I'll even leave a number to contact in case of emergencies this time." His words hang in the air between them, souring.

"You're leaving your cell phone behind again? How stupid are you, Isaac? I'll buy the fucking satellite phone for you if there isn't cell service—I told you that." Abby stands up, scraping the stool back under the counter. At the high-pitched sound, Gordita jumps down from Isaac's lap. It's a well-worn argument with little left to say and even less that can possibly change. Still, Abby feels like she has to play the part, try and be the voice of reason that Isaac despises so much.

Abby gestures at the candle wavering in the sunlight. "I don't want to light two of these, you dipshit." Isaac puts his head down on the counter, one eye up, the other smushed against the granite. She wonders if she'll ever get so tired of being the big sister, the with-it firstborn, that she'll stop harassing him. She doubts it.

"It was mostly a joke, okay? I'm not going anywhere anytime soon. If you must know, I have had my heart torn out of my body and put through a wood chipper and there is nothing left of it. I broke my own oath to never get serious about a woman, and it bit me in the ass. Me being here, in your kitchen, is what one might call a moping period, a rebounding era, me running home with my tail between my legs. Let me be a sad, dejected reminder to you to never break your promises to yourself."

He peers up at her. Abby looks down at him, the anger slow to diffuse. He has scared her enough times with his flagrant disregard for his own life that his self-deprecating humor takes a while to soak in. He groans and picks himself. His eyes are wet. Her chest goes tight. Her brother isn't much for emotions—feeling them or showing them. She, on the other hand, is what he would call a sucker. She can tell these tears aren't alligator, though. He's wounded. She forces a smile.

"I don't think crying matches your carefree aesthetic. Come on, let's go for a walk. Gordita loves it when you walk her because you're so terrible at it." Abby pulls Isaac up.

He pats Gordita on the head. "You're the only good woman."

Outside, the sun is quickly heating up the pavement. The air doesn't stay cutting for long in balmy LA. Isaac ambles aimlessly with Gordita, who pulls at the leash in all directions, taking advantage of his distraction to dig at every flowerbed they pass. Abby lets them set the pace.

"Do you want to talk about what happened?"

"Does that sound like me? No." Isaac turns a corner onto San Vicente, bustling with morning traffic.

"All right, so you want to hear about what I brought up to Mom? The story?"

"Sure. You've been acting pretty weird about it. What is it, a sex cult or something?

Because if you need an undercover operative, I am willing to volunteer."

Abby smiles. Nothing can take Isaac's humor from him. They pause at a stop light. Abby isn't sure how to begin.

"You heard about that photographer who took a picture of a dead body, and it ended up helping the police solve the case?"

The light turns and they hustle across the wide road to the neighborhood opposite. Isaac actually pays attention to Gordita for once, keeping her on a tight leash.

"Uh, sure. I read something about it. I think in your paper. Wait, am I being an asshole? Did you write about it?"

"No. Well, before the photo was used in the criminal investigation, I was writing a culture piece on what happened and the reaction. I met with the photographer, Viv Klein. The interview didn't go well. She figured out that I hadn't actually seen her photo."

They reach a quieter street, lined with bungalow-style apartment buildings. Gordita avidly works to unearth some hydrangeas. Abby takes the leash from Isaac and pulls her away.

"Abby didn't do her homework? That doesn't sound like you."

Abby turns around, starts heading in the direction of home. Walks with Isaac are always short; the dog always adopts his devil-may-care attitude and becomes unmanageable. At least Gordita pulling on the leash gives her the excuse to avoid his gaze.

"I think I'm so burned out that I'm getting circumspect in my job, if you really want to know. I thought the picture would upset me, and that I could bullshit my way through another piece without seeing it. I was wrong. She saw right through me."

"You always wanted to be a journalist so badly and now that you are, you don't seem very happy. Not that I think Mom would ever have called *you* the happy one. But you seem even less happy than before, when you were in school." It seems like there's more he wants to say, but he stops.

"Yes." She doesn't know what else to say.

They walk most of the way back in silence, Isaac trailing behind. Occasionally, he hums a few bars of off-key rock music. As they turn up the walkway home, Isaac seems to remember that the conversation isn't finished.

"So, the story didn't happen, then? Because of the photo?" He almost seems relieved, which confuses Abby. "See, sometimes I do actually listen to what you're saying."

"No. But that's because it was reassigned after the criminal investigation came to light. But I went and spoke with the photographer again, after I looked at the photo. It's kind of disturbingly beautiful, Isaac. Definitely the kind of thing you would enjoy. I think I even see why she took it. So, I feel like there's something there, a story about what led her to take that photo. Her side of what has happened since then. But I haven't pitched it to the paper yet."

Abby unlocks the door and they step inside. Isaac lingers in the doorway, kicking off his shoes.

"Why?" he asks absentmindedly, fiddling with his socks. Abby kicks him softly with her bare foot. He barely glances at her, focusing on readjusting his pant leg. His mood seems muted, dampened by concern.

"Why are you being so odd about this?" she asks.

He stands up abruptly, peers at Abby like he is divining some vital information. "You brought this up a while ago to Mom, but you haven't pitched it to the paper. You're being cagey about it. I'm just worried you're getting a bit . . . obsessive again."

The world falls away around her, and she can feel her cheeks turning red. "That's absolutely not what this is." She turns quickly and marches to her room, slamming the door behind her like a disgruntled teenager. It's amazing how quickly she could fall back into mortifying patterns with Isaac. He said something that embarrassed her, so she fled. There were a couple of years he only referred to her as Jackrabbit, until she kneed him so hard in the nuts he still swears he saw God despite being an atheist. She misses the days when physical violence could resolve issues between them. Now, he's in the other room, certain that her reaction confirmed his concerns.

Of course, this is not like the Harvard-Westlake situation. Not at all. That was an unfortunate circumstance based entirely on time and place and could never be repeated in any way. Abby sinks onto the bed, picking at her fingernails. A nasty, old habit that resurfaces whenever her guilt does. That's the problem: She still feels guilty. Years of therapy and still she knows deep down that it's her fault, what happened. Guilt and shame instead of indignation and rage. That's why something like that will never happen again.

The image of Stacey's lips curled into a playful smile floats into Abby's head unbidden. No. Not Stacey. Mrs. Fern. That was the first sign—that she, a teacher, let her sixteen-year-old students call her by her first name. Innocuous by itself, but a warning that boundaries had always been blurry for Mrs. Fern. What personal beliefs to espouse or not espouse in AP American History. What to confide in students about. What to do with students after hours.

Abby can still remember so clearly going to meet with Mrs. Fern to discuss her article on sexism within the teaching staff. Most of the students were gone; it was late afternoon and the hallways were eerily quiet. Abby had been alone in the library for hours. The prized two-thousand-word document rested heavily in the flash drive in her pocket. It was her big piece—what she was most proud of to date. She was almost finished, just needed some clarification on Mrs. Fern's damning quotes, which Abby was sure were going to bring the administration to their knees. She envisioned a massive structural change, being lauded as the feminist icon who saved Harvard-Westlake. Sometimes, she still fantasizes about what the article would have done, if it had been published.

Instead, she looked through the door window, and all those hopes and dreams crumbled in an instant. She knew, instantaneously, that the article, which rested so heavily on Stacey's testimony, would never be published. Horribly, the first feeling that seared through her body as she stepped back from the door was jealousy. Then, horror at that jealousy. Then, she didn't feel much at all and found herself crying in the second-floor girl's bathroom for the better part of the next hour.

The image of Dylan Wylock—seventeen years old, a gangly center midfielder who Abby mainly remembered for always bragging about his ape index—on his knees in front of Stacey, head obscured somewhere in the folds of her dress, would never leave her brain. Worse was the image of Stacey herself, perched on the edge of her desk, legs wide open, leaning back on her hands, triceps in stark relief as she braced herself, head thrown back. Her lips parted in a confusing, infuriating way that sent blood racing places that made no sense to Abby.

She confronted Stacey the next day. She tried to stay hard and logistical, to come across as understanding of the complications of the adult world, but also unswerving in what needed to happen. Instead, she immediately started weeping, begging Stacey to stop seeing Dylan Wylock for the sake of Mr. Fern, who Abby remembers as a middle-aged, balding algebra teacher with little charm and less intellect. When Abby left, she admonished herself for sounding like some kind of wounded lover. She was ridiculous, a farce. Of course, the article had to be placed on the back burner until this was all settled. Of that, both Abby and Stacey were sure.

The next month went by in tense agony. Stacey seemed to sense something about Abby that she herself couldn't put a finger on, and the tone of their afternoon tutoring sessions changed, almost imperceptibly at first. A brush of her hand as Stacey passed a paper back to Abby, a hand on the back as she leaned over Abby's shoulder to look at what she was writing. Somewhere, in the back of her mind, Abby understood she was being led somewhere, but she couldn't seem to stop the slow progression down that path. Then, finally, it was stopped for her.

Stacey had not taken Abby's discovery as a call for greater restraint in her rendezvous with Dylan Wylock. Nor had she lessened the frequency with which she asked the teenaged boy to meet her after hours at school. It was only a matter of time before someone who didn't idolize her, as Abby did, found out what was happening. From there, action was swift. Dylan Wylock's parents decided not to press charges so long as Mrs. Fern was fired immediately. Dylan had pleaded with them that no one could know what had happened. Sadly, he was a teenager, and while he had been coerced and preyed upon by an adult, none of his fellow soccer teammates were going to see it that way.

So, without any fanfare, one day, Stacey was just gone. Mr. Fern served out the rest of the term before leaving the school, too. It was then, when he told the class he was moving to Colorado, that Abby got the idea for the *new* piece—a scathing investigation into what made a teacher seduce a student. Of course, no one was going to give her the go-ahead to write such a piece, especially as it required interviewing Mrs. Fern to obtain the teacher's perspective, but Abby got it into her head that this was how she could rectify the situation. She had known what was happening and did nothing. She was therefore *implicated* in the wrongdoing.

Abby didn't let herself acknowledge that she also missed Stacey. Very much. And she wanted to speak with her again. She couldn't accept that Stacey was a bad person, that she could have coerced a minor into a sexual relationship in order to maintain his grade point average. That maybe Abby herself had been placated, rewarded for not telling, with increasingly flirtatious behavior. That, especially, could not be true. Her relationship with Stacey couldn't be categorized in such a gauche way.

So, Abby showed up on Stacey's doorstep, notebook in hand, a tiny tape recorder at her hip. When Stacey opened the door, she looked at Abby. Like she was a stranger—worse than that, even. Like she was an unwanted telemarketer. Stacey had said six words: "You'll get me in trouble, Abby." Spat them with venom before closing the door in Abby's face. Abby made it a block away before collapsing on the curb, hands shaking. She called Isaac to pick her up, making him promise he wouldn't tell their mother where he had found her.

If only that were the end. But it wasn't. Abby kept tabs on Stacey Fern for years. In her mind, she always told herself she would find a way to write a piece about what had happened. It fluctuated between whether she would exculpate the woman or damn her. Isaac saw the Google alert set up on her phone a couple of years later and flipped out. He made her delete it. He had known Dylan Wylock marginally and saw the damage caused to both him and Abby. After that, slowly, the whole episode faded into the background.

Over the years, though, whenever Abby seemed particularly invested in a story or passionate about exploring the psyche of a subject, Isaac would worry she was headed down a similarly obsessive path. Especially if that subject was a woman—something she repeatedly cried homophobia about. Isaac maintained it had nothing to do with her sexuality and everything to do with her obsessive nature and need for people to be heroes. He insisted that she couldn't stand that everyday, flawed reality of anyone she admired, himself included.

Sometimes she suspects he's wiser about her than she would like. When she's especially vulnerable, she worries that she never truly pursued investigative journalism—despite her professed goal—because she can't handle the depths of cruelty that can exist within people. She saw it in Stacey and still can't compute it. Doesn't want to compute it. There were markers of that cruelty of the soul in her father, in the boys that used to beat up Isaac after school. She runs from it every time, searching instead for some portent of light in the darkness. Some assurance that someone is good in the midst of all that bad. And yes, sometimes she deifies people in order to make sense of the madness.

But this? Studying Viv Klein? This is nothing like what happened at Harvard-Westlake. For one, Viv Klein isn't some kind of predator that has Abby under her spell. Yes, Abby is intrigued by her in more than just a journalistic sense. But there's nothing wrong with finding a subject attractive. If anything, being intrigued by a subject just makes the whole experience of writing about them more pleasurable. And she knows that Viv Klein is no hero—she knew that well before she even met her.

In an effort to prove to herself how aboveboard this whole endeavor is, Abby whips out her phone and dashes off an email to her editor, asking to pitch an opinion piece on Viv Klein. There, it isn't some kind of nefarious secret. She just didn't know the direction of the piece and so waited till she was able to formulate some kind of through line. She had gotten a Google alert over the weekend about Viv Klein saving a hiker out in Joshua Tree. With that and the Elmes murder case, there's enough to write a piece about Viv as an inadvertent good Samaritan. Not all Google alerts are signs of unfettered obsession.

In fact, maybe she should go tell that to Isaac right now. It's not his job to take care of her, anyway. That's what she's been doing for him for years. Her phone buzzes and Abby lets out a humorless chuckle. A text from Viv Klein. Spooky how the universe works.

When do you want to talk again?

VIV

The mistake was mailing Cole his hat back. Or, arguably, the mistake was taking the hat in the first place and therefore feeling the need to mail it back. Either way, it resulted in an uptick in her name being mentioned again across social media platforms. This time, it's a small uptick. Not many people outside of the immediate Joshua Tree area have actually heard of or read the coverage on Cole Martin's unlikely savior. But some people have, and a couple of Reddit threads were revived. People are commenting again on her old social media posts, but this time, they aren't posting death threats or insults. Her number of followers surged during the period right after the Elmes photo, and a lot of those previous hate followers are now sending her well wishes. People are so fickle.

Everything being said about her now is undeniably positive. Still, Viv doesn't like the feeling of her name being bandied about on the Internet again. For all of her dreams of being a well-known photographer, this is never what she imagined. She feels gross getting credit for doing the right thing in Joshua Tree. She feels even grosser that it somehow validated her character to herself. That feels inexcusable, that she didn't trust herself.

She's been forced to put the gross feelings aside, though, to a certain extent, because the publicity has turned her prospects around. She woke up to a text from D offering her a gig in two days' time at the Echoplex. She tried to seem busy, nonchalant, texting back a calculated hour and a half later with a simple *I'll check my schedule.* She can feel the tide turning. There is a nugget of hope that the storm has been weathered and she can continue on as if nothing ever happened. She can continue to hustle and scrounge and maybe even make a full-time career of photography one day.

Then, a text from David buzzes through. Viv's stomach immediately tightens. After the money transfer went through a few days ago, she hasn't heard from David or anyone else involved in the Hollywood Hills shoot. After expelling the contents of her stomach, Viv drove home and went to sleep, and by the time she woke up, the whole experience felt like a dream. The money in her bank account felt real, though. Very real. Rent wasn't going to be an issue in the immediate future.

She forces herself to look at the text. His message is cryptic, simply asking to talk. For a second, Viv worries that Jeremiah somehow knows she took the print, but the only way he could know would be if there were cameras in the room and someone watched the footage. But then again, that seems completely plausible for someone of Jeremiah's stature and level of paranoia. Viv can feel the onset of an anxiety attack. She presses the call button—no use prolonging the inevitable.

David picks up, sounding distracted and a little annoyed. "Hi, babes. I'm out and about right now, so I don't have long. I just wanted to check in on you after your little adventure?" Loud bass echoes from the other end of the line, and he shouts over it.

Viv jumps to her feet, starts pacing. She never has been able to stay still on a phone call. "It was definitely something I won't forget. Is that it? You just wanted to know how it went? Did Jeremiah say anything?"

"Should he have?" David pauses, and Viv can hear him whispering to someone on his side of the call. "If you're worried he isn't satisfied, don't be. I've seen the photo hanging above his mantel. It inspires a lot of questions, which he seems to love."

Viv allows herself to take a deep breath. "How does he answer the questions?"

"I don't know. Honestly, I wasn't paying too much attention when I was there. Look, it's loud here. I wish I had time for small talk, but I don't. I wanted to see if you were available for a last-minute photo shoot this afternoon?"

Viv stops her incessant pacing. She's uncertain if she's making up the slight rise in the pitch of his voice. "I don't know. I was going to speak with that *LA Times* reporter this afternoon. I also have a shoot in a couple of days I need to prep for."

"Reschedule with the reporter. You're going to want to take this. The money is very good." The dull thud of the bass seems to emphasize his words.

"Fine. You were the one who told me I should try and get a handle on my public image,

but I can reschedule. Maybe. What do I have to do?"

"Show up with a camera and take photos. They don't mind if it's digital. You'll just need to edit there and dump the media cards before you leave." *Thump, thump, thump*. The bass knocks in time with her heart.

"David, what am I taking pictures of?"

"They are fiftieth anniversary photos for the parents of a good friend. A good, high-paying friend." David must have left the space with the loud music, or else it's been turned off. The other side of the line is crisp and quiet now. Eerily so.

"Why do I feel like that isn't the whole story?"

David ignores her. "I'll send the details your way. I'm actually quite the good agent. I've set your price for this kind of work, and they are willing to maintain it, though what they want is a lot less elaborate than last time. Also, there isn't the same kind of *Infinite Jest*–length NDA. Jerry told me how that scared you. Discretion is important, but these are just normal people, Viv. Normal people who would love your help, so rein in the neuroticism. I'm getting in a car. I'll send the details." With that, he's gone.

Viv stands there, the muted whoosh of the traffic below the only sound in the apartment other than her quickened heart. Then, her phone buzzes. The details are sparse. An address, a time, and that figure again: fifteen thousand dollars. She sinks onto the bed, absentmindedly petting Connor and counting the white Teslas that drive by outside. That's always a favorite when her anxiety peaks. There are always so many damn white Teslas. One of the few certainties in life.

One. Two. The money is so good for such a short shoot. Three. Four. Basically, it's four months' pay in one day. Five. Her stomach roils again at the thought of staging more stiff limbs. Six. The image of the body bobbing in the tank seems so physically present in front of her she can't even see the road below. Viv falls back on the bed, eliciting an indignant squeak from the cat. Counting isn't working.

What scares her most is that she already knows what answer she'll give David. She's drawing it out, but she knows the unshakeable curiosity and pull will win in the end. It feels inevitable, like taxes or adult acne sprouting up before an important event. The sound of the doorbell jolts her upright. She checks her watch. She lost track of time plodding through the well-worn arguments in her head. Of course, she forgot to cancel on the journalist.

There's a lurch in her stomach, like cresting a hill while hydroplaning. Meeting with Abby Katz is starting to feel like a mistake again, but she felt so hopeful about the reporter last time. Maybe someone doesn't see her as the villain. Maybe that will help her see herself as something else, as well. She pulls out her phone, stares at it for a second.

Thinking isn't helpful. Viv sends a quick confirmation off to David and straightens herself up hurriedly, flicking on lights as she heads to the door. Abby is dressed in newsroom best, as always, a button-up and carefully pressed chinos, which Connor immediately starts rubbing against. Viv shifts uncomfortably in her ratty jeans—she didn't even think of changing, but now she feels ridiculous standing in her doorway in a chemical-spattered T-shirt. She can just imagine Abby writing some *GQ* style color about her "bohemian disregard for appearance." But then again, this is the *LA Times*. Not a lifestyle magazine. She's just being paranoid, as always.

"Come in."

Abby follows her inside. They sit at the kitchen counter again. This time, Abby accepts a coffee. Viv tries to ground herself in the space, in the moment. "Thanks for meeting me here. I just think better in my own space. Ever since the photo, I haven't felt entirely comfortable in public. I know it's ridiculous to think anyone recognizes me, but it seems unbearable that someone could."

"It's not so ridiculous when you keep ending up in the news. Speaking of which, I'd love to start by talking about what happened in Joshua Tree. Would that be okay?" Abby has her phone out on the counter, ready to record. Viv checks the time.

"Sure. But, I'm sorry, I don't really have much time today now. Something came up last-minute. I should have rescheduled with you. But yes. We can talk about Joshua Tree. I can give you about thirty minutes."

A look of annoyance mixed with something like disappointment flicks across Abby's face, but then she hits record. "I'll get right to it, then. Let's start with why you were there in the first place." Abby takes a sip of her coffee, looking expectantly at her. She seems more focused on business than last time. For some reason, this frustrates Viv. The banter was distracting, fun even. This is a bit more intimidating.

"I went to Joshua Tree to clear my head and escape everything I was hearing about myself online in the wake of Karen Elmes's death. I turned my phone off and tried to just exist separate from everything waiting for me here. Perhaps that's selfish, to run away like that, but I felt it was what I needed at the time."

Abby nods, waiting to see if Viv will elaborate further. When she doesn't, she asks the next question, "Can you tell me what happened with Cole Martin?"

"I was going for a hike—something I did daily there. The day was very hot, and I noticed a hiker behind me was struggling. He collapsed, so I hurried back to a phone and called for help as quickly as I could. Luckily, he was able to get the assistance he needed. That's all. There were other hikers behind us on the trail. Someone else would have found him and helped if I hadn't. I was just there at the right time, wrong time, whatever you want to call it."

"I think Cole Martin would call it the right time. So, tell me about the photo you took and sent to Mr. Martin after the fact. The one that you showed me last time I was here. You must have gone back to where Mr. Martin collapsed. Why did you do that?" Abby looks at her with careful neutrality.

"I don't fully know why I went back. I was distraught." Viv fiddles with her mug, twisting it back and forth, moving the coffee grounds at the bottom like she can divine some wisdom from the wet patterns they make. "It was the first photo I took since the incident, remember? I told you."

"By the incident, you mean the photo you took of Karen Elmes?" Viv looks up sharply. "I'm sorry, I just have to clarify."

"Yes, that's what I mean."

"And why is that?"

"I think I take photographs to help process moments in my own mind, sometimes," Viv says, surprising herself that she has an answer. She hasn't thought through the photo really at all since Joshua Tree. Like so many photos she takes, it wasn't an active choice; it was like breathing. A sense of something interesting, and then a click. Conscious thought isn't part of it. That's one of her issues.

"Would you say that's what happened with Karen Elmes?"

"I would say that when I find something fascinating, or beautiful, it's hard to resist. I have poor impulse control." Viv looks defiantly at Abby, whose impassive expression doesn't betray what she thinks about Viv's words.

"And you would call Karen Elmes's deceased body beautiful?"

"I would call the photo I took beautiful." Viv rubs her eyes. "Obviously, by putting the photo out there for the world to see, I hurt the family. I caused harm. I regret that."

Abby sits back, draws out the moment before the next question. "Do you regret taking the photo?" This is her pièce de résistance. Viv can tell she's writing the story in her head. Her eyes look hungry. Viv feels the perverse desire not to give her what she wants.

"What I did seems to have really gotten under your skin. You can't let it go. Why are you so interested in me?" Viv pushes the empty mug away from herself, places both hands on the counter. Abby looks nonplussed, but her answer comes out clipped.

"I'm not. If you'd answer my questions, I wouldn't have to keep meeting with you." She gives a slight, involuntary wince.

Viv stands and turns from Abby, carrying the two mugs to the sink. She takes the time to wash them before turning back. She speaks clearly for the voice recording. "I don't regret taking the photo at all." Viv pauses to let that sink in. She feels disappointed. This isn't how this interview was supposed to go. The reporter was supposed to illuminate something for her, or at least distract her. "I'm done with the interview. You can either make something of what I've said or not. I leave that to you and your journalistic faculties. I need to get ready now for a shoot. Let me know if you end up publishing something, if you don't mind. I'd prefer to have some forewarning next time I'm in the news. But for now, I think we're done."

Abby stops the recording and gathers her things—a notepad and pen she hasn't touched—while Viv busies herself pulling camera gak out of various cabinets. Viv could cry from frustration, which both embarrasses and angers her. Abby is almost to the door before Viv puts down a tripod and turns to her. "That is, unless you want to see something you will definitely find interesting."

ABBY

It'd been a while since she last came to Pasadena. The wide, well-land-scaped streets winding through quiet residential neighborhoods remind her of high school and visiting friends on the Eastside, which always felt like a million miles away. Viv parks under an oak tree on the corner of yet another deserted intersection. A lone peacock struts diagonally across the street, feathers fanned out behind him, unperturbed. He stretches taller as he reaches the other sidewalk, looking behind him with beady eyes. Abby looks away.

The drive was mostly silent. Viv had been cryptic about what exactly Abby would be observing—just that she would have to sign an NDA and it was better if no one knew she worked for the *LA Times*. Viv said she would introduce her as her assistant. Though Abby protested she didn't know anything about photography, Viv maintained it was nonnegotiable. Then, she turned on NPR at a piercing volume. Abby, uncertain of what to do, spent the rest of the drive looking up photography terms online.

Now, Viv pulls cases out of her trunk and doesn't turn to Abby until the trunk is closed. She looks nervous, like she's second-guessing bring-ing Abby along, which is exactly what Abby is doing, as well. Her curios-ity led her accept the invite, but Viv's agitation disconcerts her. She isn't supposed to mention that she works for the *LA Times*? What does that mean? That this is something illegal, something compromising? She can call a car and bail right now. Then, the only thing hurt would be her pride. She can picture the look in the photographer's eyes, judging her for running away instead of staying to see . . . whatever it is. The weak journalist, who wouldn't look at the photo, who wouldn't stay because she got scared. She curses herself for always caring so much about appearances. What does it matter what Viv Klein thinks of her?

"This job is a lot of money for me. Nothing can go wrong. Your part will be pretty easy. I'll ask you to bring me something or set up a stand. It's okay if you're slow. We aren't telling them you're a *good* assistant." Viv shoots her a quick, nervous smile.

"If this job is so important, maybe I shouldn't be here. I don't know anything about what you do."

"No, you don't," Viv concedes. "I don't really know what I was thinking, asking you to come. I thought you would find it interesting, maybe. You can leave, though, that's fine. This can't even really help with your article." For a second, Viv almost looks scared. Like she doesn't want to be here alone. That, unfortunately, is enough for Abby. She's staying, like the sucker she is. She grabs a couple of cases from Viv, looks around.

"No, I'm interested. I'll try not to impede your work. It'll be good to see you in your element, to write about your process in general. More background always helps me write. Which way is it?" Viv checks her phone and they make their way, clumsily lugging the cases, up a brick path to a Craftsman-style house. As Viv rings the doorbell, she turns to Abby, about to speak. But the door opens abruptly, like someone was waiting on the other side. Abby wonders if they've been watched this whole time. The inside of the house is dim, and the overpowering smell of roses wafts out the open doorway.

The woman leaning against the doorframe looks tired, middle-aged. She's white, with graying blond hair overdue for a touchup. She pushes a pair of cheap readers up on her nose. She looks back and forth between Viv and Abby, obviously not knowing who is the photographer.

She clears her throat. "I was only expecting one of you. David told me you worked alone." Her hand protectively clenches the door, which she holds mostly closed behind herself.

Viv nods, but before she can respond, Abby takes a slight step forward, holding out her hand, which the woman hesitantly takes. "I'm Abby Clark, Viv's assistant. We felt things would go smoother today if Viv had a bit of help. I know this is very important to you, so we want to make sure everything runs as efficiently as possible." She looks over at Viv, frowns. "I called David and let him know things had changed. I'm sorry he didn't inform you." When she goes full bullshitter mode, it's hard to rein herself in.

Viv peers at Abby for a split second with an indiscernible look, then turns to the woman in the doorway. "I know you're having to deal with a lot right now. I promise, with both of us here, things are going to go very smoothly. Now, I want to start by saying I am so sorry for your loss."

The woman lets go of the door, letting it swing open behind her. "Right, well. Thank you. We should get started." She turns and heads back into the dim house. As an afterthought, she calls over her shoulder, "I'm Carolyn. My mother will want to talk to you before we get started."

Abby and Viv follow her inside, shutting the door. Without the draft of outside air, it's stifling in the dim hallway. Carolyn leads them to a stuffy family room, which smells even more suffocatingly of roses. She pulls back a couple of dusty curtains and the room falls into a dull half light. On the sideboard is a piece of paper and a pen. Carolyn gestures to it before heading to an old desktop computer in the corner. "I only printed one. Give me a minute."

As Carolyn starts up a loud, boxy printer next to the desktop, Viv reads over the NDA. Without looking at Abby, she hands it to her. It's one page—probably the first result online for an NDA template. The verbiage is simple, relatively nondescript. Basically, by signing it, Abby forgoes her right to speak about anything said or seen within the house.

After both Viv and Abby sign the NDA, Carolyn leaves them on the pastel couch, promising her mother will be in momentarily. The house is silent, the only sound the squeaking of the couch as they shift on the vinyl furniture cover. The furniture is old, out-of-date, as is the computer and the TV set into the bookshelf across the room. There is a sense of money, though, to the décor. The shelves are full of knickknacks from various countries, the walls covered with paintings. Abby is almost certain that the large piece next to the door is a Hockney.

Heels clack on marble, and a woman in her early seventies appears in the doorway, leaning on a cane. She is much more put together than Carolyn, sporting a lavender blazer and dress pants. She has foregone dying her hair, instead styling her gray curls into an impeccable short bob. Her high, arched eyebrows match those of her daughter, though. The resemblance is undeniable. Viv stands, and Abby follows her cue.

"Sit." The woman's voice is fragile, small. It doesn't match her appearance at all. She joins Viv and Abby, sinking slowly onto a chair facing the couch. Her eyes are disconcertingly clear, like they should be set in a much younger face. She takes her time looking over both of the women in front of her. She leans back in her chair, tapping her cane on the floor. "I met my husband when I was twenty-one. I was older than a lot of my friends when they got married; not everyone waited to finish college. But I was determined to get my degree, and I didn't give many men the time of day. Meeting Ollie was a fluke. He walked into the restaurant where I was serving part-time and that was it. We were married three months later.

"It was Ollie's second marriage, something my Catholic mama hated. But we were in love and didn't care what anyone thought of that. Or the age difference. Fifteen years wasn't that much, back then, though. People didn't see it the way they do now. I liked it, how much more he knew about life than I did. He taught me so much. I hadn't even been outside of San Francisco. He showed me the world. And, whatever they thought, we had almost fifty good years together. Next week would have been our golden anniversary. Are either of you girls married?"

Viv shakes her head. "No. I can't imagine being with someone that long. I'm so sorry you didn't make it to your anniversary." The woman raises her hand dismissively.

"A week is a week, my dear. I don't need to make it to any milestone to prove how well I knew my Ollie, or how strong our love is. The only reason it makes me mad is that he loved parties so much. When it became obvious that he wasn't going to make it, I promised him we would celebrate anyway. That's what I want." She stares hard at Viv, then at Abby. "I want it to feel like a celebration." Abby works hard to keep her face neutral as she attempts to decipher the woman's words.

"We felt the time might come last night, and so we dressed him in his finest. He left this world in perfectly tailored Armani. And I'm not my mama—I don't believe in any other life than this. Ollie's gone. But he left *well*. And now, we're going to celebrate."

A rough sense of what is happening begins to formulate in Abby's mind, but it isn't until the woman leads them into the dining room that it all fully clicks into place. The room is as dimly lit as the rest of the house. The smell is overpowering, rose petals strewn everywhere—the floor, across the dining room table, on the sideboards. There is the form of a man reclining at the head of the table. It looks as if he simply fell asleep at dinner. In the faint light, it's hard to make out his face. The woman clacks slowly across the floor and rests her hand on his shoulder. "When you are ready, you can have Carolyn call for me. I'm going to go lie down." She exits through a door on the far side of the room, behind the man.

Abby waits for Viv to meet her gaze. She refuses to look surprised, disturbed, any of the myriad emotions flashing through her mind. She feels that Viv wanted to shock her a little, and she doesn't want to give her that. "Well, this is definitely interesting. You've done this before?"

"Once." Viv looks away, almost shyly. "Let's see if we can find the overheads. I can't see at all to set up." Abby searches the wall by the door for a switch, and the room flicks into light. Viv is already moving her cases into the dining room, unlatching them and pulling different bits and pieces out. Abby avoids looking at the table and the man on the other side of the room. The rose scent is making her dizzy.

Viv puts her to work quickly, setting up stands for LED lights to supplement the giant chandelier above the table. Viv screws the lights onto the stands, uses some kind of device to match the color temperature of her lights to that of the chandelier. She explains what she's doing briefly as she moves, but mostly it goes over Abby's head. Soon, the room is transformed into a bright, but somehow still shaped, space. It feels almost romantic, homey.

Viv works deftly, calling to Abby in a clipped tone to bring her a case, plug something into the wall. When she does look at Abby, her mind is clearly elsewhere. Like she's seeing the space as she wants it, not as it currently is. She improvises well, moving chairs to elongate the space, pulling curtains to add a bit of negative fill on one side of the table. That is one term Abby retained from the quick Google photography crash course in the car: negative fill. If Viv would slow down enough for Abby to speak to her, she would try and slip the term in, show that she understood some of what was happening. But Viv doesn't slow down.

Abby makes mental notes on Viv's style of work—frenetic yet focused, single-minded. Her movements adroit, assured. The space became hers as soon as the older woman left, and she's confidently shaped it into something special. She is skilled at lighting. That's something Abby didn't know from Viv's street photography. She ignorantly chalked those photos up to interesting framing and the right timing to capture the natural light. But Viv is not only good at finding interesting lighting, she can mold that light herself. It's like watching a painter, but Viv's canvas is the three-dimensional space in front of her. Enthralled, Abby works hard to keep up.

Finally, the space seems set to Viv's liking, and now there is only the subject to deal with. Viv straightens, looks uncomfortable. Abby watches from a distance as she approaches the end of the table. For the first time, Abby gets a clear view of the man. She tenses a little as she realizes his eyes are open. He looks small in his black Armani suit, leaning back against the tall head chair. A couple wisps of white hair are plastered down on top of his head. Viv holds her fist up in front of his face.

For a moment, Abby worries she's about to punch the body. Instead, Viv looks at her hand in the light, moving it this way and that, and then she turns around to look at her light sources. Abby must not look right, because Viv stops, frowning. "Are you okay? You can step out if you need to." Viv herself looks a little ill, but she seems determined to mask it. Abby shakes her head, which is starting to pound from the all-encompassing smell of the roses. "All right, we're ready for Carolyn."

Abby finds Carolyn in the kitchen, smoking. She didn't peg the disheveled woman as a smoker, and maybe she isn't usually. The cigarette looks funny in her hand. Carolyn surveys the dining room once, gaze fluttering quickly past the table. Then, without a word, she disappears down another dark hallway. A moment later, the already familiar clack of the older woman's shoes can be heard approaching. Abby realizes she still doesn't know her name.

She appears in the doorway, holding a box of party balloons, which she promptly hands to Abby, looking around the room in appreciative silence. "This is getting there. If you don't mind, I think the balloons will make the whole thing a bit more festive." Abby gets to blowing.

In the box, along with about thirty party balloons, is a large bag of confetti. While Abby inflates the balloons and places them around the room, Viv is in deep, quiet discussion with the woman near the head of the table. Abby tries to listen in but can't hear anything over her own breath and the rubbery squeak of the latex as she ties the balloons off, one by one. By the time all the balloons are placed, the woman is seated on the arm of the man's chair. Viv fiddles with her camera settings. The woman has turned the chair slightly and angled herself so it appears like she and the man are turning in toward each other. Abby can't see how, but the man has been propped up straighter in his chair. A wine glass has been placed in front of him, where his hands rest on the table. The woman holds one of his hands, a wine glass in her other.

The most surprising touch is the sparkly gold party hat that has been perched atop his head. The woman wears a matching one. With their formal attire, it looks to Abby as if the couple has been caught seconds before midnight at a fashionable New Year's Eve party. There's really only one problem: He still looks dead.

"All right, we can start with the confetti, and when we run out, we can try some other poses. I was thinking we could try cheering with the wine glass for the confetti falling? Does that work for you, Cynthia?" The woman nods from her perch on the man's chair. So, her name is Cynthia.

Viv puts her camera down and walks over to Abby. She didn't even realize she'd stepped back into the shadows in the corner.

"How are you doing?" Viv looks at her—actually looks—for the first time since they started setting up. Abby isn't sure how she appears to Viv, but it must not be good, because she looks concerned.

"I'm fine. The rose smell is just a lot. What can I do?" All of it is a lot, but the smell really is what's too much in the moment. After the initial discomfort of being in the room with Ollie's body, she sort of forgot he was here.

Watching Viv work is interesting. Seeing how this could possibly come together in a non-horrifying way is interesting. Yes, it's unconventional, but Cynthia wants this. It seems like part of her strange grieving process. But, then again, all grieving processes are a little strange. Abby didn't eat dulce de leche ice cream from the shack on the corner by her house for five years after Abuela died, because she couldn't stand to be reminded of her favorite flavor. This is, of course, a bit more unusual. But, truthfully, it doesn't feel outside the realm of understandable to Abby. Not when she looks at Cynthia's small smile. Viv explains to her exactly how to throw the confetti right outside of the frame, and Abby takes her position.

There is really only enough confetti to supply three rounds of double-fisted throwing. Each time, Viv clicks away on her camera rapidly, taking a series of photos as the confetti rains down. The first two throws,

Cynthia raises her wine glass, turning to look at Ollie, whose eyes look out unfocused over the dinner table. After each, Cynthia downs her wine glass and pours another one. It looks stilted, not at all like the celebration Cynthia professed to want to throw.

Viv sets her camera down, going to Cynthia's side. She speaks to her in a quiet, respectful tone that is unlike anything Abby has heard from Viv before. "That was great. How about we try something else for the last one? Whatever you want. Whatever feels celebratory to you."

Abby takes her place and throws one last round of confetti. As the paper begins to fall, swirling down around the chandelier to join the multicolored array already spread across the dining room table, Cynthia throws an arm around Ollie and leans in for a kiss. She approaches him slowly, tenderly, from an angle that almost makes it look like his eyes are focused on her. Viv pivots in tandem, leaning around the side of the table to get Cynthia and Ollie more in profile. As the last paper flutters to the table, Cynthia pulls back.

"Wonderful." Viv puts her camera down. She sounds moved. "Let's try something else."

The shoot goes quickly, Cynthia dutifully following Viv's directions. Within half an hour, Viv seems satisfied. They keep shooting for another fifteen minutes for Cynthia's benefit. Finally, Viv puts her camera down on the table with finality and gives Abby a curt nod.

"Let me see something—whatever you think is the best photo." Cynthia reaches for the camera. Viv hesitates. "I know they aren't edited. I don't care. Show me." Abby silently looks over Cynthia's shoulder as Viv flips through the photos on the camera's tiny LCD screen. She stops at a photo from the beginning, with the confetti falling. Ollie and Cynthia are in profile, her lips an inch from his.

Both of their party hats gleam in the chandelier's glow, while confetti floats out of focus in front of them, obscuring parts of their faces, but not all. Cynthia's eyes, full of joy and love, are trained on Ollie. His eyes are covered by a piece of confetti, but his mouth almost looks like it's pulled into a smile. It looks like a candid photo taken during a raging party. A private moment between two lovers. Cynthia lets out a deep, painful sigh. "Well, that is really quite beautiful. Thank you. You have a good eye. Ollie looks very handsome." She takes another long glance at the photo, then turns the camera off. "You can get going now."

Viv takes the camera back from Cynthia gingerly. "What about the editing of the photos? Don't you want me to do that here?"

Cynthia pours herself another glass of wine. "Just pack up and leave, dear. I don't need the photos edited. You can leave the cards here—Carolyn will pay you for them."

Viv hesitates. "I always edit my own photos. It isn't my work unless I see the process through from beginning to end. I really don't feel comfortable leaving you raw images, for your sake as well as mine. Please, let me edit them for you. It's part of my fee."

Cynthia turns slowly around, wine glass in one hand. "No one will ever see these photos. I got what I wanted—a celebration, a photo shoot, a moment to commemorate fifty years with this man. I don't need edited editions, as lovely as I am sure they would be. You've already given me what I wanted."

Viv looks like she is going to protest, but then she relents. She packs up in silence, leaving Abby to mostly stand by awkwardly as Cynthia drinks down another glass of wine, then another. Eventually, the packed cases are ready to head to the car, and Abby jumps at the opportunity to do something other than wait, eyes trained away from Cynthia and her deceased husband.

Cynthia acts like they don't exist, seated on the arm of Ollie's chair. Occasionally, she murmurs something under her breath. Abby realizes she is talking to him. The cases dwindle down to none, and Carolyn reappears with a check. After a quick exchange with Viv as to the cost of the cards, she writes an amount on the line and hands it over.

Abby and Viv check the room over, preparing to leave. Cynthia takes a small, clear baggie out of her pocket and examines the contents in the light of the chandelier. It's full of white powder, not particularly fine, closer to sea salt in texture than to cocaine. Abby has seen her fair share of party drugs in her day, but this doesn't look quite like any she has seen before. Cynthia scoops it gingerly into her hands and sprinkles it over her wine. She calls over her shoulder. "Carolyn, it's time. You can call the paramedics." Her voice is hoarse but calm.

Carolyn doesn't respond, but the quiet beep of her punching numbers into the home phone can be heard from down the hall. Bizarrely, Abby can smell almonds, even over the rose scent. She stupidly wonders for a second if Cynthia put some kind of almond powder in her wine.

Viv stops in the doorway, placing a memory card on the sideboard. "What is that, in your glass?"

Cynthia gives her a sad, steely smile. "I've had a wonderful celebration. Thank you. I don't think you'll want to have to answer the paramedics' questions when they arrive, so you'd best be off." Cynthia raises her glass to them, then clinks it against the glass in front of Ollie. She hesitates for an infinitesimal moment, then drinks the contents in one gulp. Viv stands frozen in the doorway, her hand still on the memory card. Abby looks from Viv to Cynthia and back again. Time almost seems to have slowed down, but her brain can't keep up.

Cynthia sighs impatiently. She turns her clear, ice-blue eyes on Abby. "Please. Let me be with my husband alone right now. Just go."

Abby turns, not really in control of her own body, and drags Viv out of the room, down the hall. She doesn't let go until they are outside, mercifully free of the scent of roses. Viv seems to come to in the evening air and hurries to the car, Abby close on her heels. Without speaking, Viv flips the ignition. NPR immediately blares from the speakers, Ira Glass shouting at them in soothing tones. Abby slams the volume knob hard, and the radio cuts out.

Viv shifts into drive and slowly heads down the block. Five houses down, she pulls quietly over to the curb and turns off the car again. She watches the empty street through the rearview. Abby understands. They are waiting. The paramedics take a surprisingly long time, but perhaps time isn't moving as it usually does. The women sit without talking, both riveted to the rearview, eyes on the ambulance pulled up in front of the Craftsman. After a while, two Pasadena Police Department marked vehicles arrive and park in front of the ambulance. Three officers enter the house. Viv shifts lower in the driver's seat.

It could have been minutes or hours, but eventually the door to the house opens again and a couple of paramedics come out, lifting a covered gurney down the stairs and wheeling it to the waiting vehicle. Carolyn exits, leaning on the arm of a police officer. It seems the officer is trying to comfort her. Another paramedic ushers Carolyn and the officer to the side, and a second covered gurney is lifted down the stairs.

Two bodies. The answer to the unasked question. Still, Abby and Viv don't move. They wait until the paramedics pull away, no need for sirens. There isn't any rush. Carolyn gets into one of the police vehicles, and they leave, as well. The street is empty other than parked cars. No people in sight. Abby feels a rising urge to get away. She looks at Viv, who, without returning her gaze, turns on the car and accelerates down the street.

The drive back is excruciating, both women sitting in a daze in the rush hour traffic. Viv misses the exit to her apartment and has to go a half mile up the road, fighting her way back through even more traffic to the underground parking garage where Abby left her car. Viv pulls to a stop, unlocks the doors. She still hasn't looked at Abby or said a word. Abby tries to think of what to say. Her mind shuts down, turns to self-preservation.

"There are going to be questions. The police are going to see the photos, and they're going to want to talk to both of us. It's not going to look great for you, after Karen Elmes. You need to get a lawyer."

Viv finally turns her eyes to Abby. She has been crying. She shifts in her seat and pulls something out of her pocket, holding it out in front of Abby. In her palm are two memory cards. "Only if Carolyn mentions us being there. I'm fifty-fifty on whether that will be the case. I don't know if . . . if she knew what was going to happen. I feel like she may have. I'm so sorry I got you involved in this. I swear I didn't know. I don't know why she did that in front of us." Viv's voice cracks, and she stops speaking. She trembles as she shoves the memory cards back into her pocket.

"It isn't your fault. You couldn't have known." Abby hears her voice saying the words, and then is surprised to find she means them. She believes Viv, for some reason. "It's just been a shocking, upsetting day. You should call someone. Don't be alone tonight, okay?"

Abby opens the passenger door, unbuckles her seatbelt. Viv is sitting, looking straight forward, both hands trembling on the wheel. The confidence, the imperceptible glow she had while shooting is completely gone. She looks like a hollowed-out shell. It makes Abby illogically angry, to see her look so dull. She finds herself thinking that beautiful things shouldn't be made to look so decimated. Then, that thought embarrasses her. She shakes her head a little, straightens up.

"Okay?" Abby repeats. Viv's red eyes flick to her, and she nods with a minute jerk of her chin. Abby reaches across the console and grabs one of Viv's hands, pressing it hard to the wheel, steadying it.

"Okay." Abby nods. It feels like something inside her is cracking. She simultaneously feels so numb and so angry and so something else she can't put words to.

Words aren't working. She leans forward, catches Viv's chin with her other hand and turns it toward her. Viv's pupils dilate in surprise, but she doesn't pull away. Abby closes the remaining distance between them. The kiss is quick. Viv smells faintly of roses, still. Before she can really think at all about what she's done, Abby pushes herself out of the vehicle and closes the door.

She hurries to her own car, without looking back. She hears Viv's car pull away as she closes the driver's door. Abby emerges from the underground garage into a faint pastel afterglow. The sun is set, and the street is lit by blurry white and red lights streaming past in both directions. She wipes her eyes, and the lights get slightly less blurry, the traffic more defined. The numbness takes over.She turns left onto Hollywood Boulevard, an hour to go before she can collapse into the safety of her own room. She turns NPR on, raising the volume until she can't hear anything else.

DAVID

The gaudy silk curtains become more and more repugnant as the sun rises behind them. They look like they should be wrapped around Vivien Leigh, not hanging in the home of a man of supposedly good taste. That man's name escapes David for the moment, but he definitely remembers leaving the club with a stocky Hispanic man. David rolls over quietly, observes the sleeping shape beside him. Stocky, yes, but with the bright-red hair and pale, freckled complexion of a Celt. He doesn't look particularly familiar.

David slides out of the bed without a sound, looking for his damned pants. He always flings his clothes everywhere when undressing drunk. Usually, his dates find that amusing. The Celt probably did as well, since there are two defined hickeys on his neck. David finds his pants half behind the armoire, another unnecessarily ornate piece of décor. His shirt is in the living room. Within five minutes, he is dressed and out the door. Outside, he tries to orient himself. Looks like he ended up in the Palisades. Wonderful. The ride back to West Hollywood is going to take forever. He calls a car.

The driver takes him home in merciful silence. David's head is pounding. The sun is glaringly bright, more so than usual, and he must have left his sunglasses at home. Rookie mistake. There was going to be a ride of shame home from somewhere this morning, and he was going to be hungover. Two undeniable truths he knew the night before. Usually he prepared—sunglasses and Pedialyte in his jacket pocket. Actually, they probably are in his jacket pocket. That seems to have disappeared. Damn it. That shit was vintage.

The driver pulls to a stop in front of the apartment complex. It's one of those old stucco buildings where all the second-story apartments are walkups. Getting his king-sized bed up the stairs was almost impossible. It's one of those places where everyone knows everyone and can hear everything through the thin walls and ceilings. During the pandemic, that felt like a blessing at first. David made fast and easy friends and lovers. They tired of him quickly, though. People always do. A shiny toy to be used and thrown away when they find out that what's beneath the hard plastic isn't just a receptacle for their hopes and dreams—it's flesh and marrow and need. That's less sexy, apparently. The place is rent-controlled, though.

Inside, he doesn't bother turning on any lights. He pops an espresso pod in the machine and changes into gym clothes, plugging both his phones in to charge. He sits in the dim light of the kitchen with the tiny cup of caffeine, enjoying the minimalist décor, the muted colors. It's always so comforting to come home to his meticulously crafted space after a night of hedonism.

He never allows anyone to sleep over. In fact, for the most part, he prefers to have no visitors here at all, not even his mother or sister. The last time anyone was inside his place may have been during the Black Lives Matter protests, when he and Viv were going marching together. She sat at the kitchen table and looked at him and really saw him for the first time. For the first time, she realized what it meant for him to be a large Black man. She looked afraid, asked if he thought it wise for them to go out and protest. The police were using tear gas, rubber bullets.

He both hated and loved seeing that fear for him in her eyes. It also made him incredibly angry, that she had the luxury of being able to forget how he was perceived by other people on the street. Sure, that day there were rubber bullets and nightsticks, and she was aware of that tangible danger after it was broadcast on social media, but what about his run every morning? When he walked his ex's pit bull? Even here in LA, it wasn't inconceivable that he would be seen as a threat by some gun-happy patriot and never make it home. Every day. Being large and Black was nothing new to him, and it shouldn't have been for her. She'd been in his life long enough to see how people acted on the street at night when he walked past.

But that's Viv, lost so fully in her own thoughts, in her good intentions, that she never really sees how fragile and ill-made the world around her is. She never sees how much the people in her orbit are hurting unless they shove it in her face. And David isn't one to shove. Not if it means showing a weakness, a fear. And that's what fear is, a weakness that makes it easier to try and get the better of him. That's the best lesson modeling has taught him. He knows what the world is made of, and he refuses to be afraid of it. That makes him strong.

David shakes his head, rolls his shoulders. He's aggravated. His mind keeps drifting to Viv, their contentious relationship. He missed a couple of calls from her last night, but today is about rest and relaxation. It was an incredibly long week of repeated overtime on set with a particularly pretentious French director constantly snapping at him. To top things off, he was fighting with Jerry again. So, he's promised himself that today will be about taking care of himself. Not anyone else. Zero communication. Of course, he can't fully turn off his work phone, but the thought is there. And the intention, any emergency calls notwithstanding.

He hops up, making another espresso and grabbing pen and paper. He's still a bit too nauseated to work out, so he may as well work on his stand-up routine. The paper sits blankly in front of him, an aggressive void staring back at him. He's unpleasantly on edge for no discernible reason. All right, it is discernible, but that doesn't make it any more in his control. Jerry will call or he won't; it's not worth the stress. Perhaps David pushed too far, trying to establish himself as a business partner, not just a plaything. It was a gamble that would pay off, lucratively, or it would end things with the hotshot producer with finality this time. Fine. One less fire to manage. Modeling is enough of a shit show without adding yet another side hustle.

Jerry is too arrogant, anyway. One day, he'll certainly get caught doing something idiotic and criminal, and reality will finally crash down around him. And when that happens, it won't be Jerry feeling the consequences. David doesn't need to be involved in that. He has no compunctions about illegal activity himself, if approached with care, but Jerry has enough money and clout that he's never careful. He collects speeding tickets like baseball cards, flaunts his illicit drugs in public, and treats labor laws like suggestions. He'll always be able to get himself out of most situations—unlike David. That lack of care, that power, is intoxicating, as well as dangerous. Unfortunately, this is the type of man he's most attracted to. Best not to dwell on that too much.

David forces himself to put pen to paper, attempting to brainstorm ways to tighten up his "tight five" for open mic night at the corner bar. The set is mostly about his interactions with other male models at auditions, a setting ripe with content. His last joke—a meandering story about seeing another model's dick at auditions and getting self-conscious—always earns a decent amount of laughs. Still, he hasn't performed in a while, with how busy things have been since he signed with his agent. He feels like he's losing a bit of himself, letting his dream drift along behind in his current, more a shadow or an afterthought than a buoy in the storm. It's so easy to get caught up in trying to make a living, support his family, maintain his weight, further his connections, and strengthen his brand. This body won't last

forever. If not a full transition into comedy, it'll need to be into *something*. Or many things.

God, it would be so easy to continue plodding on for ten years and suddenly realize stand-up was nothing but a dream he never really allowed himself to pursue. Like a five-year-old who says they want to be an astronaut. Just talk, no follow-through. David slams the pen down. The fatalistic thinking isn't helping his comedy. He isn't deadpan, nihilistic. He's always felt most comfortable in the old bitchy gay schtick, playing into the sassy bottom stereotype. Sure, it sometimes feels a little forced, but it gets laughs. Maybe he should just give up for now and go for a run, even if it means puking. Better to just get out of his head completely.

He stands, checking his phones before heading out the door. Nothing from Jerry. Another missed call from Viv. As he looks on, she calls again. He's about to send it to voicemail when he pauses. Perhaps it's better to talk with her and get it over with, have the rest of the day to decompress. He answers.

"Viv, you're blowing up my phone. Maybe take the hint when I haven't called you back yet." There is silence on the other end of the line. "Well, you have me now. What's going on?"

"So, you don't know what's going on?" Her voice is strained, high-pitched. She's always in some kind of anxious dither.

David sighs in frustration, starts slipping on his running shoes. "Please don't make this some cryptic thing, Viv. What is bothering your pretty little mind?"

"The shoot yesterday ended with bodies on stretchers being loaded into an ambulance, David. Carolyn didn't call you?" Viv bangs around on her end of the phone, maybe opening and closing cabinets. He puts her on speaker and tosses the phone on the side table next to him. He starts his pre-run stretching.

"Well, I asked her to spare me the tawdry details, so no, we haven't spoken. But yes, I would assume after your shoot, there would be a body to take care of. Death portrait and all."

"Stop being snippy at me and listen to my words, David. I said *bodies*. As in two. The wife, Cynthia, took something after the shoot was done. I could tell it was bad, but I didn't know what to do. She said to leave. We waited outside for a while, down the street where no one saw us, and watched the ambulance come. And the police."

David rises from his lunge, fully listening now. "What do you mean, *us*?" Silence again. "Viv?"

"I brought an assistant with me. It's fine. She signed the NDA."

"Whoa, I never said you could bring an assistant! I can't believe you didn't pass that by me. Actually, I can, because you obviously didn't tell me because you knew I would say no."

"Why is it up to you who I bring? I thought you were just the middleman, organizing this for friends of yours?"

David ignores that, pulling his shoes off again violently. He won't be running anytime soon. "So, you've been questioned by the police?"

"No, I took the SD cards with me. Unless Carolyn says anything, it looks like Cynthia had a party with her husband's corpse and then killed herself. Which is exactly what happened, just omitting the fact that I was there taking photos. But it doesn't look great when this is my second crime scene in a month." Viv sounds a little crazed. David can almost sympathize, but this isn't the time. There is damage control to be done, and Viv Klein is not the one to do it.

"All right, well, that was the right thing to do. I'm going to make some calls, all right? You aren't going to get into any trouble, okay? Just stay home and think about applying to a day job." David hangs up before she can respond to his empty placations. He makes his way restlessly back into the kitchen, pops another espresso pod in the machine. He can feel the familiar sear of shame in his gut, heating everything up from the inside out. This is his fault, for feeling some sort of loyalty toward Viv, wanting to help her out because she seems so incapable of toughening up herself.

If he had left her out of this, found someone else, then there would be no loose ends. Someone else would have acted responsibly. No one else would have brought an assistant to such a delicate job, especially without running it by him first. She was careless—always is. But she won't feel the brunt of this; he will. If they miraculously make it out of this without legal issues, it'll be his hard work that salvages the business.

The suicide . . . that could maybe be written off as a loose-cannon client. It might not dissuade further interest. But a photographer who can't be trusted to leave the photos behind, who would bring someone along and share confidential information without vetting them, is a major liability. Jerry doesn't work with major liabilities. He doesn't sleep with them, either. David put his neck out, organizing this shoot without Jerry's knowledge. It was supposed to be a show of his worth, his ability—not a giant, incriminating fiasco.

His phone rings. He jumps a little. It's the wind chime of his business phone. Jerry. He grabs it off the counter, takes one deep breath, and as soon as he answers, he feels his overeagerness to please Jerry bubbling up. He isn't ready to give up on the man, which makes him furious. It sounds like someone is mowing the lawn on Jerry's end. David pictures him lying by his pool, a smug expression on his face. The image is so visceral, it feels real, like David can see it through the black screen. Jerry whispers to someone, probably gloating to his assistant Andre that he was right about David's mettle, or lack thereof.

"Hey, David. I just heard about how your little foray into producing went. We all fall flat on our asses sometimes. Why don't you come here? Let's talk it over." His voice isn't completely unfriendly, but it contains a warning. David decides to respond casually, with his signature riposte, to test Jerry's emotional state.

"Some would say going behind your back to try and put together another photo shoot shows initiative. You're welcome." The pause on the other end makes David's insides lurch.

"I don't know who 'some' are, but they're imbeciles. Get over here now." Now his tone is dark.

Jerry hangs up. So much for relaxing. David's head is pounding too hard to drive, so he changes into something sleeker and calls another car, downing the espresso on his way out the door. He wishes he could put aside his fury at Viv, but it just sits there, festering. It makes him sweat, and not in a sexy way. Facing Jerry after this shit show will be a lesson in patience and poker faces. He'll want to put David in his place, make him feel small. That's how it goes. Then, if David's lucky, he won't get cut out of the game—or Jerry's bed.

For now, there's nothing to do but try to center himself, get himself out of the never-ending Escher-esque scheme of probabilities dancing in his head. Nothing is as meditative as the gym, but he can at least try the breathing exercises his therapist suggested. He closes his eyes. Sitting there in the back of the sedan, breathing through his nose, crawling toward the Hollywood Hills, his mind settles, thoughts congealing on his stand-up routine.

He runs through the jokes one by one, envisioning the audience's reaction in real time. He gets to the final story and his mental picture stutters. Something just isn't working. He breathes slowly, in and out, in and out. Finally, the punch line comes to him in a jolt, as ideas always seem to when they are good. He pulls out his personal phone and jots down a note:

Call it dick dysmorphia, not penis envy—i.e. I'm fine not being a skinny twink. I'm fine with my thick ass. It's just my dick. I don't have body dysmorphia. I have dick dysmorphia, which is like the opposite but on a smaller scale. I look at myself in the mirror, and I look way smaller than other people see me down there. What do you all think? Does my dick look small in these jeans?

David snickers, letting out a little hiccuping sound that only happens when he's overly tired. The driver glances at him in the rearview. David doesn't feel embarrassed. He rarely has to, when his good looks can get him out of most socially sticky situations. He should be able to laugh if he wants to, if something is funny. He can tolerate people treating him like he's small, if it gets him somewhere, but for now, in this car, that isn't the case. He resolves himself, sets aside his pesky anxieties. He isn't giving up on anything—not his comedy career, not his business interests, and not his romantic predilections for pompous men. He's still on the right path, and he's determined to tell Jerry that. To *show* Jerry that what happened in Pasadena is only a blip on the path to what they can do together. He closes his eyes and breathes in and out, smiling.

LOS ANGELES TIMES

CYNTHIA AND OLIVER LEITH, RENOWNED
PASADENA PHILANTHROPISTS, DIE
AS THEY LIVED: TOGETHER
By Fred H. Johnson | Staff Writer Oct. 23, 2023
Updated 2:34 PM PT

Cynthia and Oliver Leith, pioneering California art connoisseurs and co-founders of the Leith Arts Foundation, died Wednesday at their home. He was 86. She was 71. Early the next morning, a photograph of the couple, seemingly celebrating their 50th anniversary, appeared in the main gallery of the Leith Arts Foundation building in South Pasadena without the knowledge of the staff.

No one, as of yet, has taken responsibility for placing the photo in the gallery, or for removing the Keith Haring piece that had been hanging there beforehand. The Haring was found in the staff bathroom by Curator Elles Bean early Thursday morning. No damage was evident to the piece. The Leith Arts Foundation permanent collection has been taken to storage for temporary safekeeping while the incident is investigated.

"I'm gutted to think we will never see either of our inspiring, loving, trailblazing founders walkthrough these doors again. But it's also impossible to think of one of them without the other. As you all know, they were incredibly romantic, in love with each other even more than they were in love with art. It seems right that they would leave this world together," Bean said in a statement to foundation patrons last night. The museum will be closed for the foreseeable future as the security system is upgraded. No security footage from Wednesday night was recovered.

The Pasadena Police Department has not yet released the cause of death for Cynthia or Oliver Leith. Both Leiths were pronounced dead at their home late Wednesday evening. The *Times* will continue to report on their passing as more information becomes available. Over their 50 year marriage, 40 years of which were spent in Pasadena, Cynthia and Oliver Leith traveled the world, curating a collection of international and Indigenous art that sparked the creation of the Leith Arts Foundation in 2010. For decades, they were central to the LA arts community and worked tirelessly to bring the work of local artists to the foreground of the art world. "If we can leave anything behind, I hope it's art that the next generation can enjoy. Art that will inspire and that will show the most powerful force we have—love," Cynthia Leith told the *Times* for a 2016 profile of her work as chairwoman of the foundation.

Cynthia and Oliver Leith are survived by their daughter, Carolyn Leith, chief financial officer of the Leith Arts Foundation. She declined to comment on the passing of her parents at this time. A vigil honoring Cynthia and Oliver Leith is scheduled for Oct. 24 at 7 p.m. in front of the Leith Art Foundation's east entrance.

ABBY

Abby has been dreaming of her terrible and imminent death. In these dreams, someone always tells her how terrible and imminent her death is. Now, in her waking hours, she finds herself acting out of character. It embarrasses her how on the nose her fears are, and how ill-equipped she is to face them. Logic and facts pervade her life. Not much time for existential dread. It's been this way since her abuela died, when she figured out her relationship to the cycle of life—one of studious disinterest.

The last time Abby went to church before this week was sometime in college. Occasionally, she would slip in on a Sunday and attend a mass, just to be reminded of the days when she used to trail Abuela into the uncomfortable wooden pews of Saint Martin of Tours. She never learned her Hail Marys, never confessed after the week of Abuela's passing. Still, there was something comforting about being present in the space her grandmother had cared so much for. It made her feel a bit more tied to the heritage that had seemed to die with her. Sitting in the back of the church, no one knew she didn't belong, that she wasn't just another devout Catholic. That was, until it came time to take communion and the pews emptied except for her.

Gwen said that Saint Martin's stood on land that used to be owned by Gary Cooper, one of Abuela's favorite actors. It had been an orchard in a previous life, during the pre-Hays Code, Wild West days of LA. Gwen says it should have stayed that way—that at least an orchard brings something practical to the people who give their time and effort to it. Of course, Gwen studiously attends temple three times a year, once for Rosh Hashanah, once for Yom Kippur, and once to drop off her donation check. It isn't that she wants Abby to be more of a devout Jew, just that she sees Catholicism as her ex-husband's purview. Anything tied to his identity is immediately perverse and beneath the remaining Katz family.

Abby has never told Gwen that she sometimes attends mass. She wouldn't understand. Not that Abby fully understands, either. She doesn't really believe any of it—her idea of the organization of the universe is nebulous and terrifying, not structured and plot-based. Still, here she is yet again, the third time in as many days, trying to look as unobtrusive as possible in the last pew. Even after so many years, the rhythm and rhyme remains the same. *Et cum spiritu tuo.* The only time those Harvard-Westlake Latin classes ever pay off.

So far, it hasn't made any discernible difference to her low mood. *In nomine patris et filii et spiritus sancti.* She keeps toying with the idea of confession, but what does she have to confess? She goes over and over the whole afternoon and evening of the photo shoot, parsing through every jumbled memory. What they did wasn't wrong, exactly. And there was no way they could have known what the woman had been planning. She can't shake the image of herself rewriting history, running at Carolyn, giving her the Heimlich maneuver, scolding her for attempting to end her life in front of them. Saying life is a precious gift that shouldn't be thrown away so thoughtlessly.

A gift? From whom? The same God whose priest stands at the front of this congregation? That priest wouldn't let her father take communion after he remarried. That priest would shame her for kissing Viv, though perhaps she should be shamed for that, for reasons other than sexual impropriety. Either way, she doesn't seem in great standing with the Catholic God, and it feels almost hypocritical to be doing His work for Him when she wasn't even confirmed in His church. So maybe life is a gift from the Jewish God. Isn't it undue suffering a sign you're favored by Him?

The priest glances her way, as if he can hear her sacrilegious thoughts. His voice seems to beckon to her, the lost lamb who has wandered away from the herd. Listen, my child, to the eternal words I speak. She averts her gaze. Maybe it's better to keep the specifics out of it, leave it nonpartisan. Life is a gift from an unknown sender; you don't choose to receive it but you can't give it away. There. That's what she could have said to Cynthia. In her imagination, Cynthia would have nodded sagely, admitted a lapse in judgment, and thrown the cyanide away. No, not thrown it away, flushed it down the toilet, where no rat or human or anyone could get it. Abby and Viv would have left unnerved, but all right. Viv would have thanked her for her help as an assistant, and for saving Cynthia's life.

Viv would have dropped her off at her car and shaken her hand, telling her to write a great story about the experience. The photo wouldn't inexplicably end up in Cynthia and Ollie's gallery. No boundaries would have been crossed with Viv. Abby wouldn't feel oddly betrayed, wouldn't feel that Viv must be responsible for the photo's appearance.

Of course, the truth is that there's a great story to be written about the experience as it actually happened. Even more so with how it ended, brutal as that sounds. Yes, she signed the NDA, but maybe Carolyn would be willing to waive it, to talk about how everything unfolded with her parents. If she isn't willing, though, there are surely other stories like this to be told. This is the tip of the iceberg of this bizarre world. Viv said she'd done this type of photography before. Someone must be willing to talk about it. A lot of people would be interested in reading about it. Modern-day death portraiture. People would have a morbid interest. Abby's interest felt almost empowering before it went so horribly wrong. Now, it haunts her and pushes her to attend religious services she doesn't even believe in.

The mass ends with Abby retaining nothing more than that she is sent forth in the world in peace and love. Parishioners file past her into the bright light outside while she remains, in no hurry to drive to El Segundo to meet with Fred at the office. She called him last night in a moment of weakness, feeling a bit in over her head. He'll know how to approach this potential piece. It's worth getting his perspective, as the much older and more accomplished journalist, even if she does ultimately have to share the byline. Deep down, she knows she needs help on this. She's never approached a story like this before, and it would be selfish pride to refuse to collaborate on it with him.

Abby is so lost in her own thoughts that she doesn't notice the priest until he is upon her, leaning into the pew. He sits down creakily beside her.

Up close, she notes the smattering of gray in his black hair, the desaturated pallor of his face. He looks tired, like he has been for years, even though he can't be more than forty or fifty. His eyes are dark brown and cryptic, though that could be her editorializing. It's hard to tell the pupil from the iris. She isn't sure if he's here to admonish her for dawdling or to engage her in conversation. She hopes it's the former. She isn't looking to be converted. Same as during the service, it seems his eyes bore into her.

"I've noticed you here the last couple of days. We haven't been introduced. I'm Father Juan." The priest sticks his hand out of the long sleeve of his alb. Abby shakes it.

"Abby Katz." His handshake is firm. "This was my abuela's church," she adds as a sort of half explanation, half apology. She's certain he can tell that she isn't Catholic, that she doesn't belong here. He's probably confused by her last name, but he nods and leans back in the pew. Apparently, he plans to have a conversation with her. Wonderful. "When did your abuela pass?"

"Years ago. Father Pete was rector. She knew him pretty well. He said some beautiful words at her funeral. We all appreciated it." Abby tries to maintain his deep eye contact. Speaking with religious leaders always leaves her a bit on edge, like she's somehow disappointing them by simply existing.

"What made you come back after all this time?" His expression is more curious than anything. He holds up one hand. "And don't feel like you have to open up to me if you don't want to. I'm just interested whenever I see new faces. I want to know what I can potentially do to help them find what they are seeking."

Abby shifts on the pew uncomfortably. Here comes the conversion. "I'm not really seeking anything. I just find comfort being here, where my abuela found a home. It brings me closer to her memory. When I am particularly missing her, it's nice to be here."

Father Juan clasps his hands in his robed lap, giving her a sympathetic smile. She notices that he's wearing black Nikes, which seems incongruous with the rest of his outfit. She can't help but wonder what priests wear under their robes. Is he just in complete athleisure under there?

"Sometimes I think we can find ourselves closest to the dead when we allow ourselves to feel their joy, even if it is not ours. When I miss my father most, I lock myself up in my room with his favorite vodka.

It always does the trick." His face breaks out in a crooked grin and he laughs, closing his dark eyes for a moment. Abby tries to parse if he is serious or not. His eyes open and fix back on her. His look isn't unkind. She decides to open up, if that's what he wants so badly.

"I keep having dreams of my terrible and imminent death. If that sounds ridiculous to you, it does to me as well. But that's what people keep telling me in my dream. That my death is terrible and imminent." She isn't sure why she says it, maybe to shock him, maybe in some sort of faint hope he will be able to talk reason into her. He doesn't look fazed. He's a priest. People probably say wild things to him daily.

"And is it?"

"Is my death terrible and imminent? I hope not."

"I mean in the dream, do you experience your death? Does it meet those criteria?"

"No. I always wake up before that."

"But you're still scared. Of course you are." He turns toward her in the pew. The space between them is very small. Abby leans back a bit.

"What do you think you're more scared of, the fact that in these dreams your death will be a terrible one, or that it is about to happen so soon?" Abby stares at him. "You don't have to answer. But dreams have always interested me a great deal. Joseph's ability to interpret dreams brought him great honor and a chance to see his father again before he passed. Dreams can be a blessing. Even those that terrify us."

Abby nods politely. But her neutral façade clearly isn't working—he can tell she is placating him, as she would a small child explaining magic to her. He smiles in amusement, shaking his head. "Even if you don't believe dreams are auguries of anything at all, they can tell you something about yourself, if you will listen. Our subconscious feeds off of our daily thoughts and experiences. That's science meeting the divine."

"Respectfully, I don't believe my dreams are representative of much at all other than that I should have taken a melatonin before I went to bed."

"Humor me and answer my question, if you don't mind." Father Juan's small smile irritates her more than it should.

"All right, I guess I'm more scared of my death being imminent. This can't be the sum of my life. I don't think I would mind a terrible death so much if it came when I was one hundred. I haven't done anything worth being remembered for, worth having someone try and remember me through my joy. Death isn't as terrifying as being forgotten."

Father Juan taps his fingers on the back of the pew in front of them. He looks reflectively at the crucifix illuminated at the front of the church. "Thank you for indulging me. I can be too nosy, sometimes." Abby waits but he doesn't say anything else.

"Well, what do you think my answer means?"

He looks back at her, surprised. "Does it matter?" But before she can respond, he waves his hand. "No, no. Don't answer that. I'll tell you. I love talking; it's my cross to bear." He gives her a small, secretive smile. "Let me respond this way: We don't always see what others do in us. I doubt there is no one who would want to remember you through your joy. But maybe that's true, maybe you are a dreadful person not even a mother would mourn. I just met you. I don't know. But I doubt it. Very few people are.

"If I were to speak to you religiously, I would tell you there is something greater, *someone* greater, who does care about your life, no matter what. If I were talking secularly, I would tell you that sitting here, not listening to my sermons, isn't going to make your life meaningful. I wish I had faith it would—but it won't. I don't know what will, but it seems like you are thirsting for that, so I have faith for us both that you will find it." Father Juan stands up, patting Abby on the back. "Please, feel free to keep coming. I'd love to see your face in the pews. I am already late to confession, so for now, I need to rush off."

With that, he leaves Abby alone in the pew, more discombobulated than before. The empty church is disconcertingly quiet. Abby is silent the entire drive to El Segundo. Speaking with Father Juan ruined the peaceful nostalgia of visiting Saint Martin's. It wasn't meant to be a spiritual or even philosophical experience, just a soft, nostalgic one. Instead, she feels called out, unjustly so. The sweet bubble of memory popped and reality rushed in, unwanted. It's pathetic how she opened up to Father Juan. This is the pernicious danger of religion, drawing her in, making her reveal her soft underbelly. And for what? She vows she won't return, sending an apology to Abuela into the ether. Maybe Gwen is right about the orchard.

She parks and straightens her hair in the rearview mirror. Going in to the office feels foreign after so much time spent at home during the pandemic. With hybrid work schedules, she almost feels like she could disappear and no one at the newspaper would even notice. She pushes that out of her mind for now, far far away where she has shoved the thoughts of religion and loss and oranges. She doesn't need to come off as trepidatious in front of Fred. This is her story. She found it. She deserves to be here.

Inside, the newsroom is all beige, whites, and blacks, color only coming from the knickknacks on the desks. Screens hang from every pillar, descend down from the matte black ceiling, cover every hard white surface below. Despite the clutter, the space feels huge. Too huge for the couple of people hunched over desks today.

She finds Fred, as expected, by the coffee machine. He's leaning on the counter, scowling at the coffee that drips slowly into his mug. When he sees Abby, he straightens, rubs his hands over his bald head. It's a habit that never left, even when his hair did. The sleeves of his ill-fitting button-up are rolled to his elbows, revealing pen stains—a sign he's working on a new piece. He always writes first drafts with pen and paper, hunkered down like he's guarding a secret. His favorite ballpoints are some shitty off-brand version that bleed everywhere.

"Just let me get my coffee and we can find a place to sit and talk." Fred turns back to the coffee machine, brusque as usual. Abby grabs a mug and gets her own coffee, tense in the silence. She has never spoken one-on-one with Fred before but knows he doesn't suffer small talk. Coffees in hand, they find a place to sit at a communal table. Fred has his own desk, but he never seems to be at it. Months ago, after writing a masterful article on gun violence, he installed a tracker on his desk that tallied the number of mass shootings this year. It got so depressing the editor asked him to take it down for morale. He refused on principle, but he also started avoiding his own desk.

Fred takes a long gulp from his mug and leans back in his rolling chair, hands crossed over his belly. He looks expectantly at Abby, absently picking at where the buttons are pulling on his shirt.

Abby takes a deep breath and begins, "I know you personally knew the Leiths. I'm sorry for your loss. Like I said on the phone, some of what I have to say involves them and is rather delicate."

Fred slowly swivels back and forth in his chair. "I doubt you can shock me. Just tell me what you know and we can go from there." Abby takes a sip of her coffee and explains everything that transpired with Viv Klein, minus the kiss. His expression stays neutral as he continues to drift back and forth, back and forth in his chair. Finally, when Abby finishes, he leans forward to put his inky arms on the table.

"How online are you, Abby?"

The non sequitur surprises her. "Excuse me?"

"We're just delivery nurses. Most everything is gestating somewhere before we find the pulse, bring it into the world. I mean, that isn't the case for certain breaking news stories, but we're not talking about a hurricane here, we're talking about ideas that have been fomenting somewhere, right?" Fred's tone is that of a patient kindergarten teacher. She tries to conceal her rising ire.

"You're telling me that you aren't surprised by what I just told you? Because it's been 'fometing' somewhere?"

"I've read everything already. But that's only the first part. Then, you have to figure out how much of it is true. Most of what I read is bullshit. One percent of it is gold. You deliver the gold." He leans back in his chair and struggles to pull his phone from his pants pocket. He squints at the screen. "Here." He hands her the phone. A Discord channel is pulled up.

"What is this?"

"This is how I've been writing this story for the last twenty-four hours before you came to me with it."

VIV

Time as we know it is a construct. No one interprets it objectively, because there is no objectivity to be found. Five p.m. in L.A. is 8 p.m. in Salt Lake City. A blood draw takes eons while an orgasm is gone in a blip. It's all experiential, or else fake. Most things are ephemeral; that's time's only rule. Still, Viv feels like she's been waiting forever. Nothing about it feels fake as the minutes tick by and her heart rate continues to climb. Jeremiah—or Jerry, as he told her to call him—asked to meet with her at nine.

Andre met her at the door. It felt out of place to see him in casual attire, in dark jeans and loafers. He deposited her at the infinity pool, where she sits, idly watching the shadows shifting across the pool, slowly getting sunburned. She has no idea how Jerry is involved with the Leiths or their photo shoot. It seems like he is, though, and he isn't happy. He was so insistent about meeting that Viv felt like she couldn't say no. Not after the SD card had gone missing.

Viv has never been one for sitting with her thoughts, especially recently. Especially after watching Cynthia Leith kill herself and then taking off with the photographic evidence of the evening. Especially after that photographic evidence somehow ended up printed for the world to see the next morning—and Viv had nothing to do with it. She seriously doubts Jerry will believe that baffling and inexplicable fact. She's certain Abby Katz won't believe it, either—though, she also doubts they'll ever talk again. What do you say after something like that?

Viv replays last night's concert in her mind. She finally made it across her threshold at 3 a.m., greeted by a very alert Connor, who promptly absconded with a lens cap, and this kept her up for another half hour as she struggled to get it back from under the bed. Even then, though, she lay in bed, staring at the ceiling, going over and over in her mind what Jerry could possibly want from her. She tried to focus on the concert—the photos that would need to be selected, edited—but she couldn't. Even at the concert, with the bass thumping so loud it reverberated in her bones, her mind had kept wandering to the meeting in the hills the next morning. She felt disconnected even as she pushed through the mosh pit, at least half a dozen people touching her on every side at all times.

By all accounts, the concert couldn't have gone much better. D had sold out the Echoplex. Every square inch of real estate was draped with hip-looking Eastsiders sweating through their flannel, alternating between beer and canned water. The place stank of marijuana, and the energy was as high as the audience, and everyone in the band could feel it. D gave his sweat and tears, and a couple people in the audience gave their blood when the mosh pit got too rowdy. Luckily, the worst of the injuries were a couple of scraped knees. Viv spent her night weaving unobtrusively through the band members, a frenetic shadow. What she was getting with her camera was good, intimate yet grand. D exuded charisma and pop god sex appeal. The whole show seemed to have more gloss and glitz than any of his previous ones. The energy was different. The zeitgeist was turning in his favor. And in the end, D's careful and authoritative handling of the incident led to him trending online for half an hour in the greater Southern California region of the Internet.

Before the concert began, D had pulled Viv into a rum-and-tobacco-scented hug and told her how happy he was to have her back with the band, like her absence had been her choice. She played along, telling him how happy she was to be back where she belonged. And in some ways, it felt true. Just not completely true. The concert was electric, but it felt less like an exciting opportunity to flex her eye and more like a repeat of something she had already done before. Even the potential career boost of the high-profile show didn't particularly interest her.

Sitting in the rising heat, watching shadows cross the infinity pool, the Echoplex felt like a different lifetime. Before Viv can delve too far into what that means, she hears a door sliding open, and finally Jerry's confident voice calls to her from across the patio. Unfortunately, he is not alone. Next to him stands Abby Katz, avoiding eye contact with Viv. The journalist's presence sends Viv into another confused spiral.

She stands, uncertain whether to go to him or wait. After a moment, he turns to call something inside and then jumps out onto the patio, gesturing for Viv to meet him next to a covered table.

She makes sure not to look at Abby but is hyperaware of sitting right next to her. Best to act as casual as possible. Jerry sprawls in the chair across from Viv, leaning back in his board shorts and moisture-wicking shirt. He looks tanner, leaner somehow, despite his already wiry frame. It's something about the wealth he seems to exude; on a man like him, skinny looks like an aesthetic choice. Like the past few weeks have treated him well.

"Well, things have been interesting since we last met, haven't they?" he begins, voice neutral.

Viv can't help it. She looks at Abby. Abby stares at the ground. The pieces aren't quite fitting together. Why is the journalist here? Viv swallows and addresses Jerry. "Sure, that's one way to put it. I'm a bit confused—were you a friend of the Leiths? I'm not sure I understand how you're connected to what happened?"

Jerry grins, but it doesn't quite reach his eyes. "There's a bit for us to talk through. Starting with the night you asked Abby here to accompany you on the job. It seems everything kind of went downhill from there, didn't it? I was hoping you could tell me a little about what happened." Jerry looks right at her. Abby is still studying her own knuckles.

"Right . . . respectfully, what do you have to do with any of this?" She winces internally at how whiny she sounds. Something about Jerry puts her off-balance.

"I'll explain more after I hear your side of things. Just understand this has everything to do with me. And I don't know if I can trust you."

Viv relents. He surely has already heard everything from Abby, so she may as well reiterate it. "We did the shoot, things went sideways, so we left. I'm sure you know that already. I don't know what happened with the SD card. I took it with me. I put it in a drawer in my apartment. Then it was gone—the print was made, the photo was everywhere. I don't know what happened, who stole it or how. I certainly don't know who printed it. I don't expect you to believe me, but it's true." She looks Jerry straight in the eye, and he almost looks like he believes her. Viv gains a little courage. Why is she trying to explain herself to this man, anyway? She lifts her chin.

"Can you explain what happened then? I'm just confused as to how you took the memory card you were told to leave behind and then misplaced it." Jerry leans forward on the table, his face disappearing into the dark shadow of the patio umbrella.

"I took it with me because I could tell things were going south. It felt like the right thing to do in the situation. I still stand behind that."

"The right thing for the situation, or for yourself? It's not difficult to imagine you took the SD card to protect yourself from becoming embroiled in another police investigation. Then, you go home and the artist in you feels the urge to have your work seen. It's a bit of a familiar refrain for you, isn't it?"

The white wall behind Jerry reflects the sunlight straight into her face, making it impossible to read his expression. Abby leans back into the sun, sunglasses obscuring her eyes. No one has acknowledged her presence or explained it, which irritates Viv.

"Like I said, I don't know what happened. I don't have any connections to the Leiths' foundation, which I'm sure you already know. There's no way I could have gotten the print in there."

"No, I don't think you could have." Jerry leans back and pushes a button on the blindingly white wall behind him. It's like he has just switched off interrogation mode. His posture changes, relaxes. Viv wonders if he ever really thought she was behind the photo surfacing in the Leith gallery. Seconds later, Andre appears from inside. "I forgot to ask if either of you wanted anything. Andre, I'll take another kale juice." He looks from Abby to Viv. They both shake their heads. "I guess nothing else then, Andre. Thanks." Andre promptly disappears back into the house.

"Why is *she* here?" The question comes out more rudely than Viv intended, but oh well. She's waited close to an hour only to be hounded with questions and given no answers.

Jerry looks between the two women. Again, he doesn't really answer. "Right, that's the other aspect we haven't talked about. You invited a journalist to come with you."

Viv stands, the patio chair screeching on the stone. She's had enough of Jerry's opaque replies.

"I am under the impression that I worked for you one time on a freelance basis and that our work together is finished. You called me here to seemingly interrogate me about my work with other clients, and I think I've already told you more than I should have, seeing as it doesn't involve you. If you don't have more of an explanation for me, I'm going to leave."

Jerry looks up at her, infuriatingly bemused. "Sit down. There's no need to get worked up. You aren't in trouble." Viv stands awkwardly for a second, trying to decide what to do.

Curiosity wins and she sits. Andre reappears with a highball glass of chunky green liquid, which he sets in front of Jerry. Everyone is silent until the house door closes softly behind him.

"When I asked you to shoot for me, I had two goals. First, and more importantly, I knew how I wanted to commemorate the person I loved most in this world and I felt like you were the person to do it. Second, I'm a producer. Part of me is always thinking about what's marketable, what people want and how I can fulfill that need. I have a sixth sense for the box office, and that talent doesn't end there. I can't just turn it off. It permeates everything I do. I was my own first client; you were the first freelance artist I employed. Didn't you check where your latest payment came from? It was transferred from the same place."

When the money came in from the Leith photo shoot, Viv couldn't bear to look. It just brought back the mental image of Cynthia telling them to leave.

The money had come a few days after the shoot, and she was surprised she'd been paid at all past the check for the SD cards.

"I don't understand. What are you getting out of this arrangement?"

"It's a photography business. I'm sure you're familiar with those, yes?" Jerry smiles patronizingly. "Part of the appeal of a luxury good is the cost. Photography of this nature is delicate, special. It's an amazingly lucrative market that no one is delving into. I don't want to be crude; it's not just about the money that can be made, but think about it. It's an exciting frontier. I intend to be at the forefront of it."

"Why didn't you tell me you were technically my boss? I was under the impression that I was working for the family directly, not that there was some sort of . . . business I was hired under. Customarily, an employee knows who is employing them."

Jerry takes a deep swig of kale juice before answering. "Does it change anything? I told you now. As I did with Abby earlier this morning. I knew a journalist wouldn't be able to resist trying to investigate this little operation. And that's fine. I'm not opposed to some free marketing. I'm all for her writing about our work here." Jerry glances at Abby. "Not that I want to manipulate your story at all. I just want to make sure you have the truth." He turns back to Viv.

"Anyway, I'm a businessman, but I'm also a romantic. I love a good story, a good piece of art, anything that can truly touch me. So, even though this last shoot was a little rocky, I don't want to end our arrangement, Viv. Your photo of my mother brings me joy every day.

You have a knack for this. I can see us all working together in synthesis. You shooting, Abby

shadowing you for the time being, me vetting our clients a bit better. No more suicidal ideations. Just us bringing some peace and comfort into a challenging time for people."

Viv is flummoxed by his cavalier attitude. She addresses Abby for the first time. "You agreed to this? Why?"

Abby looks back at her, probably, from behind her sunglasses. "You told me you would show me something interesting. You did. There's a story to tell here, and Jeremiah is offering me access. In exchange, I won't reveal any names in the article I publish. I'll shadow you. I'll keep your anonymity and just watch what you do in order to report on the unique art of death portraiture."

Jerry nods emphatically. "I have a high profile, Viv. You know this. I didn't feel like I could comfortably reveal to you what was going on right away. It was better to test you out, see if we were a good fit, and then really open up to you about the opportunities we can explore together. I'm sure it's not the first time you worked a job not knowing who helmed the organization that hired you. Now we can move forward with greater honesty. I trust you didn't steal the SD card in order to print the photo. Can you trust me to lead us in this?"

Jerry finishes his kale juice and slams the glass down on the table. "There is so much we can do to help people here." He looks expectantly at her, like he already knows what she's going to say. Unfortunately, she already knows, too. A job like this is hard to resist, red flags be damned.

She has been consistently paid for her work, and paid well. The same can't be said for some of her previous projects. The idea of working while Abby Katz watches intrigues her, too. It's hard to turn down a chance to show the world her artistic point of view, even behind a pseudonym.

"All right. I'll keep shooting for you, as long as I have a better understanding of what I'm walking in to each time. I want a chance to consent to the specifics. That will help me do my job better on the day, too."

Jerry claps his hands and nods, immediately all business. "Of course. That's only reasonable. Now, let's get inside. We may as well get started. I have a couple of clients for you to look over." He gestures to the door. When Abby stands and turns away, Jerry leans in to growl in Viv's ear, "Do not go behind my back again." He claps her on the shoulder, and Viv shivers involuntarily. He rises and, beaming, opens the door for Abby.

"Are you sure you don't want something to drink? Seriously, Andre makes the best smoothies." Viv shakes her head, wondering if she will regret her decision to stay. She trails them into the house, trying to avoid eye contact with Andre, who stands in the living room, staring at her with a funny expression. She wonders if he saw the interaction between her and Jerry at the table. He closes the space between them, conspiratorially hands her a smoothie. She takes it almost involuntarily. Andre pats her hand.

"You look like you need some refreshment. There's a little twist in there. You're welcome." He winks and lingers a second, like he wants to say something more. He thinks better of it and turns on his heel, gone. She takes a swig, her throat immediate burning.

PRIVATE DISCORD SERVER

LOS ANGELES FORUM FOR CRITICAL
THINKING CHANNEL: # DEADMANWALKING

CONNOR B. (HE/HIM) 10/25/2023 2:25 PM
Y'all, my girlfriend works at the Leith in Pasadena,
and I totally got the tea on the whole painting
deal. Anyone interested?

PABLO D. (HE/HIM) 10/25/2023 2:30 PM
Duh, we're interested. Don't be so annoying, Connor.
Just tell us what "tea" you apparently got from
your "girlfriend."

TED H. (HE/HIM) 10/25/2023 2:55 PM
Typical Connor—says he has something to say,
completely logs off.

ZACH W. (HE/HIM) 10/25/2023 3:10 PM
Lol "girlfriend."

CONNOR B. (HE/HIM) 10/25/2023 3:20 PM
My dudes, some of us are at work and can't respond immediately. Okay. So, yes, my **girlfriend** told me this. Not all of us are incels like Ted. But, basically, she told me that everyone who works there is convinced Ollie (that's what they call the old dude) is unalive in the photo. They've, like, really studied it, and they knew him really well. So, I think we have another confirmed death picture on our hands.

TED H. (HE/HIM) 10/25/2023 3:31 PM
Death portrait, not death picture.

PABLO D. (HE/HIM) 10/25/2023 3:35 PM
That's all she had to say? We basically already knew that.

CONNOR B. (HE/HIM) 10/25/2023 3:56 PM
First of all, stop hating on me. Second of all, that isn't even the spiciest part, all right?

TED H. (HE/HIM) 10/25/2023 4:00 PM
I'm dying of suspense.

CONNOR B. (HE/HIM) 10/25/2023 4:10 PM
Fuck you, Ted. This is interesting stuff, okay? There was apparently a "glitch" in the security cam, and there isn't any footage of when the picture was put in the gallery. We knew that, right? Well . . . guess what! The convenience store across the street has some grainy-as-shit footage of a guy all in black walking up out of nowhere, wheeling a dolly with a giant-ass parcel on it. Like a big, rectangular, picture-shaped parcel. He disappears around the side, and it's like 480p video, so you can't tell anything else, but they have him on camera! How's that for tea?

PABLO D. (HE/HIM) 10/25/2023 4:14 PM
Damn, Connie B, that's a good cuppa. So, we're looking for a man in black. Hell, that could be me right now in my sweats.

ZACH W. (HE/HIM) 10/25/2023 4:16 PM
Piping hot!

TED H. (HE/HIM) 10/25/2023 4:21 PM
How can you tell it's a man, if the video quality is so low?

ZACH W. (HE/HIM) 10/25/2023 4:26 PM
Yeah, maybe it was your girlfriend.

CONNOR B. (HE/HIM) 10/25/2023 4:44 PM
Ignoring that, Zach. I'm trying to have a mature conversation here. It was obviously a man. He was, like, tall and wide. And that picture is heavy as shit. It took two of the office staff to move it the morning it went up. No offense to any women, but they would have to be, like, a powerlifter or something.

TED H. (HE/HIM) 10/25/2023 4:47 PM
I'm not hearing any hard evidence it has to be a man. Maybe the perpetrator tried to conceal her natural appearance? Wore tall shoes? Bulky clothes? Maybe she's just stronger than the pencil pushers who work at the art gallery. Dare I say, stronger than you, Connor?

ZACH W. (HE/HIM) 10/25/2023 4:55 PM
Doubt it.

CONNOR B. (HE/HIM) 10/25/2023 5:04 PM
Well, Ted, do the Leiths make it onto your spreadsheet now?

TED H. (HE/HIM) 10/25/2023 5:07 PM
They were already on there, which you would know
if you ever checked the spreadsheet. It's a shared
document for a reason. I will move them from the
"Possible" to the "Probable" category, though, and
enter your secondhand accounts under the "Hearsay"
column. All of this, by the way, you could have
already done.

CONNOR B. (HE/HIM) 10/25/2023 5:10 PM
Probable??

TED H. (HE/HIM) 10/25/2023 5:14 PM
You know the rules. Only firsthand accounts given
directly to a member of the **# deadmanwalking**
collective (by the way, I let you pick that asinine
appellation) move a suspected death portrait into
the "Confirmed" category. Then, and only then, their
data can be aggregated with that of the other
confirmed cases in order to give us a clearer picture
of where and how frequently the rich partake in this
custom. There's a reason we don't have any confirmed
cases from the last couple of years. It's called
due process.

ZACH W. (HE/HIM) 10/25/2023 5:32 PM
Eat the rich!

PABLO D. (HE/HIM) 10/25/2023 5:39 PM
For sure, man, until you are them.

CONNOR B. (HE/HIM) 10/25/2023 5:44 PM
Endless cataloging for no reason whatsoever. That's
what this is. Ted would catalog how often Bill Gates
shat if he could. I am giving you cold, hard facts
here. Spreadsheet that.

TED H. (HE/HIM) 10/25/2023 5:49 PM
You are all children. Probably literally, since we maintain a modicum of anonymity here. I would have no idea that I was in discourse with a bunch of prepubescent boys other than by the way you speak. You know what? I have no need to continue this dialogue.

TED H. (HE/HIM) 10/25/2023 6:52 PM
I'll update the spreadsheet accordingly. Maybe try to check it from time to time.

ABBY

The producer insisted they meet on his turf—something Abby has taken particular note of. This actually isn't the first time she's been to Jeremiah Fink's Hollywood Hills house, though she's certain he doesn't remember. She was fifteen when her mother designed the costumes for *Skywanders*. Jeremiah hosted a big party for wrap, with all the cast and department heads invited. At the time, Gwen was so impressed by him—he really won her over by inviting the lowly costume designer to the party with *People*'s sexiest man alive. Not all producers would have done that.

She had been given a plus one. It was right after one of her unsuccessful attempts to rekindle things with Abby's father. She decided the only date she wanted was her daughter. Abby wore her fanciest dress and tried to get a quote from Samuel L. Jackson for the Harvard-Westlake paper. He told her she could print that the film was a "motherfucking good time." The cinematographer gave her a puff of his joint in the backyard. She didn't feel a thing. She felt like the universe revolved around Jeremiah's house, and she reveled in her moment at the center. For once, she felt special. It was the highlight of high school for her, though she was ashamed to admit it.

This time around, she is greeted at the door by Jeremiah's assistant,

Andre, who leads her to the living room and deposits her on a ridiculously low-to-the-ground, slate-gray couch. In many ways, the house is how she remembers it—modern, cold, surprisingly spacious for a place tucked up against the hillside. But now she thinks the whole room looks laughably new-moneyed. The modern sculptures on the end table would easily pay ten times over for the new washer and dryer she desperately needs. Flagrant consumption. Both distasteful and enviable. She wonders how good Jeremiah's contract lawyers and agents are. She's seen big-name producers' homes before, but this is surprisingly lavish.

Directly across from the couch, alone above the fireplace, hangs a framed print of an old woman swimming. It isn't the largest or most ostentatious piece of art in the room, but it draws the eye in a way nothing else does. The woman wears a one-piece, goggles, and an enigmatic smile. She looks powerful, graceful in her movement. It looks like Viv Klein's work. Which of course it is. When Jeremiah called, asking to meet, he explained his connection to Klein. Abby still has questions.

Jeremiah doesn't leave her waiting long. He strides into the room, crossing the space in a few long steps, while taking off a pair of aviators. He pauses in front of Abby, pulling a pair of wire-rimmed glasses out of his back pocket. He puts them on and blinks. His energy and sinewy frame don't match his faded hair and the subtle crow's feet around his eyes. His black T-shirt pulls on his thin arms. Other than the length of his shaggy beard, he doesn't look much different than Abby's vague memory of him from a decade and a half ago. He's apparently leaning into the mountain man aesthetic now, though. He sticks out a large hand and tells her to sit.

The only thing Jeremiah says about their past connection is that her mother "defined *Skywanders*—what a shame it never became a full franchise affair." She immediately dislikes him this time around. She remembers how he took credit in the media for creating the Skywanderer's iconic look—something her mother had researched and meticulously melded from depictions of Bedouin tribes and medieval descriptions of samurai. Of course, he claimed *Variety* had misquoted him, but he never had it corrected. Gwen gave him the benefit of the doubt, but they never worked together again.

Jeremiah starts in on a winding story about his life, going all the way back to his childhood and his strong bond with his mother. Abby can hardly get a word in. He has ideas, goals for this death portraiture business.

And that's what he calls it: a business. Abby listens politely, and the more he speaks, the more convinced she is that he's somehow behind the photo of Cynthia and Oliver ending up in the Leith gallery. It isn't anything he says, but more the cavalier manner with which he holds himself. Now she's even more confused about how Viv factors into all of this. If Viv was truly as clueless as Abby in the aftermath of the photo shoot, then Abby's feelings of betrayal aren't substantiated. If she doesn't need to feel betrayed, she doesn't know how she feels about what happened the other night. She decides to parse that out later.

For now, she smiles and nods, the awe of the teenage girl at her first Hollywood party completely gone. With her fully formed frontal cortex, Jeremiah strikes her as a bit of a pompous ass, albeit a smooth one. Gwen always joked that you could tell a true producer by how quickly they compliment themselves by complimenting you. Jeremiah didn't even gone so far as to compliment her, just her mother, and briefly at that, before immediately spinning it around to himself—a consummate producer. Part of her wants to tell him off for Gwen's sake. But of course she won't. After her talk with Fred, which lasted hours, she is determined to find her in for this story. Jeremiah seems to want to hand it to her on a silver platter.

He suddenly stops himself mid-monologue. Abby opens her mouth, ready to ask her first question, but Jeremiah clears his throat, evidently not done. Then, he casually suggests they go check on Viv. Apparently, while they've been discussing Abby's desire to write about what happened with the Leiths, with numerous digressions into Jeremiah's life story, Viv has been outside baking in the sun the entire time. Abby guesses he did this as some kind of power move but agrees amiably, hiding her frustration. He's already agreed to let Abby shadow Viv on a shoot or two—exactly what she wants for her article. But she would have liked a chance to make sure everything is copacetic between her and Viv without Jeremiah.

Obviously, that isn't going to happen. In this circumstance, the best plan seems to be to exchange as few words as possible with Viv until they have a chance to speak privately. The photographer is a loose cannon, though. What if she mentions the kiss? When Jeremiah opens the back door, though, Abby can't tell which one of them Viv is most unhappy to see: her or Jeremiah. Abby keeps her expression neutral.

Luckily, Viv seems to be avoiding her. As Jeremiah speaks, Abby's discomfort only grows, and nonsensically, part of her hopes Viv will turn down his business offer. Even though she wants to shadow Viv, follow this story. She asked for it ten minutes before. It was the best-case scenario she and Fred had discussed. Still, there's something embarrassingly intimate about sharing their night at the Leiths.

After some petty admonishing, Jeremiah turns on his salesman charm. Viv agrees to work for him and to let Abby shadow her. Abby's anxiety spikes. She needs to get ahold of herself. She can't help feeling a bit out of her depth. Her pocket vibrates repeatedly—no doubt Fred impatient for an update. Abby puts her phone on silent.

Jeremiah leads them both up to his monk-like office. From an old-fashioned file cabinet, he pulls out two manila folders, tosses them on the steel table in front of them. "These are the two we're currently on deck for. Of course, the actual date of the shoot is up in the air. I hope you don't mind me speaking so directly, but it's easiest that way. When they die, we show up. The quicker the better." He looks excited to be sharing his filing system with someone. Like he needs someone to validate that he's a clever boy.

Viv is all business. She opens both folders, parsing through them casually like they contain something mundane. Abby can see pages of biographical data, photos. "You said you're making sure there are no more suicide risks. How are you doing that?"

Jeremiah sits down in his oversized office chair and looks at her with relish. He was obviously waiting for this question. "Background reports, including psychological information, on all potential clients. It isn't 100 percent. It can't be. But it's as close as we can get."

Abby jots notes on her phone. Per her deal with Jeremiah, she can never record his voice. Vic glances at her, then turns back to Jeremiah. "I don't want a repeat of what happened with Cynthia and Oliver. Ever. Those reports are very important to me. I'd like to look them over in detail."

"That's fine." Jeremiah says it with a cutting edge. Like, *you are replaceable.* There's tension between them that Abby can't completely understand. She reaches for the files.

"Do you mind if I take a look at your next clients?"

Jeremiah opens his hands in acquiescence. Viv slides her the folders, and they make eye contact for a brief moment. Abby clears her throat and flips open the first folder. The first few pages are a printout of an email chain between what must be one of Jeremiah's accounts—no name is mentioned—and the prospective client. In it, the client details what they would like from the shoot, some specific positioning and props. There's also a lot of fluff, unnecessary back-and-forth that doesn't tell much at all. It seems ridiculous to be looking at a printed version of an email chain. It's like Jeremiah just wanted the folders to be thicker, which he probably did.

After the emails, there are the results of the background check, some private investigator–style photos, some information from the client's psychiatrist that seems highly illegal and unethical to possess. It's too comprehensive—like it's all made-up or he had to step over some lines in order to gather so much data. Abby can't help but think it all feels like it's for show; she's just not sure if it's for Viv's sake or her own. Maybe both.

"So, what are the next steps?" Viv asks Jeremiah. He takes the folders back, holds them up on either side of his face.

"We wait. See which comes up first. That is, if they both seem satisfactory to you?"

Viv nods slowly. "Yes. I would like a bit more time to look over the information, though."

A look of aggravation flits across his face, but then he smiles. "Look at you, doing your research. Sure. That can be arranged." For now, he tucks the folders away again in the filing cabinet. "Obviously, the shoot will come up very last-minute. That's part of why you're being compensated so highly. You need to be available whenever the call comes. I'll let you know when that is. Ms. Katz, I hope that the special nature of this chance to shadow Ms. Klein allows you to clear your schedule and be there as well. I think we can get some pretty compelling stuff for the *LA Times*."

With that, the meeting is over. Andre appears at the push of a button to escort them to the door. Abby grew up around a lot of rich people, but this is a bit too *Upstairs, Downstairs* for her. She can only hope that Andre is getting paid generously for this. He closes the door silently behind them before she can thank him.

Back in her car, she immediately calls Fred, fills him in on everything that has transpired. He agrees that the files feel over-the-top, performative, but he doesn't think she should read into it. "This is the golden ticket for us. He's giving you access. Of course, don't trust the bastard. But take what he's given you and run with it."

Fred already spoke with the editor the day before, getting the green light to work with Abby on this piece. Everything is going as well as it can this early into the process. Abby doesn't want to jinx it. As Abby turns out of the neighborhood, another call comes in. Her stomach lurches. "Viv Klein is calling me."

Fred's voice comes through the speaker a little garbled. "Well, answer it. Call me back later." Abby hangs up on him and answers the phone.

"Hello?"

"Hi. I just got off the phone with Jerry. The call literally just came in for the first client—Amy Lee. Don't worry— not the singer. I think he sent you the address. It's in the San Gabriel area. We can either meet there, or, I mean, I know you're going to be observing for the newspaper, but I could use some help loading and unloading my car. This is the one who wants the whole rainbow effect, according to the file—not that I really got to absorb what it said. I'm going to need to bring a lot of lights. We could meet at mine and go together? I could explain my ideas for the setup on the way. Up to you." Abby hasn't had time to go through her notes, consolidate her thoughts on the morning, let alone get herself into a headspace to speak with Viv Klein. Hell, they just left Jeremiah's house minutes ago.

She hangs a left on Barham and starts toward East Hollywood.

VIV/EVELYN

The setting feels fuzzy, like an out-of-focus photograph, like the edges are rounded when they are supposed to be square. Maybe they are—it's hard to focus on the architecture behind the rush at the intersection as the light turns and the throng presses forward. At first glance, it's a normal, bustling city day. Men in suits and felt hats, women clacking by on heels that peek out beneath their peacoats. Their clothes look a little funny to her, but she can't place why. She tries to remember who she is, why she's here. She crosses the street before the light turns again, because it seems the sensible thing to do. She was standing on the corner. She must want to be on the other side.

The buildings around her feel incredibly small, or maybe she feels incredibly big. She looks down. She doesn't look incredibly big. Sensible tan skirt, blouse, coat. Kitten heels. In fact, she doesn't remember being this small. Everything feels slightly askew, like looking into a mirror and seeing your twin reflected back at you. It's when the cars start popping out of the storm drains on Fifth Avenue that she realizes this is a dream. One of those funny dreams where you know you're dreaming but you can't stop, can't derail whatever's coming next. In front of her towers the Empire State Building. Everything else shrinks in comparison.

She vaguely feels of this time and not of this time, whatever time this is. Frustratingly, she can't remember her name, let alone put a finger on when there were hardly any skyscrapers in Manhattan except the art deco behemoth in front of her. She must be existing in a previous iteration of New York, but that's irrelevant. She's here now. Details slip out of her grasp before she can interpret them. She is a person in a sensible tan skirt buying a ticket to the observation deck of the Empire State Building. She is a person riding more than one thousand feet up and up in an elevator and stepping out onto a floor where she can see all of Manhattan, but this isn't Manhattan. She looks south—no World Trade Center. Not again. No, no, there's nothing this high up. It's like the city was bombed, or disappeared, or was never really there. She feels invincible. She feels peaceful. She feels the nothingness of the height and space and air.

She leans on the railing now. She knows what's coming. It doesn't particularly scare her. There is still some other potentiality that could be, other than this. But she doesn't want it. Didn't choose it before coming up here. What is it? Gone in the wind pushing toward the Hudson. What's the use in trying to pin down these pesky details, when really what matters is she didn't care to pursue them? She wants this. The nothingness of the height and space and air. There is no in-between, between the other and this, not for her. She knows that much about this odd, flattened Manhattan.

She sets her purse down on the railing, loosens her scarf, and straightens her back. One foot slips out of the shoe, plants on cold concrete, then the other. The movement is quick, decisive. There can't be any waffling or she won't clear the building itself. Then, she flies. In this odd, unreal Manhattan, she truly does. She unfurls her arms and soars up past the top of the building, coasting back down in a spiral to the eighty-sixth floor. Her scarf floats behind her on the breeze.

She nose-dives and lets the wind whistle past her ears. She does a couple of corkscrews for good measure. At the twentieth floor, she slows herself, pulling up short to look for a good spot to land. The gleaming black hood of a Cadillac parked alongside Thirty-Fourth Street. Welcoming, warmed by the sun. She sets her body down. The metal crumples around her like satin sheets. She can finally rest.

It's hard to rest, though, when everything and everyone is so loud. Cars screech to a stop, their idling turning to a frustrating drone.

Then, there's screaming, more annoying than the cars. The sounds of people running. Cameras clicking. That's the loudest. It's impossible to rest with that infernal sound in her ears. *Click. Click. Click. Click. Click.*

Viv shoots upright in bed. Connor jumps to the floor, poofy. Her shirt sticks to her sweaty back. She picks up her phone, checks the time. Four a.m. She's barely been home an hour from the shoot and already managed to have a dream that will keep her up the rest of the night. She runs a hand through her hair, debating the age-old question: coffee or whiskey? She decides on whiskey, pouring an inch into a coffee mug. Back in bed, Connor jumps up next to her again. She pulls out her laptop, aimlessly clicks through emails just to have something to do with her hands.

She thinks about texting David, then thinks better of it. He's probably awake but would be self-righteous about comforting her. It would be unbearable. She decides to text Abby Katz instead. The shoot went well. Any awkwardness between them faded as the night went on. There was a job to do. Abby was only observing, but she was enthralled, and it pleased Viv. It's the artist's quandary of balancing extreme vanity and a constant, aching need for validation. Abby Katz fills that need, at least partially. It's more than just the fact that she's writing about Viv for the *LA Times*. There's something vindicating about Abby's personal interest in Viv's work, and yes, in Viv herself.

Viv opens a new message.

I just had a dream that I was Evelyn McHale.

Then—

Do you know who that is?

Viv tosses her phone to the side. It's probably too late to text. She closes her eyes but can still see the crumpled black satin of the Cadillac, hear the clicking of camera shutters. She feels wobbly, half-stuck in the dream. She takes a drink, opens her flagged emails. There's one from an unknown address—someone who apparently found her via her website— that she's been avoiding for the past few days. Now is as good a time as any to finally open it.

The sender is looking for an event photographer for an engagement party. If all goes well they also hope to work with the same photographer at their actual wedding. Viv has done weddings before. She's done everything before. Wedding photography pays well, even if it's not where her heart lies. She always likes seeing people so happy, and it feels like a job that's actually important—documenting a turning point in people's lives. Maybe that's her schtick. Maybe she can market herself as a photographer who records all of life's big moments, from birth to death.

But the idea of agreeing to the photo shoot feels odious. She hates to think of her current work as exciting, artistically fulfilling, but it is. That's the truth of it. Whether or not she wants to love it, she does. She doesn't want to hustle from gig to gig, shooting tepid work that pays the bills and nothing more. She wants to capture people's purest essence—that moment when, despite the elegant lighting and perfect framing, they let their guard down and say something interesting by accident. The nexus of beauty and meaning. Surprisingly, she found an avenue to that kind of work through subjects that don't say much at all.

Unfortunately, this only confirms the feeling she's always had that she is somehow separate, other, responding to the gravity of a different planet. Sometimes she forgets how this world works, or tires of it too quickly, or never really cares enough to play along. Her parents used to teasingly call her a troglodyte, but that's unfair, on top of being a ridiculous thing to call a child. Her cave has never been one of her own making. Though she feels clueless, she tries to play the part, but somehow people still see through her. Jerry Fink did. He sees her as different, flawed, someone who would do something like this. The truth is she's always run in an alternative groove. Now, that groove has diverted even further from the norm, but this is the track she's always been on. She wants to continue working with Jerry. She needs to.

Viv leaves the email flagged in her inbox and shuts her laptop. She doesn't have the heart to shut down the possibility of a gig she would have leaped at a month ago. Not yet. She picks up her phone and whiskey and heads to her makeshift darkroom. Sitting and thinking is only taking her to worse places than Fifth Avenue and Thirty-Fourth Street. She needs

to do something with her hands. Per usual, she nabbed some of the outtakes from the shoot today on her way out the door. She developed the majority of the film back at Jerry's, where he had set up a more permanent darkroom for her in the garage. Abby saw Viv slip the roll of film into her bag but didn't say anything. Viv doesn't know why, but she feels like she can trust her not to tell Jerry. She's less sure Abby won't tell the audience of the *LA Times*. Now, she places a negative on the enlarger and snaps it on, turning the focus knob slowly. In the dim red light, Amy Lee comes into focus. Viv's phone buzzes in her pocket.

Your photo of Karen Elmes was compared by a lot of news sources to the photo of her, so yes. It may shock you, but I did do my research. Why are you awake?

Then, moments later—

"I have too many of my mother's tendencies." That line from her note stuck with me. I guess I'm no better than the rubberneckers hypothesizing about Karen Elmes on the Internet.

Viv types out a quick response.

Which photo did you look at first? Don't tell me you saw the photo of McHale before you ever looked at mine.

And why are you awake?

She shoves her phone back in her pocket and returns to the enlarger. The setup was hard to achieve in the house, but the results are undeniable: Amy Lee got her rainbow. It arcs out from both sides of her like wings. The photo is from the top down, directly above, barely doable with a twenty-foot ladder and a tall garage. Not that you could tell it was taken in a garage.

Everything fades into black on the edges, nothing but the ebb of red, orange, yellow, green, blue, indigo, and violet rays into nothingness. Viv let the colored lights stay slightly overblown in exposure, blossoming out from themselves through the medium of her vintage lens.

Viv had a neutral-colored white light with her on the ladder, but the result on Amy is subtle. It just adds clarity to her form—which takes up about half the frame. It creates a focal point, a brightness to her face, like Amy is lit almost from inside, with the rainbow arching around her, and she is radiant. Her peaceful expression helps. Her son said she was glad to go. She looks young, midsixties at most. Her face is so clear, so set. Now, it makes Viv think of Evelyn McHale wanting to fly. The freedom of the wind beneath her outstretched arms.

She took the first roll she'd shot, back during the trial and error of figuring out how to position the ladder and herself on top of it. The resulting photo on the enlarger is a little off-kilter, askew. Most of the roll is. Viv switches off the enlarger and carefully replaces the photo with another negative. This one is slightly blurred. The ladder shook while she was leaning out over the top. Still, there's something compelling about it, the arch of the rainbow on either side of Amy almost like wings in flight.

An idea tugs at her brain. This blurry image alone won't work, but paired with the focused photo, she could put Amy Lee in the air. Give her the freedom of the wind. If she scans both negatives and does her post work digitally, combining them into a double exposure, there might be something of interest. She's already turned off the enlarger and is flitting about the bathroom before the idea is fully formed. Her pocket buzzes again.

I will tactfully refuse to answer that question.

There's something comforting about bantering with the reporter. Viv shoots off another response as she flicks on the overhead bathroom lights.

Sometimes no answer is an answer.

Why do you think I dreamed I was her, not the photographer? That feels strange.

Then, she puts her phone on Do Not Disturb and gets to work. For the next few hours, she scans, combines, and edits her two photos, meticulously layering the blurry image on top of the focused one, experimenting with opacity and contrast. She scoots back from her laptop as the sky begins to brighten, scraping her rickety chair so loud across the kitchen floor that Connor hisses. She turns her laptop's brightness as high as it goes and full-screens the final image.

The composite is ethereal. Amy Lee's tranquil face is the focal point of the picture, a slight smile creasing her lips. For the center portion of the image, Viv left the overlay very subtle. The slightest softening of lines, the slightest doubling of angles. On either side of her sprout rainbow wings, seemingly in motion, both in focus and not, a heavenly spray of color. It's as if she's been caught in motion, mid-flight, a moment of stillness between the beating of wings. Just her and the nothingness of the height and space and air and color.

Viv holds back tears. She wants to share this with someone, to not be the only one who has seen it. She sends a copy of the photo to herself on her phone and opens her conversation with Abby Katz. There's a new message.

Someone told me recently that dreams tell you something you need to hear about yourself. Don't know if I believe it. Do you feel enlightened?

Viv sends her the photo of Amy Lee.

Before I do something stupid like post this online, I feel like you would appreciate it.

It's silly to think Abby will respond immediately, hours after her last message. It's daybreak, for God's sake. She puts the phone down and goes to the window, basking in the moment of clarity that comes with creating something satisfactory. The sky is rosy over Mount Hollywood. There's something so hopeful about the start of a new day. She starts to heat up water for her coffee. Before she can think better of it, she opens up her email and clicks back to her flagged messages. She types out a reply to the request for an engagement photographer, citing her busy schedule as the reason that *unfortunately, at this time, I can't commit, but I hope the wedding is a huge success!* She hits send as the water begins to boil.

DAVID

Jerry called late in the morning when David was still at the gym, finishing a set of squats. He let the call go to voicemail. The last time they had seen each other, Jerry gave him a furious verbal castigation, leaving David in a sour mood, turned off both sexually and as a potential business partner. Still, when Jerry called a second time, David knew well enough to answer. Jerry wasn't one to be ignored.

David's pride had been hurt by their last conversation, but then again, he had gone behind Jerry's back with the Leith photo shoot. It was supposed to have been a brilliant move to show his competence and value to a man who was rarely impressed. And in some ways, Jerry respected the balls needed to do what David did. But there would be repercussions. That much he made very clear. David needed to prove his loyalty and how hard he was willing to work. If he did, it could potentially be very lucrative for him, doors could open. Jerry was always vaguely hinting about this sort of thing, but never was willing to make good on it. Yet. David tried to neutralize his emotions. This was the danger of mixing business and pleasure. He had to be patient.

Jerry was brusque on the phone. Apparently, there wasn't much time to spare. The next client was ready. Though the family had insisted there was no way she would pass away outside the home, that was exactly what happened. Now, David was on retrieval duty. This had never been formally established as part of his job description, but Jerry told him he was on "the shit end of the stick for this next one, if it comes to it." Well, it had come to it, and it was truly shit.

He drove out to Santa Clarita at once, shirt sticking uncomfortably between his back and the car's leather seat. He hated not showering after a workout. Hated the feeling of being sticky. It only exacerbated his foul mood. Of course, Amy Lee had chosen a horrible place to die. Not only had she passed in Santa Clarita, an hour drive away, but she had left this earthly plane in a *dog park*. Apparently, he was not only retrieving her, but also her bereft son and a purebred Yorkshire terrier named Constantine. The son couldn't deal with the body on his own, so David would be chauffeuring them all back to Arcadia.

David had never understood the concept of man's best friend being an incontinent, slobbering beast. The idea of a dog in his car pained him. He wasn't an overly ostentatious person— he prided himself on that— but he was meticulous and careful with his things. He found flashy items to be a stupid way to spend his hard-earned money, unless having them led to making more money. That was the case with his physical appearance and what clothes he wore. Attention to fine detail there was what made him desirable, got him work. No one but him cared about his car. The car was American-made, nice but reasonable. Nothing special, but he treated it like it was. That's how he treated all his things. No one rode in the car. No humans, and definitely no dogs. Not until now.

There was the requisite traffic on the way to Santa Clarita, giving him plenty of time to think about the last time he saw a dead body. He'd been five and had hardly known his grandfather, only met him a handful of times before the funeral. David filed through the line of people paying their respects, his oversized, hand-me-down suit jacket almost covering his fingers. At the front of the line, he stepped forward and looked into the open casket. It looked like his grandfather, but not. He compulsively touched his hand—spurring a horrible, visceral image of meat hanging in a cellar. When David's other grandfather died three years later, he made up a lie about mandatory standardized testing in order to skip the funeral. David wondered if Amy Lee would remind him of meat hanging in a cellar.

The dog park was small but well-maintained. Not quite the disgusting menagerie he expected. A young woman was semi-successfully trying to train a lab to run through the pipe-like tunnel in the middle of the park. Along the edge, two people sat on a bench, a Yorkshire terrier lying quietly in front of them. David took a moment to compose himself, then made a beeline for the bench. He hoped the young woman wouldn't find it bizarre that he didn't have a dog.

David sat down as casually as he could on the bench, scratching the dog's ears for good measure. Slowly, he turned and took in Amy Lee on the other end of the bench. She was leaning back, head lolled to one side, mouth in a half smile. She could have passed for deeply asleep, probably, if one didn't look too hard. Finally, he turned to the ashen-faced man next to him. "I'm David."

The man nodded with vacant eyes. "She wanted to visit her favorite tea shop one more time, so we came up here with Constantine. She used to live up here, you know. I was walking the dog when it happened. I came back to the bench and she was gone. Then, that woman showed up." He looked down at the dog and then back at David, like he had forgotten something. "I'm Zachary."

David didn't reply, just watched the young woman and the lab. Luckily, they seemed oblivious. Unfortunately, they also didn't seem in a hurry. David and Zachary passed the time in silence. At one point, Constantine stood up on shaky legs and came over to David, putting his front paws on his lap. The young woman didn't seem to be looking, so David ignored him. Eventually, he lay back down.

After dozens of unsuccessful attempts, with the lab going halfway through the tunnel and then stopping to obsessively lick the plastic tubing, the young woman gave up. She never even looked over at the bench as she pulled her dog back to her car. As soon as she drove off, David was on his feet. "All right, can you carry her?"

Zachary looked at him blankly. In the end, David had to carry Amy Lee to the car and lay her in the back seat. Zachary and Constantine sat dumbly in the passenger seat, waiting. David was careful never to touch any exposed skin, and later reflected that she reminded him more of a sack of potatoes than meat in a cellar.

He sweated more on the drive down to Arcadia than he had at the gym. What if he were pulled over by a cop, the body found? He would be shot on the spot. The news would use it as an example of why police *did* need to racially profile drivers. You never knew—they might have innocent old women dead in their back seats! Perversely, he found himself thinking about the incredible sob story his sister would have for college applications. She'd probably go Ivy with that one.

And once he made it to Arcadia, he had to wait for Zachary to pull Amy's SUV out of the garage and onto the street. The car was disturbingly silent without him. Once the garage was clear, David pulled in and waited for the garage door to close again. In the dim, warm light, he removed the body from the back seat, placing it carefully on a waiting sheet stretched out behind a pile of boxes. He guessed the boxes had been placed there deliberately to obfuscate the view of Amy Lee once the garage door opened again, though he wondered who had done this. There seemed to be voices inside the house, but he didn't stay long enough to find out. As soon as the body was out of view, David drove slowly out of the garage and turned back onto the street without another word to Zachary.

Now, a day later, after several attempts at rigorous at-home detailing, the car still isn't clean enough to David. It looks fine, smells fine, but it isn't fine. He decides to take it to the full-service car wash down the street. He noticed the place on the corner many times, prided himself on the fact that he didn't pay other people to do what he could easily do himself with some time and a hose. Funny how easy it is to shell out thirty dollars and rid himself of any need to think about why his car feels so unclean. The joys of modern capitalism. He shifts uncomfortably on the plastic seat in the tiny waiting room, listening apprehensively for his number to be called.

This feels like a low point, a place both metaphorical and physical, that he must make sure never to visit again in future. Jerry made a show of punishing him with Amy Lee, and he can't let that happen again. He won't be relegated to moving dead bodies. It's just the same as the social dynamics of the modeling world. You can't let someone walk all over you, or soon everyone will. You have to show yourself to be strong, to command respect. The problem is that Jerry doesn't see him as an equal. Then again, Jerry doesn't see anyone as his equal. That's also very like the modeling world. Inflated egos have to be managed or else they'll bite you in the ass.

David's course of action in these types of situations had always been to show himself as a formidable ally. With people who were just looking to use people, he had learned to show himself to be very useful. If you can't be seen as an equal, you can at least be seen as worthwhile. He didn't get into business with Jerry to be a grunt—and definitely not to ferry deceased women and dogs from Santa Clarita. He admires Jerry's acumen and dedication. He knows they could work well together, that it could be lucrative. Also, he likes sleeping with him. It's such a pity the man always seems to underestimate him.

He decides to send Jerry a message:

I feel like I've been working very hard. Where's my reward?

The reply comes through almost immediately.

Why don't you come over and find out?

David doesn't respond. He stares dully out the over-tinted window of the car wash, mindlessly tapping his foot to the Top 40 song playing through the speakers. He's gotten good at waiting, after all the endless casting calls. His next step is planned out, he just has to bide his time until he can execute it. Replying isn't necessary. He knows what Jerry wants. It's better to pretend to leave Jerry guessing, though they both know there isn't a world in which he doesn't go.

The car wash bathroom isn't the ideal place to fix his hair, but if he breathes through his mouth, it's tolerable. He's in workout clothes again—he was planning to hit up the gym after getting the car cleaned. Fortunately, Jerry likes the gym rat look, the grungier the better. He likes his men to look like they get their hands dirty. It's part role-play, part truth—the silver spoon–fed aristocrat and the everyday Joe. It's better than if Jerry were to pretend to be someone he isn't. That's one thing Jerry never does. He is unabashedly and unapologetically himself. He doesn't have the faux shame others would have about his money, his privilege. There's something equally appealing and appalling about a man so willing to outwardly relish in his white-gloved life.

Eventually, the car is as clean as thirty dollars can buy, and David decides to pretend the overwhelmingly pine-scented air freshener is enough to erase the memory of Santa Clarita. He rolls down the windows and heads to the hills. The driver's seat is uncomfortably oily, probably staining his shorts. Oh well, they won't be on long once he gets to Jerry's house. Traffic is bad, and he feels a bit like he is suffocating in a national park. You would have to shove your face inside a tree to get such an overpowering smell in the wild. He makes a mental reminder to never get pine-scented air freshener again.

Maybe there's a bit to be written about this. Super relatable: How do you get your car feeling clean and untainted once you've used it to transport a dead body? He could use it to audition for *SNL* one day. By the time he pulls up to the gate at Jerry's house, he has run through the entire scenario of Lorne Michaels turning him in to the police while also offering him a season contract. The gate opens silently, and David pulls slowly up to the house, attempting to clear his mind and nasal passages.

Andre is waiting with the front door slightly ajar. David always feels uncomfortable around him. He's much closer in age to Andre than to Jerry. He doesn't find him unattractive. In a different life, they might be friends, lovers. But maybe not. Andre always seems to be judging him. They're both here hustling in their own way, but one's in Jerry's bed and the other responds to the ringing of a bell like a well-trained dog. David slips past him into the house without making eye contact, knowing Andre notes his stained shorts.

David lets himself in through the double French doors at the end of the second-floor hall. Jerry is nowhere to be seen. The blackout curtains are drawn over the floor-to-ceiling windows. David fumbles in the dark for the remote, tripping over the foot of the California King. Cursing, he raises the curtains. With a slow buzz, they fold up, revealing the far-reaching view out over Hollywood toward Downtown. As always, his gaze inadvertently turns to the lacquer case on the side table. He can't help it. The antique pistol makes David uncomfortable—any gun would. His discomfort is only exacerbated by the fact that Jerry refuses to lock it up. He loves to pull it out at parties, explaining that it used to belong to some mob boss. David always tended to excuse himself from the conversation sometime around then.

Jerry argues it's safe enough—he doesn't keep ammunition in the house, never points it at anyone. Though he's never said it outright, Jerry clearly thinks David's dislike of the gun is race-related—even though David never saw a gun before this one and his life was far removed from any kind of physical violence. David doesn't care to explain himself to Jerry, who's a silly boy playing with his toy, completely untouched by consequences. If he wants to think it's a race issue, so be it. Add it to the many topics best left undiscussed between them. So long as no ammunition passes through the doors, David has decided to ignore the firearm.

He pulls his gaze away and notes that the bed is, as always, so flawlessly made-up that it looks like it should be in a department store showroom. He feels the urge to bounce a coin off of the perfectly taut comforter, like in some cheesy mattress commercial. He has no idea who makes the bed every day. It's hard to imagine Jerry doing it, but then again, he's so detail-oriented that maybe he does. It's an endearing thought. That's what he is, endearing and infuriating. Someone to envy, to lust after, to want nothing to do with. A heady mix of intense feelings, often diametrically opposed.

David sprawls across the bed, intentionally messing up the clean lines. Jerry likes to leave him waiting sometimes, wants David to sit with bated breath, obedient and eager. David doesn't feel like it today. He starts to strip. If Jerry wants to take his time, then he'll start without him. Sometimes this pisses Jerry off, sometimes it turns him on. Sometimes both. David slingshots his shorts across the room.

He rips the comforter down, sliding his skin over the silk sheets underneath. He takes his time, languidly gazing out over the city beneath him, hands roaming as they see fit. He can feel himself getting hot, hard, feelings of hunger mixing with feelings of anger. He slows down. His heart is starting to race, the silk sheets painfully cool beneath him. The French doors open and Jerry steps inside, leaving the doors wide open behind him. David almost asks him to close them, but what's the point? Let Andre watch if he wants to.

Jerry smirks. "You aren't a very patient boy, are you?"

He saunters over to the bed in his dress pants and black sweater. He kicks off his shoes and unzips his pants.

"Turn over."

David complies. It's quick and rough, but not entirely impersonal. Jerry remains standing over the bed the entire time. As he finishes, he runs his hand through David's hair once. Then, he zips his pants back up, smooths his own hair back from his face. David rolls over, leaning back on his arms, not satisfied but content to observe how he has undone the other man. Jerry puts his shoes back on, adjusts his belt.

"Going somewhere?"

Jerry turns to him like he forgot he was still there. Instead of the act of sex relaxing him, like most men David knows, it always seems to send his mind into overdrive. Sometimes David finds that to be one of his endearing qualities.

"I have to go over to the studio in a bit. Do you want to have a coffee together before I go?" Jerry always loves a postcoital espresso, says it keeps the heart rate up longer and improves the cardiac benefits of getting laid. It sounds like bullshit to David, and he definitely doesn't need any more caffeine pounding through his system, but Jerry does tend to be more present, more open to talking in those fleeting moments after sex, over a coffee.

"Sure." David slides off the silk sheets, starts to retrieve his clothes from where they landed across the room.

"No need to cover up the view," Jerry says, hitting the button for Andre next to the bed.

David ignores him, pulling his shorts on. "I don't need you distracted. I want to talk business. This was a lovely bonus for my hard work, but we still need

to talk."

Jerry sighs, looking out the windows over Hollywood. "Alas, I do love to mix business with pleasure. If you want to talk shop, who am I to say no?" More like he can never let business go for more than an instant. It's something David likes a lot about him, when it doesn't annoy him.

They're both relentless in their obsession with upward mobility and don't see any shame in it. They both want to live the good life. What's wrong with that? David respects anyone who respects the hustle, and enjoys the occasional commiseration with like-minded individuals. They're both dreamers in their own ways.

Jerry, however, loves to wax poetic about the trials and tribulations of his money-making endeavors. His diatribes tend to be generic and make him out to be a martyr. David usually leaves feeling a severe lessening in his attraction to Jerry, at least for a couple of days. Jerry making money is sexy. Jerry talking about money is borderline Republican.

Jerry starts in with his usual refrain. "Business is so tenuous, though, to talk about. Especially now. You have no idea the stress I'm under trying to keep this damn ship afloat with the superhero schtick. I'm always two steps behind, trying to fund my own creations. I've told you this before, but basically one angle is never enough—not when the entire convoluted shape of the thing is bent against you. You have to keep contorting yourself until you break through. It's how it's built for people like you and, yes, people like me."

This is a well-worn theme with Jerry, the mystifying fact that he sees himself as an underdog, his uncle's position at Warner Bros. be damned. It tempers his personality, makes him not a complete asshole. He thinks the world of himself, but he also thinks the world thinks nothing of him. "I know I've told you I come from nothing, but I don't think you've ever really understood what that means—it's so easy to see everything I surround myself with now and have that seem to absolve everything from before. It doesn't. I never even had the love and support you feel from your mother and sister. Nothing like that. I envy that so much." He's on a roll now.

"What I have is what I built for myself—that's as American as it gets, love it or hate it. If you want to be a winner—yes, I know, what an odious desire to admit to—you have to diversify your interests outside of one pathway, one goal. For me, producing isn't enough. It wants to take up all my time, all my energy, but it can't be allowed to. It can't sustain itself. I'm already sweating over here, solving this never-ending Rubik's cube of how to make money and stay out of trouble. How to take care of my dreams, my friends, myself. I have to get my hands dirty. I have to be the first to attack. You don't have to worry about that. Don't choose to. Let me take care of you. We tried to go into business together. Maybe that isn't for us."

Andre appears in the doorway, studiously looking anywhere but at David. "Two espressos, please, Andre." He disappears, closing the doors behind him. David pulls his shirt over his head and joins Jerry at the window, trying to discern what he's staring at so intently. Whenever Jerry alludes to getting his hands dirty in order to stay at the forefront of the filmmaking game, it always seems to upset him and then he shuts down.

Jerry's jaw is set hard, a muscle popping out in his cheek. David wonders if he's grinding his teeth again. The only person David has ever heard get away with expressing disappointment in Jerry was the dental hygienist on the phone after Jerry refused to come pick up the mouth guard that he had ordered. He had changed his mind and decided it wasn't necessary– an opinion not held by the dental authorities that be.

"The view has changed a lot since I bought this place. You haven't been around long enough to notice, but if we keep enjoying each other's company, you will. The city morphs and changes and becomes something entirely new so quickly. Oftentimes, it's imperceptible in the moment.

A second story added on here, a restaurant bulldozed and rebuilt there. Then, one day, you realize that it's like you're living in some parallel reality, looking out some similar but different window at some foreign LA."

David looks sideways at Jerry, at the muscle working in his cheek. He's so earnest. It's hard to not want to placate him. "Or maybe you just aren't very observant, , so when you finally notice something it surprises you."

Jerry laughs, jolted from his reveries, and turns to face David. "Maybe. So, what did you want to talk about? You're so unrelenting, David. It's insufferable, sometimes. I feel so burned-out constantly, and you're so full of grand ideas. There's so much you want to do, want to achieve. I'm impressed by that."

Jerry waits for some kind of thanks, so David gives him a tight smile.

"I'm sorry, partially, about sending you to Santa Clarita, by the way. I'm sure that wasn't pleasant, but you do understand the need to prove yourself to me, yes? You stepped outside the bounds of our arrangement, circumvented me with the Leiths. Actions have consequences—that's fundamental to how I run things. This isn't going to work if emotions get carried into it. What we do in this bedroom can have nothing to do with how I treat you in regards to anything else. That's what makes me nervous about us being in any other kind of partnership."

"I never asked for special treatment. And actions do have consequences. Which is what I want to talk about." There's a quiet knock on the door, and then Andre steps inside again. He places two espresso cups on the nightstand closest to the window and retreats. David waits for the almost imperceptible click of the door fully closing before continuing. "We both take our vocations very seriously. You're a producer, a businessman. You give your all to all you do. I know you have a lot of high aspirations, things you still want to achieve. You know I do, too. I have a mother and a sister to support. I want to be able to do that without sacrificing what I love."

"The stand-up." It isn't a question, just a statement. Jerry's lips curl upward, though he tries to mask it. He likes being seen with a model; he doesn't understand why David would ever want to give up that sexual status to become a comedian. They don't discuss it much. If they were in a relationship, Jerry would try to forbid it. However, they aren't, and it's best left alone most of the time. One of a million omissions that make this work between them.

Now, David looks Jerry in the eyes petulantly. "Yes, the stand-up. You know that alongside my modeling, I hustle however I can to make some more money. Partially to help out with my sister's school, partially so I can take comedy classes and afford to keep evenings free for open mic nights. You understand the need for multiple revenue streams. You know that I feel firmly that I need to pursue this. So, I do what I can."

Jerry breaks eye contact, lazily crossing to pick up the espresso cups. He makes a big show out of walking carefully back to David with them and hands him one. "I don't give friends loans. I'd feel bad fucking them over with my idea of an interest rate." Jerry drinks his coffee in one long sip, avoiding David's eyes.

"You know I wouldn't ever ask you for money. Don't offend me by acting like you think that's what I'm doing." David downs his coffee and grabs both cups, setting them down on the side table a little too hard. "I want us to keep working together. I want to be considered as integral to this photography endeavor as I am."

Jerry finally makes eye contact. He sighs a long, affected sigh. "To be honest, I hoped this last job would dissuade you from that. It feels tricky, us combining work and . . . everything else. This photography thing was partially your idea, I'll grant you that. But do you really want to continue with it?"

David closes the distance between them quickly, grabs Jerry by the hips and turns him so they are nose-to-nose. Jerry looks surprised, slightly pissed, but he is listening now. "I'm not looking for emotional fulfillment through our work. I'm looking for money. I know how to separate parts of my life. We work well together—you know this. Who has spoken with all these photography clients, gotten them on the books? Hell, who got you Viv Klein? I'm a good frontman, a good salesman. I know how to pick a target and how to follow through. I picked you, didn't I?" He takes a slow step back, shoves his hands in his shorts pockets, and tries not to worry about the stain on his ass.

Jerry stares at him before a broad smile spreads across his face. "Did you practice this pitch? It's a bit corny, but pretty good, nonetheless." David opens his mouth, but Jerry raises his hands in mock surrender. "No, you're right. You've been integral to the process—the success of the photography project so far can absolutely be, partially, attributed to you. You know I'm very reticent. I move slowly when it comes to business relationships. But you're right, if you want in, you deserve it. We can figure out what that means for us."

David relaxes his shoulders. "All right. So no more asking me to pick up dead bodies?"

Jerry chuckles, picks up the remote for the blinds. He never likes to leave them up when he leaves home. He clicks the button. As the room slowly descends into darkness, he walks past David, patting him on the ass. "No more picking up dead bodies. I'll send Andre next time."

Jerry throws open the French doors, letting light spill in. David hesitates, then says what he's thinking. "You know, you can tell me what's bothering you, if you want. I don't know anything about producing and not much about listening, but I'll try."

Jerry laughs, considers it for a moment before his expression closes off again. "Maybe I will take you up on that." David follows him out into the hall, where they part ways. Jerry hurries to the garage, where his electric sports car is already turned on and waiting, making the fake engine noises that David always finds absurd.

David makes his way downstairs alone, where he finds Andre standing in the middle of the living room, staring at the portrait of Jerry's mother. Part of him wonders if the other man was listening, then ran downstairs to pretend to be busy with something else. Part of him feels guilty, but he doesn't know why. David hurries to the front door, pretending not to see Andre. As he turns the door handle, he hears Andre call out, "Goodbye" faintly from the other room. His voice sounds slightly off, strained, but that could be his paranoid imagination. David can't tell if Andre's speaking to him or someone else, so he decides not to answer, closing the door behind him.

ABBY

Per usual, Fred wants to work at a communal table, this time in an unused conference room right by the coffee machines—which Fred has already visited twice. At this point, Abby has almost gotten over the feeling of having to prove herself to him. She even teased him about his caffeine intake. He's listened to her from the beginning, always been respectful. The gruff, hard-boiled reporter attitude runs deep, but he's a soft man at heart. She feels like her investigative and deductive skills are getting better just by talking to him. She's glad his name is going to be on the byline with hers.

He's buried in his Discord server, sipping his third coffee of the day. The Internet conspiracy theorists have been hard at work trying to identify the person who planted the photo of the Leiths at the gallery. Much to Abby's fascination, they seem to be exceedingly productive compared to the police. Fred seems to think they'll find the person within the next day or two—if he doesn't first. Abby hasn't failed to notice that he is always a step behind the Discord participants. While that leaves him drastically ahead of the police, it seems unlikely that he will find the perpetrator first. Fred doesn't seem too concerned about that.

The goal is to poach the conspiracy theorists' find—immediately reach out to the person, secure their story before anyone else can. The mysterious print captured the public's imagination, and an explanation of what happened with the photo will, hopefully, draw interest to the greater scope of what they plan to report on. Fred is confident he's the only journalist on the server. He seems very proud that he looks for stories where no one else does. Abby has to admit that she admires his dogged search across the bowels of the Internet.

He's been furiously trying to track down any other people shooting death portraits in Los Angeles, or outside of it. He's found nothing from the last five years. Before that, there are rumors, but nothing substantial enough to even follow up on. For all appearances, it seems that Jeremiah Fink has cornered the market. That being said, it feels like the burgeoning of something bigger. So far, Abby has been at two of three sessions. There are ten more on the books for the near future. Jeremiah's business seems to be on the cusp of becoming one of the most successful photography businesses in LA, monetarily, while circumventing the law and public mores at the same time. But they don't want to treat death portraiture like a singularity only to discover it's more common than they thought.

Hence, Fred's manic scrolling on Discord and Reddit. He's even spoken on the phone with one or two of the most vocal participants. Despite their mistrust of the media, Fred got them talking. Abby asked if he wanted her to speak with some of them, to lighten his load, but he delicately said no. She isn't sure if he doubts her ability to draw anything out of them, or if he doubts they'd be willing to open up to a woman.

Both Fred and Abby have spoken to Carolyn Leith, who didn't know death portraits existed until David Le Clerc reached out to her mother. Le Clerc seems to be Viv Klein's connection to Jeremiah, as well. As of yet, he hasn't returned any of Abby's calls. She pushed Viv a little on the subject after the last shoot, but she didn't offer up much information on the man other than that he's apparently a stand-up comedian.

The plan is that Fred will continue to search and make sure that Jeremiah isn't copying anyone else. If that can be more reliably stated and the Leith gallery intruder found, they'll have enough to go to print. While those pieces fall into place, Abby will continue to shadow Klein. She also has a more formal interview with Jeremiah scheduled, which she is dreading. She doesn't like his calm, irritating smile. But he's an important source. Maybe the most important source.

Fred finishes his mug of coffee and slams it down on the table. "We need more from Klein, you know. If we want people to understand the artistic ethos of it all, it's got to come from her." Abby shifts in her chair, fiddling with her own coffee mug.

"Is it our job to make people understand the artistic ethos of it all? Do we, even?"

Fred scowls at her, shutting his laptop. "Motivations are interesting. Motivations are part of the story. I've also heard you talk about the photos—you get the artistic factor. Don't act so obtuse just because the photographer scares you." Abby opens her mouth to respond but thinks better of it.

Fred grunts as he stands up, readjusting his belt, which is unsuccessfully circumnavigating his stomach. "We have a *why* from Carolyn Leith, which we can and need to get backed up by other clients, by the way. We have a *why* from Jeremiah. The photographer doesn't like to speak straightforwardly. We don't have her *why*. People want that. I want that. It's literally journalism 101. You need to get it."

Abby almost asks, "*Why* me?" but she doesn't need to come across as a whiny child. Viv doesn't like to talk too much about her thought process, but it's Abby's job to open her up and get her to divulge. She doesn't want to send in Fred. She needs to stop being so . . . what? Intimidated? Fascinated? By their subject. For the first time, Isaac's warning about her involvement in the piece worries her. She hasn't felt this invested in a subject in a long time. Then again, she's spent most of her time writing cultural fluff pieces. Perhaps this is what it feels like to write the kind of work Fred writes. Then again, she doubts he's ever spontaneously kissed a subject. She can't stop thinking about that, or the photos, or her terrible and imminent death. The dreams haven't stopped; if anything, they're getting worse.

"I'm getting more coffee. Walk with me and tell me why your face looks like that." Fred heads out of the conference room. She hurries after him.

"I don't know what my face is doing. I was just thinking about trying to get Viv Klein to speak more openly. She's very self-conscious about the photography. She becomes antagonistic easily. She deflects."

Fred doesn't reply until the coffee streams into his mug. He wrestles to open a packet of half-and-half. "Your face wasn't saying, 'Yes Fred, no problem, I can handle her.' That's what I wanna see. Instead, it's saying, 'Fred, I'm deathly afraid of this woman.' That's not what I wanna see. I know she's a little off. But if it's too much to get through to her, you need to let me know."

"Not at all," Abby says too quickly. She either sounds like she's lying or overeager to please him. It's cringy. She amends her answer. "She can be a lot. I appreciate your offer. But I think getting another reporter involved would only spook her more. I have it handled. Really." Fred nods once, tersely, and pours the half-and-half into his mug.

"Then try a happy face. Your expression is depressing me. Or is that bad to say nowadays? Telling a woman to smile? You know how I mean it. I want to be reassured that my writing partner can handle this. I don't give a shit if you look pretty while doing it." And with that, he brushes past her back to the conference room. Abby's frown deepens.

She debates making herself another coffee, but she already feels wired. She pulls out her phone and texts Viv.

I'd love to sit down and talk some more for the article. Observing your work has been great, but we're lacking some perspective we think you can lend to the story.

The response is almost immediate.

My perspective is invaluable, I'm sure.

Then—

I feel like I've told you a lot already, but okay. Come over.

Come over. It's open-ended. It doesn't have to mean now, but why not? Fred's in a Reddit deep dive. She may as well show her initiative. She puts her mug in the overflowing communal dishwasher and rejoins Fred in the conference room. She clears her throat to get his attention, but he's too absorbed in his laptop to notice her.

"Fred." He looks up, distracted, and grunts. "Viv Klein is open to speaking right now. I thought I might go over to her and try and get a more comprehensive follow-up interview than we've been able to get so far. Does that sound good?"

He looks at her blankly. "Why does it sound like you're asking my permission to do your job? Go." He looks back down at his laptop and starts typing something. Abby gathers her things as quickly as possible. She hates feeling inept. She isn't. She was the one with the lead in the first place. Her work observing and detailing the photo shoots has gotten compliments from Fred, as well as from the editor. It was her compassionate touch that got Cynthia Leith talking.

From the beginning, though, she hasn't been on top of her game with Viv Klein. Something about her knocked Abby off her footing before they even met. She always does her research, yet, for some reason, she didn't look at Klein's photo before the interview. She's starting to think that was the fatal mistake. It set a precedent where Klein didn't really take her seriously. That must be it. And she hasn't given her a reason to change her mind. She sees her as a friend, or something else, not a reporter. And the banter hasn't helped. The lines are just too blurry.

Abby spends the long drive from El Segundo to East Hollywood fortifying herself. She doesn't want to come off as overly hostile—she knows she made Klein go on the offensive the last time she tried to do an official interview. That being said, putting Klein on edge did lead her to try and prove herself to Abby by inviting her to the Leith photo shoot. Still, it doesn't feel like the right tactic this time around. The key is to command respect while also creating a safe environment in which to speak openly.

By the time Abby finds herself walking down the ill-lit hallway to Viv's door, she feels calm, ready to make Fred proud. She almost smiles at the thought, but then forces her lips down. She refuses to smile for him. She rings the doorbell. Abby's eyes almost have time to adjust to the low lighting before the door swings open and Connor the cat comes running out to twine around her legs.

Viv stands in the doorway in her usual chemical-spattered T-shirt, hair in a messy bun. She's wearing glasses. She was probably working in the darkroom. "Come on in." Viv steps back and allows Abby to pass, closing the door behind her. The cat runs away into the apartment. "Before we talk, I want to show you something." Viv heads toward the kitchen, pulls up the various blinds, letting light flood into the apartment. Propped on the counter is a print, about the size of a legal pad. The same photo Viv sent her the other morning: Amy Lee in double, flying on rainbow wings.

"It's a digital print, even though the shoot was on film. I did the double exposure on my laptop after, then got it printed discreetly. Not that anyone can really tell what's going on in the photo without context. Unfortunately, I don't have a way to print digitally here."

Abby leans in close and examines the print. The colors look even more vibrant than on her phone. "It's stunning." She straightens and looks at Viv. "But what can you do with it? You weren't supposed to take any of the photos with you."

Viv looks a little shocked at the question. "I'm not going to do anything with it, I guess. That wasn't the point. The point was just to make it."

Abby pulls out her phone. "Do you mind if I start recording? That's honestly exactly the kind of thing I want to talk to you about. You seem to have this impulse that you can't really control to make beautiful things. Would you agree with that?" Viv leans against the floor-to-ceiling window, backlit.

"Go ahead, you can record." Viv tenses a little. "I want to state that any mention of my personal prints is off the record. I know you're changing names, but Jerry knows it's me, and our clients will, too. I can't admit to taking any photos home. I know you saw me take the negatives the other night, and you'll do with that what you will, but from here on out, I'm not talking about those negatives for the newspaper. I'd prefer if you never mention them, but I understand I can't tell you what to write."

Abby nods, gingerly placing her phone on the counter, facing Viv. "I understand. It's off the record. I don't want to blow up your career or get you in any trouble. Really, I just want to talk about how the same impetus seems to drive you across the board. With Karen Elmes. With all these photo shoots. Do you feel you take risks with your art?"

Viv crosses to the kitchen counter, sits stiffly, formally, and motions for Abby to join her on the rickety chairs. As soon as she perceives the setting as a formal interview, she becomes so different from the caustic texter or confident photographer. "You mean risks in making my art, not artistic risks?" Abby adjusts the phone on the counter.

"I'd like to hear your answer to both, but we can start with the former. So, you think the art you make is risky in its creation?"

Viv can't seem to sit still. She's up again, refilling the cat's food bowl. Abby turns the phone again. "The legality of these shoots ranges from dubious to extremely illegal. I think people would objectively say that the creation of this art is risky. That's on top of the public perception, which I'm afraid won't be favorable. I mean, that was the case with Karen Elmes. Then again, that situation was a bit different." Viv settles into the right angle between kitchen counter and wall, looking like a cornered animal.

"I know you got death threats after posting the photo of Karen Elmes. That must have been extremely hard. So, what drives you to keep shooting these death portraits, knowing the potential repercussions?"

Viv shrugs.Abby waits. Viv spits out one word: "Stupidity." With that, she is flitting across the apartment, picking up a cardigan tossed on the bed and putting it on. She makes her way slowly back to the kitchen. It's odd to see the dichotomy between Viv at work and Viv just existing. Her presence is still commanding, with her scrutinizing stare and proud look, but her energy is so frenetic. There's nothing of the steady calm she seems to exude while shooting. It makes Abby nervous herself. Viv shoves her hands into the sweater pockets and gives Abby a defiant look. "Maybe I just like to create my own personal hell."

Abby matches her look. "I don't know if you really believe that. Plus, I'm not the one to talk to about hell. I'm Jewish—we don't have hell." Viv pulls at her cardigan, looking anywhere but at Abby. "I was also partially raised by a good Roman Catholic, though, so maybe there's a *lot* of hell. Then, you might be in trouble." Viv's lips flutter upward momentarily before she can control it. It feels like a huge success, getting Viv to momentarily relax.

Abby makes a point of pausing the recording. "We really want to be able to fully show your perspective in the piece. Is there something I could do to make you feel more comfortable? I've noticed that whenever I bring up your reasoning behind the art you make, you tend to get a bit reticent." Viv's eyes flash, and Abby winces—the last thing she needs is to inadvertently antagonize her again. But Viv settles heavily back in her chair.

"I'm sorry. This is a big break for you, isn't it? I'm not making it easy." She takes a breath, then looks at Abby with startling intensity, leaning over to press start on the recorder. "I like to have my work speak for me. Then, if people want to laugh, or see me as some odd-duck

curiosity, they can. They can call my work morbid sacrilege and that's that. For me to justify what I do feels like pandering to them. I've tried to make myself, for your benefit, but I'm afraid I keep failing. I take photos—whether people think that's art, beautiful, poignant in some way, or not, isn't up to me. I choose to do what I do because I see value in it." Viv lapses into silence again, looking thoughtfully at the counter. Finally, she adds, "I think that *is* some perspective. I do what I do because I see value in it. Other people can agree or not. Is that printable?" Viv looks miserable. Her mind seems miles away, and whatever she's thinking about isn't pleasant.

Abby finds herself reaching out and grabbing Viv's hand. Viv's expression changes, swooping back from whatever distant thought she was fixated on. She looks at Abby, puzzled. Abby lurches back so quickly her chair scratches on the floor. She can feel her cheeks burning. "I'm sorry this interviewing process makes you so uncomfortable. I appreciate you still trying to be open with us. Fred and I really want to get a comprehensive picture—no pun intended—for the story." She's speaking too loudly. She looks like an absolute idiot. Viv just stares at her, like she's trying to discern something.

"Why did you kiss me that night?"

Abby's hand flies to her phone, stopping the recording. So far, she's shared each recording with Fred in its entirety and he's done the same. It feels wrong and dirty to edit the recording beforehand, but now she has no choice. Viv regards her, calmer than she has seemed so far today. Abby slowly realizes she is supposed to answer. She decides to use Viv's own explanation: "Stupidity."

Viv's expression is indiscernible. "It seems we're both pretty stupid, then, in our own ways. What a shame."

Abby forces herself to make eye contact. "It was inexcusable—kissing you. I should have apologized sooner. It's the second time my actions with you haven't reflected that of an *LA Times* reporter. Instead of addressing it, I pretended it didn't happen. That night was emotionally wrought, and I acted out of character. I can promise I won't cross a line again. I understand if you would be more comfortable speaking with my colleague instead of me moving forward."

For some inexplicable reason, Viv looks amused.

"I'm sorry—is this funny?" Abby spits, then winces again.

Viv shrugs. "I'm just not so sure it's out of character for you, is all." It's as if she's enjoying Abby's discomfort, the seesaw of the power dynamic back in her favor.

Abby snaps, "I don't think you know my character." Then, she leans back in her chair, tries to collect herself. She closes her eyes. It's easier if she can't see Viv's mirth. "I'm sorry. I crossed a boundary with you, and now I'm getting angry at you for your response. There are channels, if you feel you need to report my behavior to the newspaper."

"I know, I already have." Abby's eyes fly open. Viv raises her hands. "Just kidding. You think I don't know I could have reached out to someone if I felt threatened or anything like that? I could have told Jerry I didn't want you shadowing me. I've been initiating correspondence with you. I feel an utter lack of intimidation when I look at you." Viv looks at her like this should ameliorate things. Abby doesn't feel ameliorated.

"I've ruined any chance of you taking me seriously as a reporter. That's understandable."

Finally, Viv's amusement fades. "I've taken you as seriously as I would any reporter. I don't know why you seem to feel like you have to prove yourself to me. It's almost like you just need to prove yourself to you."

Abby scoffs. "I know I don't have to prove myself to you. You just make me feel off-balance, uncomfortable. I don't know why."

Viv raises an eyebrow, a sad little smirk on her face. "See, therein lies the problem. That's been it since before you even met me—when you wouldn't look at the photo. You can't help but judge."

Abby rolls her eyes. She knows she's being unprofessional and doesn't really care. "You're always othering yourself, but people have consistently seen and admired your vision. Maybe not everyone you wanted, but there have always been some. Even in the thick of everything with Karen Elmes. But that doesn't fit your narrative."

Viv stands, moves back into her corner of the kitchen. "Right, because it was part of my narrative to have vitriol thrown at me on the Internet. To receive death threats."

Abby follows her into the kitchen, shoving her phone into her back pocket. The interview is clearly over. "I never said that." Maybe she really is a terrible reporter. She's literally in a shouting match with her subject. This is so inappropriate, but so is everything with them.

Viv slaps the counter in fury, demands, "What do you want from me?"

What a wonderful question. Abby has no idea. She can't think of anything to say, so she says nothing. She realizes she doesn't *want* to say anything. She closes the space between them until she is inches from Viv's face. Viv turns her chin up defiantly. As is always the case with Viv Klein, Abby stops thinking. She reaches out slowly for Viv's waist. Viv doesn't stop her. She allows Abby's hands to rest lightly on her hips, barely touching her. It's discombobulating, going from such a heated argument to this softness, this slowness. Abby pulls Viv closer and leans in, pausing millimeters from her lips. She waits for Viv to close the rest of the distance. She does.

PRIVATE DISCORD SERVER

CONNOR B. (HE/HIM) 11/03/2023 9:13 AM
I have to gloat a little, my dudes, because this
is the benefit of having a girlfriend in the art
business. She handed me the key to this whole
puzzle. I called the guy at the shop she said must
have done the print and I was able to charm some
hot info out of him. Of course, we gots to keep
it on the DL, because she promised her boss she
wouldn't tell the cops the name of the printshop in
case the printmaker got in trouble. I guess he's
tight with the gallery. But, **we** know who made the
print now.

TED H. (HE/HIM) 11/03/2023 9:15 PM
Sorry, I already figured it out without the help
of a girlfriend. The man we're after is named

David Le Clerc. He made the print and planted it in
the gallery, presumably.

CONNOR B. (HE/HIM) 11/03/2023 9:16 AM
What the hell, Ted?! I told you to let me follow up
with the printshop.

TED H. (HE/HIM) 11/03/2023 9:17 AM
It's standard protocol for us to double-check each
other's sources and work. I reached out to the
printer last night. He just emailed me back.

CONNOR B. (HE/HIM) 11/03/2023 9:20 AM
Screw protocol, dude. I'm out. You make this whole
thing a drag. Have fun tracking down David Le Clerc
and living alone without a girlfriend.

TED H. (HE/HIM) 11/03/2023 9:21 AM
Wow, you just accurately stated exactly what I'm
going to do.

ZACH W. (HE/HIM) 10/25/2023 9:33 AM
Why are we fighting? This is great news! We just beat
the 12 on this one, y'all.

PABLO D. (HE/HIM) 10/25/2023 10:03
AM What do we do now?

TED H. (HE/HIM) 11/03/2023 10:06 AM
We have to find a way to get ahold of him, stat. Search
the proverbial phone book, if need be. Basically,
Pablo, start Googling. The man has quite an Internet
presence. We just have to get his attention. God
forbid the police speak with him first, because you
know the story will get completely spun before
we have a chance to parse out what we can from
this criminal.

FRED J. (HE/HIM) 10/25/2023 10:10 AM
Hi, all. I know my entrance to this server was conditional on me never posting, but I feel like I need to reach out and let you know that I would love to speak with you all for the piece I am working on. I feel like we can help each other out.

VIV

It's early for the doorbell to ring unexpectedly. Actually, the doorbell never rings unexpectedly, even later in the day. Usually, it's gig economy workers dropping off food. Friends, what there are of them, don't "stop by." So, when the doorbell rings at 10:30 a.m., it startles Viv, elicits a deep sense of foreboding. She wants to hide. Maybe she can just cocoon in her bed, even if Connor has already trotted to the door. She's felt restless, inspired but without direction, ever since Abby's last visit. She wants to shoot endless rolls of medium format film. Her subject: flowers. She wants to sit and stare at the wall. She doesn't know what she wants and that scares her.

The doorbell rings again. She feels embarrassed by her reticence. It would be nice to say it all started with the death threats, but she's always been one loud sound away from expecting the worst. She doesn't fight, it's always flight. She's being ridiculous, and she knows it. So she stands, makes her way to the door, peers through the peephole. It's David. She ignores the drop in her stomach, the disappointment that it isn't the reporter. She lets him in.

He's disheveled, his usually perfectly coiffed hair sticking out at odd angles. He's in a muscle top, but he looks too veiny underneath, like he's going to pop. He immediately heads for the coffee in the kitchen. He always drinks too much caffeine when he's stressed, which only exacerbates the problem. Connor rushes after him, leaving Viv holding the door. David bangs through her cabinets, evidently upset that she reorganized them. Silently, she joins him and starts making him a cup of coffee. He stands down, watching her, breathing heavily.

It's easy to slip back into old habits. She knows what he's like when he's this upset, knows he wants her to take care of him, so she makes him a coffee and, after that, his favorite omelet recipe—the one good thing she brought with her from Minnesota. It's chock full of cheese and mayonnaise—something he likes to swear he'll never eat. She sets it in front of him, and it's gone almost instantaneously.

Finally, once he has gorged himself, he makes eye contact with Viv. He looks ashamed to be here, to be this vulnerable. She keeps her face neutral, knowing that if she looks too happy to see him, he'll take it as her being smug to see him so distraught. He pets Connor languidly.

"I assume you don't know why I'm here. Otherwise, you probably would have kicked me out by now."

"You can pretty much assume at any given time I'm out of the loop. What did you do and how does it affect me?" Viv gives him a wan smile.

He's succinct in his explanation. There is no justification or apology. Just the facts. He put together the Leith shoot, not Jerry. Once it went sideways, he had this harebrained idea that he could salvage the business by showing off the work. He still has a key to her apartment and she still shares her location with him on her phone. He even knows where she keeps her photography gear. It was only too easy to stop by and copy the SD card when she went out. He didn't have any compunction about it; it suited him, so he did it. Now, it no longer suits him. Some online conspiracy group figured out he placed the print in the Leith gallery and has been bandying his name about on Internet forums.

Even worse, the *LA Times* reporter working with Abby Katz contacted him to obtain his side of the story. It's inevitable that his name is going to become public knowledge on a grand scale. He has some ideas to spin it, make himself into some altruistic good Samaritan. For some reason, he isn't at all worried about the police, which would have been Viv's biggest concern. Maybe he knows something he isn't sharing. Instead, he only seems to care about Jerry and what this means for their relationship and business interests. Eventually, David runs out of things to say. Without an apology, there is only so much information to convey.

Viv hasn't moved from where she is leaning on the counter. Deep down, she can't say she's surprised. The possibility David was behind the photo did cross her mind. He had access few people had; she just didn't really think he would do something that careless. "You broke into my home and stole from me. You broke into an art gallery—I don't even know how you managed that. You moved a Keith Haring painting into a bathroom, for some reason, to replace it with my death portrait. And for what? What was this supposed to do? You aren't part of some kind of international espionage, David. This is crazy. You can't just do things like that."

"Getting into the gallery was hardly international espionage. Carolyn let me in."

Viv straightens. That makes no sense. But then again, that's why he isn't worried about the police. It wasn't breaking and entering.

"I don't understand. Why would she do that? Also, why should I even believe you? By the way, give me back my key. Now." Viv thrusts her hand out so quickly her elbow cracks. David looks from her hand up to her face, eyes dull.

"I don't have any reason to let myself in again."

Viv keeps her hand out. "That's a nice euphemism—'letting yourself in.'"

David shrugs, almost apologetically. "I don't have it with me. I don't keep it on my key ring."

Viv turns her back on him. Immediately, she calls apartment maintenance to request a new lock on her door. When she hangs up, David is staring at her.

"That was really not necessary." He looks chastened, like a much younger version of himself who still gets anxious about making someone mad. Part of her wants to strike him, to see him react to anything outside of himself—and she hates him for this. She was around violent people enough back home to know them for what they are: sad and desperate. She doesn't want that to be her. She can just kick him out. But she doesn't.

"So, Abby Katz knows it was you." It isn't a question. If Fred knows, Abby knows. But David's too preoccupied with his own situation to care why she said it.

"I suppose so."

Viv changes the subject. "So, you aren't afraid anything will happen with the police? Because Carolyn let you in? But the police investigated the situation, so . . . they don't know about Carolyn?"

"I'm finding all this exposition tiresome, Viv. The police won't be my problem. Trust me. Can we move on?" He looks like the perfectly crafted movie version of a man down on his luck. Still roguishly handsome, even glamorous, with his creased shirt and wild hair. Real people don't look like that when they're at a low. Only his red-rimmed eyes and pallor give him away.

Underneath, somewhere, is a person.

"You haven't explained anything, so I don't know why you're so tired. What do you even want to move on to?"

"I'm worried what Jerry will do to me, if I don't do something first." To Viv's surprise, there's fear in his voice. Sure, she didn't like the way the producer tried to threaten her at his house, but she doesn't consider him a serious concern. Especially not for David, who seems to occupy some sort of business-associates-with-benefits role with the man. Jerry is awkward and gangly, anemic-looking. He's vain and petty and speaks grandly, but in Viv's experience, men like this can never back it up.

"What's the worst he could do, stop working with you? Break up with you?" Viv boosts herself up on the counter, hunches over so her elbows are on her knees.

He clenches his jaw, making a vein pop on his forehead. Viv instinctively reaches out and grabs his hand. He lets her. "Jerry doesn't suffer humiliation. He isn't going to just let me slide by on this one. He has to make an example. He already knows I went behind his back. The print is going to put him over the edge. I have to weigh my options here." Viv squeezes his hand and lets it go, sitting back.

She responds softly, "What do you think he can do to you?"

He looks up at her with dilated eyes, big, scared moons. "Whatever he wants to."

Viv doesn't know what to say to that, or if she even believes it. She busies herself putting David's plate in the dishwasher. Eventually, she thinks of the most banal thing to say, "Everything is going to be ok."

From there, the conversation moves away from the Leiths and Jerry and what happens next. Viv's anger has already burned itself out. She hates to admit it, but a photo like that deserves to be seen. Part of her was happy when it showed up in the gallery. It was obscene—a Keith Haring in the bathroom, her photo on the wall. It was exciting. She brews David another cup of coffee. She doesn't see why this revelation should jeopardize her position with Jerry or stop the work they're doing together. It might cause a rift between David and Jerry, and it might mean David loses out on this one particular side hustle. But he's always juggling more than he can handle, anyway. Maybe he'll be angry at her for continuing on without him, but when was he not angry with her for something?

She brings the coffee over to the bed and slaps the mattress next to her. David looks over at her from where he is slumped at the kitchen counter. "Come on. There isn't anywhere else to sit, so get cozy." He slowly gets up and shuffles over, sitting down heavily on the mattress beside her. Viv hands him the mug and opens her laptop, pulling up one of the particularly stupid reality shows that David used to watch religiously back when he stayed with her.

"Are you caught up?" she asks. He shakes his head. "Well, settle in, because we have a lot to watch, then." Sitting shoulder to shoulder in amiable silence, David's jaw slowly unclenches, his brow unfurrows, and the heat of his shoulder presses into hers. It's nice, she thinks. Sometimes, trust doesn't matter as much as just having someone around. Especially with her overactive mind. She'll get the locks changed. He'll do something to remedy the situation while only making it worse. They'll continue to bicker and fight and somehow remain friends. But for now, they'll binge-watch a whole season of television, letting their brains drift off together.

ABBY

It feels like she's always in her car these days—perpetually headed to the Eastside or home from it, leaving her feeling drained and testy. She wonders if self-driving cars are as close on the horizon as Isaac seems to think. Of course, he doesn't really have a stake in the technological revolution because he prefers his feet or, more recently, just being sedentary on her couch. He makes being home almost as draining as being out—constantly fretting about her "important article." At least he takes Gordita on walks.

Today, leaving Brentwood for the Hollywood Hills feels like an escape. Isaac spent all morning blaring his ska music on the record player. He called it soul-searching. She called it impossible to think over. She could still hear it from the driveway. He can't control himself whenever he has too much energy and nowhere to direct it. Abby, on the other hand, can never control herself when she *does* have a place to direct her energy.

When she left Viv Klein's apartment late the other night, she edited the recording of the interview and sent it Fred's way with a long, convoluted message about forgetting to send the file earlier. She made too big a deal of it, which might have raised some questions from the veteran reporter if so much hadn't happened afterward. Fred's Discord server group of conspiracy theorists identified the Leith gallery trespasser as

David Le Clerc, Viv's friend who had introduced her to Jeremiah Fink. Fred leaped so hard on the lead that he almost scared the conspiracy theorists off completely.

Fred reached out to Le Clerc but unsurprisingly received no response. From what they've deduced about him from Viv and Jeremiah, he's a tight-lipped man, despite his huge social media presence. He'll be cautious about speaking with reporters. That makes the job harder, but not by much. A lot of people don't like when Fred comes calling, and Fred doesn't particularly mind.

He was prepared to roll up his sleeves and continue on gumshoeing, but then, out of nowhere, Jeremiah called both Fred and Abby and, sounding like a jilted lover, asked them to meet with him first. He alluded to knowing something about Le Clerc that would help their story—a vague promise they had to follow up on. Hence, the drive to the Hollywood Hills this morning.

Abby isn't as certain as Fred that Jeremiah will have anything worthwhile to say. She can see him dragging them across town only to try and malign David Le Clerc's character with baseless, petty accusations. Jeremiah insisted on holding the interview at his house, which isn't convenient for anyone—he himself has to drive back from his office in midtown. But he refused to meet with Abby and Fred at his production company, saying, "This isn't business. This is me performing my civic duty." Something about that rubbed her the wrong way.

Abby knew she was bobbing in murky waters when she texted Viv immediately after learning about Le Clerc to see if she had heard the news. That was two days ago. She didn't ask from an investigative standpoint, which she was sure Viv would understand. She simply wanted to see if she was all right. David Le Clerc was supposedly Viv's close friend. She must be feeling betrayed, angry. It would be callous not to check in. As soon as she sent the message, she regretted it, but the response came almost instantly:

Let's just say I had to get my locks changed because of him. Lesson in keeping illicit photography more under wraps.

Of course, she hadn't known about the print.

Since then, they've kept in slow but constant correspondence. Viv seems fine, all things considered. Abby is acutely aware that Jeremiah didn't mention wanting to say anything about Viv during the interview.

She can't help but think about her mother and how he sidelined her when he felt he had taken what he could. She wants to warn Viv to stay on her guard, but she still hasn't found the words.So, rather than talking about what comes next—or even photography—they've just been texting about the weather and traffic and everyday annoyances.

Fred brought up the possibility of Abby asking Viv to check in with David, to see if he would be willing to speak to them. Abby's response was noncommittal. She's completely overwhelmed, unable to reconcile her job with how far she's stepped over any sensible boundaries. For now, her phone is on Do Not Disturb and her thoughts are focused on Jeremiah Fink. On him and the traffic on Cahuenga that's raising her blood pressure.

When a call from Fred comes through, her chest immediately tightens. He must have called several times already to get past the Do Not Disturb. She knows it's irrational to assume something's wrong. Maybe he wants to discuss something before the interview, but she doubts it. As soon as she answers, her worries are confirmed. He sounds agitated. Her mind flits to all the possibilities—him finding her research to be inadequate, him questioning her emotional attachment to the piece, all the way to him asking her outright about her relationship with Viv Klein.

Fred, as usual, doesn't keep her waiting. He shouts gruffly over the interference on the line. He always insists on driving with his windows down instead of using the air conditioner, even when on the phone. "Abby, what do you really know about Jeremiah Fink's character, other than the fact that he's an asshole? Your mother worked with him before. How long ago was that?" Well, that wasn't any of her suspected conversation topics.

"It's probably been a good fifteen years. Why?"

There is a pause while Fred mutters to himself, the sound of his blinker clicking through the phone line. "Sorry. I hate multitasking, but this is important. I just got a call from David Le Clerc. We absolutely should still go to Fink's and see what he has to say, but I just learned some very interesting information about him. That is, if we can corroborate it. I was wondering if you ever heard anything." For a man who's usually very forthright, he isn't telling her nearly enough.

"Things didn't end well between him and my mom, but I have no idea what you're talking about."

The wind rustles loudly through Fred's windows. He's driving fast.

"Le Clerc seemed to know that Fink was going to throw him under the bus with us today, and so he decided to share some information with the *LA Times* that he's considering taking to the police. Apparently, he has evidence that Fink has been using illegal means to research his potential photography clients. Hiring someone to break and enter, searching personal computers, that kind of thing. According to Le Clerc, he's done this kind of aggressive vetting on business associates for years. Honestly, it's hard for me to believe, because it seems like overkill. I feel like everything he would need to know about a potential producing partner is right on their social media feeds."

Despite how online Fred is to keep his finger on the pulse of the city, he stays completely off of social media in his personal life. Abby remembers him grumbling about even having to have a personal email. He isn't the sort of man to have details of his life aired to anyone, even his friends.

"Le Clerc is worried, or so he says, that Jeremiah's behavior may jeopardize our article. He claims he doesn't want the *LA Times* to get looped into 'a myriad of lawsuits waiting to happen.' You sure you don't remember anything with your mom, or anyone else on the film?"

Abby can't help it, her mind goes straight to Viv. She wonders if Jeremiah Fink has had someone search her apartment. He can't have. They would have found the photos she stole. But didn't David Le Clerc break into her place? She swallows, unsure of how to respond to Fred. "No, I don't. Sorry. Let's hope that isn't true and Le Clerc is just spouting off," she finally manages.

"Obviously, Fink doesn't know that Le Clerc called me. So, we can root around a bit today with him, but I don't want to let on that we have any suspicions about his tactics. It'll be much easier to look into this without him trying to cover his tracks. I know I don't have to tell you that, but just prepare your poker face."

Abby laughs humorlessly. "He already knows I have suspicions about him, just in general. He can't stand that I'm professional with him, but I don't fawn over him."

"Well, then, good. Do whatever you normally do when you speak to him. No sudden fawning."

"That's easy enough." The wind coming through the car speakers is earsplitting. Abby goes to turn the volume down, but then Fred starts to speak again. "One other thing. Le Clerc said that Carolyn Leith let him into the gallery and that she is willing to admit to that, both to us and the police. I struggle to believe she would keep that from me, but that's probably my ego talking."

Fred hangs up, leaving Abby in a deep silence. She almost misses the sound of the wind. In its absence, there are only questions. The traffic is both terribly, tediously unhurried and not nearly slow enough. Before she really feels composed enough for the interview, Abby is pushing down hard on the gas pedal to make it over the last serpentine hump before Jeremiah Fink's driveway comes into view. Luckily, she can see Fred's beat-up 1990s sedan in the rearview mirror. He struggles up the hill after her, one arm hanging out the driver's side window. She parks and waits for him, and they walk to the door as a united front.

Fink's assistant, Andre, opens the door before Abby even has a chance to let go of the bell. He meets them with a smile, but his eagerness disconcerts her. He leads them to the living room, depositing them on the same absurdly low, slate-gray couch that Abby had the misfortune of sitting on before. Fred grunts in discomfort.

After asking if they want anything to drink, to which Abby desperately wants to reply vodka but instead says nothing, Andre disappears into one of the house's numerous other rooms. Abby glances at Fred, who is uncharacteristically silent. His eyes are focused on the wall above the fireplace. She forgot that he's never seen any of Viv Klein's works in person. His expression is thoughtful. He leans forward over his knees, taking his readers out of his breast pocket. The tiny, round lenses glint in the sunlight and soften his look, making him look older but also less haggard. With the glare, it's hard to see his eyes.

"Well, I guess I get the appeal. She's beautiful. My mother would have loved something like that—her playing mahjong or walking her damned Pomeranians preserved for time immemorial. Sounds like I wouldn't have been able to afford it, though." He takes his glasses off and puts them back in his pocket, his fat fingers overstepping the thin wire frames, smudging the lenses. He repeats, "She would have loved something like that." He tears his eyes away from the photo and looks discerningly at Abby. "You okay?"

She doesn't get a chance to answer. Jeremiah comes bounding into the room, dressed in his usual attire, but with a scraggliness about his beard that she has never seen before. It lends him a bit of a manic air.

"I'm so sorry to keep you waiting. Everyone, down to the interns, seems to have a question for me right when I'm headed out the door." Abby highly doubts Jeremiah has spoken to an intern in years—unless he was trying to bed them. Fred begins the laborious process of struggling to his feet.

Jeremiah doesn't wait for him to stand completely, giving him a firm handshake that almost knocks him back onto the couch. Jeremiah offers his hand to Abby, who notes how cold his fingers are. He doesn't look well.

The three of them stand in awkward silence while Jeremiah stares at the ground. Then, just as dynamically as he entered, he turns on his heel and gestures for them to follow him out the sliding doors to the backyard. "I can't think inside today—it's too nice outside." Jeremiah leads them to the patio table where he, Abby, and Viv formalized their arrangement.

Jeremiah sits on the edge of the table, forcing Fred and Abby to have to lean back to look up at him. Whether or not it's a mind game is hard to say, but either way, Abby's getting annoyed. For his part, Jeremiah looks distracted, off in his own thoughts. He stares at the pool almost wistfully. "If you both don't mind, I may take a swim while we talk." He hops off the table and starts to strip.

Abby exchanges a glance with Fred.

"Sometimes I wear my swim trunks to work in case I have a chance to jump in the pool on my lunch break. I usually end up back here midday, unless I'm on location. Thank you for indulging me." Jeremiah sheds his pants. Abby can't help but notice how pale his skin is, almost translucent. His sparse, wiry chest hair sticks out straight from his bony torso—something Abby did not want to know.

He dives into the water with an ease that belies his awkward form. He shoots to the bottom, butterflying from one end to the other, a wavering shadow getting farther and farther from the table. Finally, he pops up like a seal at the far end of the pool. He calls to the journalists, watching incredulously. "Feel free to join me. I have some spare swimsuits around here somewhere."

Fred gets up and makes his way to the pool edge, looking down at Jeremiah with his hands on his hips. "No thanks," he says, an edge of irritation in his voice.

Jeremiah swims over to the edge of the pool, resting his arms on the patio deck. "I'm really not trying to get out of speaking with you. I know

I'm the one who called this meeting. I guess you could say I am just feeling a bit uncomfortable, is all. David is someone very special to me."

Abby joins them. Standing at the pool, leaning over Jeremiah while he floats beneath them, is almost more uncomfortable than him towering over them. Abby tries to ignore the odd tableau and speak as if this were a normal interview. "I'm sorry this news has been hard for you. Feeling uncomfortable with the situation makes absolute sense. We just want to do our best to understand the facts in their totality in order to report on them."

Jeremiah pushes off the side wall with his feet, bobbing backwards, out of their shadow. The sun gleams off of his wet skin.

"I think you misunderstand me. I'm not uncomfortable with what David did. I knew about that. Of course I did. I was running this whole operation. That's not the issue at all. What I'm uncomfortable with is how I'm afraid he's going to be portrayed in the news. I don't want to see him villainized."

Fred clears his throat. This is an unexpected turn. On the phone, Jeremiah sounded irate at David.

"We aren't interested in villainizing anyone." Abby quickly interjects. Jeremiah looks at her uncertainly, making a show of clamping his mouth shut.

Fred shoves his hands in his pockets. "So, why did you want to meet with us? What is it that you want to share about David Le Clerc—something you think will vindicate him?" Fred's voice is neutral, but Abby can see him stand up a little straighter. When elements don't fit together, his mind goes into overdrive, rotating the pieces a thousand different directions like Jenga on steroids. He always finds the missing piece, always rotates what he has until it fits. He's just not there yet with Jeremiah.

Jeremiah treads water, looking between the two reporters. "What I wanted to say is that he was following orders. I don't take any responsibility for any laws he broke, but I do understand that he mistook my instructions and was acting in good faith. I'd hate to see our collaboration turn sour because of this. I'd love to see both of you continue to enjoy the behind-the-scenes access I've given you to my photography business. I do really think you could write a very compelling article." Jeremiah ducks under the water, shaking his head like a dog when he comes up again. His beard floats out in front of him on the shimmering surface, reminding Abby of some floating detritus making its way to shore.

Fred sighs. "Are you trying to say you're going to stop assisting us with our research if we pursue the story of David Le Clerc breaking into the Leith gallery?" His voice remains pretty neutral, but Abby is close enough to see the ball of his fist in his pants pocket.

Jeremiah swims in lazy circles below them. "Exactly."

Fred nods once, tersely. "Well, I think we've gotten quite a lot from Abby's observations. We will be fine with what we have so far from you. Thank you for your time." Fred turns and starts to walk back to the sliding glass doors. Abby hesitates, then follows him. They have no choice; they can't have a source telling them what they can and can't look into. As much as she hates to admit it, Fred is right. They have a wealth of material already.

Fred is already half-inside before Abby hears the slap of wet feet on the patio behind her. She turns to see a dripping Jeremiah jogging carefully toward them. He halts a few feet away, a puddle of water forming around him. Water beads in his wiry chest hair, and a steady drip falls from the tip of his beard. Fred stands behind Abby in the doorway, one hand against the jamb, waiting. Jeremiah flashes them an apologetic smile. "I overplayed my hand, didn't I? You can't fault me for wanting to protect him." He looks expectantly at Fred, who remains silent.

"Forget I said anything. Feel free to observe, to talk to me, to talk to Viv Klein. I'm not trying to get in bad with the press. I'm a huge proponent of free speech."

Fred shifts his weight. "Do you understand that we will be looking into what happened at the Leith gallery, potentially speaking with David Le Clerc?"

Jeremiah wrings out his beard, overflowing the puddle in front of him, which starts to drain toward Abby. "I understand." Then to Abby, "Sorry about that." Jeremiah takes a step back, arms out. "Look, this next shoot is going to be spectacular, of a scale we haven't yet seen. I want you there. I want you to get the full story. I'm a hardballer—I'm sorry that came out in our conversation. I get that this isn't my production company. Are we good?"

Abby lets Fred take the lead. He taps his finger on the doorjamb. "We're good."

Jeremiah looks to Abby, who repeats, "We're good."

Jeremiah beams. "All right, well then, Viv will let you know when we're good to go on the next one." He starts to turn back toward the pool, then adds, as if it's an afterthought, "I'd just hate to see David get in trouble for breaking and entering. The Leith gallery isn't the end of it, you know? We've had some trouble here at the house, as well, with him finding his way in when the doors were locked. He's a wonderful guy, but he's a bit troubled. Just be careful with him." Jeremiah shrugs and jogs back to the pool, disappearing under the crystalline surface.

Andre meets them back in the entryway, asking again if there's anything they need before they leave. While she waits for Fred to return from the bathroom, Abby's eyes wander over the shelf of industry awards tucked into an alcove. A sculpture partially obscures them, making a show of modesty. Two of the awards are for *Skywanders*. When Fred finally reemerges, they walk in silence to their cars. They aren't even down the driveway yet before Fred calls.

Ten minutes later, they're tucked in a back booth at a diner that's trying too hard to be nostalgic for a time in which it never existed. They both order coffee and watch the cars on Franklin Avenue. A withered hydrangea sits in the middle of the table, drooping over the sides of a glass pebble–filled vase. Abby supposes it was meant to add some color and life to the dark corner, but instead it fits their moods perfectly. A sense of deflated energy hangs over them. Abby takes her phone off Do No Disturb—no new messages. Good. She doesn't want to talk to anyone until she's wrapped her mind more fully around the last hour. Like so many times over the last couple of weeks, she is so glad to have Fred to help her parse things.

Fred doesn't talk until he's halfway through his first cup of coffee. "I don't think I've ever told you about my garden. I grow hydrangeas, among a lot of other things." He motions to the flower in between them. "That one looks like shit. I never like it when people take flowers out of the ground. My wife used to get angry that I wouldn't pick anything from my garden for her. I'd ask her why she wanted something dead when she could just look out the damned window. Then, she divorced me." Abby can't help the expression she makes. Fred laughs.

"She had a lot more reasons than that. But yeah, me not being romantic enough was definitely part of it. I can't say I blame her. Not how my mind works." He shoves the hydrangea across the table toward Abby.

"Here, take this flower—it's a symbol of commiseration from me to you, because we have our work fucking cut out for us."

Abby picks up the half-dead flower and bats her eyelashes at Fred. "You shouldn't have." She pushes the vase back to the center of the table. "Really, you shouldn't have. I'm going to have to tell HR."

Fred finishes his mug and slams it down on the table. "My girlfriend doesn't care if I give her flowers. I'm just supposed to show up with a six-pack of beer. Speaking of which, since you're already calling HR on me, how about we get out of this depressing joint and grab a different beverage? We both need it. I know I can't deal with any more of Jeremiah Fink's bullshit today."

Abby looks at the afternoon light drifting through the windows. "It's still pretty early."

"So?"

Abby finishes her coffee. "So, nothing. Let's go."

It's no longer early when Abby puts Fred in a rideshare and sits back down on the curb, waiting for her own ride. The hours passed quickly, the street lights blooming out over the concrete while they sat in a favorite haunt of Fred's. The world spins slightly, but not unpleasantly. Abby leans back on her elbows, barely eliciting any looks from passersby. This is Hollywood. Isaac pulls up to the curb. Abby stands shakily and opens the passenger door.

"I don't want to hear it, okay? He's my boss. Well, he isn't my boss, but he's important. He's an important reporter and I'm learning from him, okay?" Abby slams the door behind her, punctuating it with a hiccup. Isaac turns on his ska music, loud, and pulls a U-turn.

"I can tell you're learning very important things." He smirks as she punches his arm.

"Excuse me, I just picked you up after you went on a bender with your boss. You could be a bit nicer to me." Abby hiccups again, trying to focus on the road ahead of them. It seems to be moving from side to side. "I bribed you with cheeseburgers if you came. Don't talk about altruism."

Isaac turns the music up louder, shaking his head. "All right, I'll just talk about one *truism*—you're more fun drunk."

Abby ignores him, pulling out her phone. The screen is a little blurry. She's not sure if she got something on it or if it's just her eyes. She eventually finds her text messages and opens them.

Seeing Viv's name is a sobering influence. It brings back David accusing Jeremiah of breaking and entering. Jeremiah accusing David of breaking and entering. Jeremiah trying to strong-arm them into not talking to David. Viv entangled with them both. The names are all soup in her head, getting scrambled together.

Where was the truth? Somewhere in the middle, probably. She's more inclined to believe David than Jeremiah, but the whole situation is too much for her brain tonight. She takes her time painstakingly typing out a text, deleting all the typos that she can find, but they keep multiplying.

Viv Klein, it Abby Katz. I do not trust David Le Cler. Ido not trust Jeremiah Finkk. I feel you are stuck n middle of it all. Do you know ths?

She gives up and deletes the text. She'll bring it up to Viv in the morning. For now, she sinks back into the passenger seat, letting the syncopated bass reverberate through her head as the road dances from side to side.

VIV

The thing about bad ideas is that they are infinitely harder to fumigate from your mind than good ideas. They sit there, perniciously scratching at your consciousness until you give in. At least, that's how it always feels to Viv. But then again, she always worries that she has a harder time than most with ironic process theory. Intrusive thoughts are constantly popping up in her brain before she even consciously decides not to think about them. She's always contemplating the white bear, somewhere under the surface. The illicit always attracts her for the sake of its illicitness.

Basically, it seems doubtful, in retrospect, that she would have ended up anywhere other than here—looking through all the photos she took from the death portrait shoots, envisioning putting together a gallery showing. Yes, she told herself the photos were for her alone, but that lie feels flimsy now. She isn't sure how she ever believed it. It's her tried-and-true Achilles heel rearing its ugly head again. She doesn't know how not to share her work with the world. These photos are something real, something special. She owes it to the subjects not to gatekeep them from the world.

She looks at the pieces she has laid out on the wood floor of the studio apartment. Jeremiah's mother is in the center, swimming up and out of the photo toward the light. On either side are two slight variations of Cynthia and Ollie as the confetti rains down around them. She slides the left-most photo over and gingerly replaces it with the double exposure print of Amy Lee. Viv hesitates, then places a print of Karen Elmes in the row. Her throat tightens. She removes the photo from the lineup. There's time to figure out if Elmes belongs. For now, that one picture seems to hold so much weight that it sucks all meaning from the rest.

The remaining pictures are replete with color, vibrancy, movement. Individually, she loves them, but with them all displayed together, something feels off. It's almost overstimulating, an inundation of saturation. It needs a palate cleanser, something to balance them out tonally. She pulls a print of the photo of Cole Martin's hat from the stack she brought out from her bathroom storage—which she was planning to organize after looking at the death portraits. There's something intriguing about pairing the death portraits with snapshots of everyday life.

She starts to comb through her work from the last year, looking for lifeless life to pair with lively death. The more she thinks about the juxtaposition, the more it excites her. So very quickly, the idea is just an idea and no longer a bad idea in her mind. She is too far down the path of working out how to fit the visuals together to want to admonish herself any longer. She won't allow herself to think it, but this is how this was always going to end. There's a reason she kept this stash in her bathroom—a reason she couldn't stop thinking about any of these photos. It's so easy to give in.

Soon, the natural light starts to fade and she has to turn on a lamp to see the photos scattered on the floor. She would have stayed that way, hunched and squinting in the diminished light, if the phone didn't ring. The number isn't saved in her phone. For some reason, she answers. Part of her hopes it's David calling from someone else's phone, checking in. She hasn't heard from him since their binge-watching night, though he did send back her key by overnight mail. The locksmith had already come and gone, but the gesture was nice.

"Hi, Viv. This is Jerry. I hope I'm not catching you at a bad time?"

She sits back on her heels, surprised. But this makes sense. After everything that happened with David, he's certainly not involved in Jerry's business anymore. Perhaps Jerry's making his own phone calls now. Viv looks down at the stolen photo of his mother.

"No, this isn't a bad time at all. What can I do for you?" Her phone buzzes against her ear.

"Good. If you said it was a bad time, I was going to have to tell you to rearrange your plans. I just sent you the details for the next shoot. The quicker you can get over there tonight, the better." Viv puts the phone on speaker and opens the message he just sent. It's a map link. The address is in Beverly Hills. She waits a moment, but no more information comes through.

"I don't remember any of our clients on the docket living in Beverly Hills. Which one is this?"

Jeremiah is silent for a second. Viv hears him rustling around with some papers. "Oh, right. I think this one didn't get shared with you. I'm sorry. If you could start heading that way, I'll make sure the information gets to you."

Viv frowns. This isn't the way the shoots are supposed to operate. "Can you send it now? I need to know what I should bring with me, lighting and camera-wise."

Jeremiah sighs. "Bring a little of everything. I'm not at home right now, so I can't send it your way. I probably can in the next hour, but time is of the essence. You know that."

Viv stands, begins to clean up her photo-covered floor. "You know I don't like it when things are last-minute. I've been working out ideas for all the clients on the docket. I want these photos to be as good as they can be. Having time beforehand is paramount to the shoots being a success. I need that prep time."

Jerry continues rustling. "Sure, that's ideal, but that's not what you have right now. What I need is a photographer who can roll with the punches. Are you telling me that isn't you? Because if it isn't, let me know and I'll make the call. I need someone there right now."

Viv feels the heat rising in her cheeks, along with the anger restricting her throat. How dare he speak like she's replaceable, like he could threaten her into doing whatever he wants? She looks out toward Beverly Hills. The window is an opaque mirror. She looks straight back at herself through her reflection. She doesn't look happy. The truth is, she *is* replaceable.

"I'll be there as soon as I can." She tries to make the words as withering as possible. Jerry doesn't seem to pick up it. Viv imagines how David would respond to him, sycophantic and smooth. She doesn't have it in her.

As soon as she gets off the phone with Jerry, she calls Abby. The reporter is already on the Eastside of town, so they plan to meet up at Viv's apartment and head to Beverly Hills together. Viv tries not to dwell on her relief that Abby will be coming with her. It's ridiculous to be nervous about upsetting Jerry. It won't bode well for the quality of her work if she spends too much energy on pleasing him. Her modus operandi is to do whatever she wants, even if it diverts from the expectations placed on her. In some ways, it makes her unfit for the freelance life, but in other ways it works. She has numerous repeat clients, after all. If they like how she functions, she works with them again. That's how it was with D— but she didn't care about the work with D.

Originally, she didn't want to want this job badly enough to compromise herself or her vision, but now she worries she's already there. She resolves to take her time tonight, to approach this shoot how she feels is best, no matter what. It's Jerry's fault he didn't prep her. In future, he can figure out the logistics of how to get her what she needs. In the end, this isn't the end of her career. She knows that now. Even if she stops shooting for him, she'll shoot again. She has to let the care go.

Viv hides her prints back in the bathroom storage before gathering her shooting equipment. There's no need for Abby to know about her bad idea for a gallery showing. Right now, that's all that it is, anyway, a bad idea—a blip in her subconscious that peeked out and found purchase in her mind. Viv finds herself caring more than she imagined she would about what the reporter thinks of her, but this isn't at all like the worry she feels about Jerry. It's exciting, freeing. She feels lighter when the reporter is around—doesn't have to compromise anything. If anything, seeing her own work through Abby's eyes is clarifying, oil in water.

But when Abby arrives, she's oddly quiet. She takes up a spot out of the way of Viv's equipment organizing and pensively pets Connor. Her mood has to be about the text she sent the other morning. She was convinced Jeremiah and David were going to implode the whole photography enterprise, and that Viv would be the one to take the fall. She seemed to think there was some kind of blackmailing component, as well, which Viv thought was ridiculous. She reminded Abby she's a photographer, not a mobster. Abby reminded her she takes photos of dead bodies. They dropped the discussion, but now, it looks like Abby wants to pick it back up again.

"Jeremiah told to me this next shoot was going to be a big deal, that he wanted me there, but somehow he failed to ever send you the paperwork so you could prepare? That doesn't make sense, Viv. Have you still not heard from David?"

Viv clicks closed another case, stands it upright. "I told you I would tell you if I did, Madam Reporter. I don't have any new information, other than that Jerry talks a big talk but forgetting to send me information doesn't seem that out of the norm for him."

Abby puts down the cat and comes over to Viv. "I still don't like it. There's something wrong with this."

Viv snaps her cases shut, lining them up by the door. She is aggravated, almost disappointed, but she doesn't want to show it. Abby can understand the importance of this work or not—that's up to her. "Don't come, then. You have enough, don't you, for the article? If you don't feel good about the situation, then stay back."

Abby stares at her like this is the most asinine thing she's ever heard. "If you insist on going, I'm going, too." They pile the cases into the car in silence.

The house is the stereotypical Beverly Hills mansion—a beautiful, whitewashed exterior with golden light spilling out of well-spaced sconces. Pillars line the porch, giving the place a grounded, solemn look. It reminds Abby of friends' houses growing up. It reminds Viv of some movie from the eighties. They park in the long, curved driveway. As Viv shuts off the engine, the garage door starts to slowly rise. A tall, lean Hispanic woman peers at them and motions for them to pull inside.

Once the garage door is shut, she introduces herself. "I'm Sandra Perez—you're here to photograph my daughter." It's a sad, quiet statement. Her eyes travel slowly from Viv to Abby. She looks too young for what she said to make any sense. Her long hair is pulled back in a simple French braid that cascades almost to her waist. Her skin is taut, blemishless. It would be hard to believe she's any older than thirty-five. Before Viv can decide whether to ask for clarification, the door to the house opens and David joins them in the garage.

"David?" It's a stupid thing to say. It's obviously David standing five feet away from her.

He nods to Sandra and then turns to Viv, eyes unreadable. "The rest of the family is still getting ready, so take your time." Sandra excuses herself, closing the door to the house behind her. "Jerry and I made up," is his explanation. Tonight, his face is flush with relief. If he isn't right with Jerry, he at least has a scheme for how he'll be all right in general. There's a hopefulness about him Viv hasn't seen in a while.

His focus turns to Abby. "Abby Katz?" She nods. "There's someone inside already from the *LA Times*." Abby looks to Viv in confusion, then pushes past him to the door.

Viv begins the process of unpacking her car as David watches. "I've been trying to get ahold of you, you know," she says. "I was afraid you were going to go off and do something foolish, like you tend to do." She gestures to the light stands. "You going to help?"

David shuffles over and helps her lift cases from her trunk. He doesn't speak until the car has been emptied. "You know me. I always land on my feet. You shouldn't have worried."

Viv slams the trunk shut. "You know me. I always worry. Anyway, you seemed scared.

Which made me scared. Everything is really okay with Jerry?" David picks up a case in each hand and walks heavily toward the house.

"Nothing a little flattery couldn't fix—for now. I'm sure he plans on lording this over me in the future, but that's just it. He likes having something in his back pocket he can bring out to make you do what he wants. I just have to make sure he doesn't have that opportunity." With that, he shoulders the door, awkwardly using his elbow to push his way inside, cases clanging into the wall.

Inside, the house is brightly lit. It looks like every light fixture that could be found is on. A mix of different color temperatures floods the home in a burnished-yellow tone. The garage opens into the kitchen, where Sandra sits hunched over the wet bar with a glass of red wine. For the first time, Viv notices that she's wearing all-white. The open floor plan lends a view out into a dining room and a living room beyond, all light-colored, modern furniture and caramel-colored wood floors. Abby is nowhere to be seen.

A man also dressed in white enters from the dining room and puts his arm around Sandra. She leans into him. He's stubby, built like a pit bull with the jowls to match. He's pale, white, with dark-purple circles around his eyes. He pulls back from Sandra and looks around. His eyes aren't unkind, just bloodshot. "Hello, you must be the photographer.

I'm Shaun Perez- Miller. I believe you've already met my wife. Thank you for coming out so quickly." He gives Viv a hearty handshake that leaves her hand aching. "The kids are in the other room." His tone is subdued, like that of his wife, but he seems a modicum more present. His gaze seems to fall on Viv, not past her.

Viv looks questioningly from Shaun to Sandra, who is staring into the bottom of her wine glass like it holds an augury. "The kids?"

Shaun slaps the side of his head like a cartoon character that forgot to share a pivotal piece of information. "Right. I'm acting like you know what we want, but we haven't even discussed it. It's a family portrait. We always get one every year. Here, follow me." Shaun leads Viv into the living room. From here, a spiral staircase comes into view.

Three children, probably ranging in age from eight to sixteen, slump on the stairs. Of course, Viv isn't very good with children's ages. They could turn out to be toddlers or legal adults and she wouldn't be surprised.

They look up with dull eyes as Viv approaches. Like their parents, they are dressed entirely in white. The youngest looks hauntingly like Sandra. The other two seem to have inherited Shaun's squat build and pronounced cheeks. All three are playing on screens of varying sizes. One of them plays music that they don't bother to turn off. Shaun claps his hands once and turns to Viv. "We really want that classic, portrait studio look. In the past, we've gone in to have these done. Sandra had the idea to line us all up on the stairs. What do you think? Can you work with that?"

Viv looks at the grand staircase, the three huddled forms. There is obviously something he is leaving unsaid. "Yes. I'd love to see what you've liked in the past." Shaun leads her to an office off of the living room. The children go back to their screens. Inside, above a large mahogany desk, is a gaudily framed family portrait. A single desk lamp illuminates this space, barely bright enough to make out the particulars of the picture. Shaun flips on an overhead light, and Viv blinks, eyes adjusting.

Within the frame, Shaun and Sandra stand with their arms around each other in a stiff pose while four children sit on a low bench in front of them. This portrait is a couple of years old—the children are all notably smaller. They are seated by gender instead of age—boy, girl, boy, girl. The second-oldest child, a girl with Sandra's tall, elegant form and Shaun's broad shoulders, sits on the far left. Her head tilts in toward the middle in a severe way that makes Viv wonder what the photographer was thinking.

Viv leans in closer, gestures to the girl. "Where is she?" It isn't a delicate question, but she can't think of a better way to ask. She has been shown three children, all very much alive. The fourth is conspicuously missing. In the past, seeing the body was always one of the first components the family wanted to get out of the way.

"She isn't here yet."

Viv turns to Shaun. "Excuse me, what do you mean?"

Shaun shifts uncomfortably. "There were some complications, taking her from the hospital. The nurses never seemed to be around when she was alive—when she needed anything. But as soon as she was gone, it became impossible to get a second alone." He laughs mirthlessly. "Anyway, someone has her now. She's on her way."

Shaun reads Viv's worried look. "They know the body is missing, but they don't believe the family is involved. The charge nurse saw the man who ran down the hallway with the wheelchair, described him to the police. Everyone is being very apologetic. You don't need to worry." It's impossible to really comprehend what he's saying.

Viv finds the words she forgot to say earlier. "I'm sorry for your loss." Shaun nods awkwardly, then leads her back out to the living room.

"If there's anything you want to move around, feel free. I'll get out of your way." Shaun exits upstairs, leaving Viv alone with the three children slouching on the stairs. She looks at them silently, then starts to take in the room, figuring out where and how she's going to light the photo. It's too much to think about what she is lighting for. She begins to set up. Abby is still off somewhere, presumably with the other *LA Times* reporter. Viv feels slightly irritated but lets it go. Abby isn't actually her assistant. She probably has more important reporterly duties to tend to.

As soon as Viv brings a light or two into the living room, the children disperse, except for the young one that looks like Sandra. She stays in the corner, watching Viv with wide eyes. Being observed like that makes Viv uncomfortable. She tries not to glance over at the girl as she bustles about, turning off lights and turning them on. It isn't a hard setup—a classic strobe light situation, à la a one-hour photo studio. Of course, she'll add her own spin to it, create a bit more contrast in the background, attempt to elevate it while delivering something within the realm of what Shaun wants.

She's practically set up by the time Abby emerges from a side hallway with an overweight, middle-aged white man who must be Fred Johnson. They both look tense. Fred introduces himself, giving Viv a damp handshake.

"You finally came to see what all the fuss is about?" Viv tries to lighten the mood a little, worried about the frown lines around Abby's eyes.

"Can't let her have all the fun," he replies. Viv figures she can just ask Abby for details later. For now, there's a lot of noise coming from the kitchen. Shaun appears, flushed.

"Gina has arrived."

Viv hasn't emotionally prepared. Upon learning the subject would be a child, she simply busied herself with other matters. Now, she's going to have to put on a neutral expression in front of that child's parents and pretend that this is completely normal. For their sake, it has to be. Someone has already managed to get Gina into a matching white outfit, a long skirt and peasant blouse. Her eyes are open—Viv notices this in a quick glance that she does not repeat. Someone, presumably Sandra, has braided her hair back off of her face. She looks small, sickly. Viv wouldn't have been able to guess her age, but she overheard it: seventeen.

For the first time in a while, Viv second-guesses what she's doing. But the father, Shaun, looks so determined. They want this so badly. Viv keeps her composure and sets up the shot. She turns off the overhead lights, lighting the candles spaced along the staircase wall in tiny alcoves. The effect is subtle, but it allows the background to fall off in a romantic way. The strobes will give the family soft, even lighting, but hopefully the look will be slightly more natural, less forced, than the photo in the office. Viv stages Shaun at the top of the group, followed by Sandra on the stair below. He envelopes her in his arms, practically holding her up. From there, the children are arranged from youngest to oldest, each resting their hands on the shoulders of the sibling in front of them.

Gina is placed with her older brother behind her and her younger brother in front, buoying her up. With a bit of shuffling, eventually the pose looks relatively unforced. It isn't perfect, but Viv starts shooting, thinking through what she can alter as she goes. Sandra looks like she'll lose what's left of her composure if she isn't given a task to focus on. For now, that's looking at the camera. The children all look incredibly uncomfortable. Viv can't blame them at all, but it does heighten the stilted feeling of the photos.

After a few practice shots, she stops. It's not working. She can feel Abby and Fred watching from the large sofa that takes up the middle of the space. David paces in the dining room, talking in hushed tones on his phone. She forces time out of her mind. Focus. She rearranges the family, having them sit instead of stand on the stairs. She places the three children where they were when she first saw them, staggered every other step. Shaun and Sandra sit together, a few steps above them all, Gina between them.

With a couple quick shifts of the lighting, Viv is set. The photos are still very conventional, but at least they're starting to look more organic. She's seen worse family portraits in her life—including the one in the office. But she still isn't satisfied. Viv continues to click the shutter in silence, the flash of the bulbs and her steps on the granite floor feeling shocking, intrusive in the stillness of the house. She finds herself trying to tiptoe. The silence is stifling. She puts down the camera.

"Is there any music that Gina loved that you would like to play? It's a bit quiet in here." She almost winces at the echo of her voice.

It's Sandra who responds, "Selena." A speaker is retrieved and Viv recommences shooting to the sounds of "Bidi Bidi Bom Bom." At first, the children remain stiff, hunched on their steps.

Surprisingly, Shaun starts crooning softly, voice cracking, about how his heart wants to sing. Sandra joins in with a clear, strong voice. Together, they rock Gina back and forth as they recite the lyrics. Slowly, hesitantly, the children join in. It's an odd, mournful rendition that melds in an uncanny way with Selena's vocals.

Sandra reaches forward and puts her hand on one of her son's shoulders. He grabs her wrist without turning around, holding on tight. There are tears in the whole family's eyes as they continue to croon, *bidi bidi bidi bidi bom bom*. It's a bizarre, touching sight. Viv glances over at the couch. David has joined Fred and Abby, who softly chants along. Viv pulls her eyes back to the Perez-Millers. There's a faint smile on the youngest daughter's lips as she beats out the rhythm of the song on the granite step next to her. Click. This is the photo.

The loud clatter in the kitchen doesn't even register until everything is over. The next thirty seconds are a jumble, a patchwork of sound and movement in no discernable order: Shaun and Sandra let Gina fall forward with a sickening thud. The youngest daughter screams shrilly, but it can barely be heard over the deafening bang, like a car backfiring directly out front. Someone drops a plate or something that breaks into tiny pieces. The overhead lights flick on in the kitchen. Viv finally snaps an acceptable photo, but she needs to change her camera battery, take a couple more photos for safety. Selena croons the last lingering sounds of her heart. *Bidi bidi bom bom.*

No, it's the other way around. Selena begins to fade out. *Bidi bidi.* Viv hunches down to grab the camera battery when the lights turn on in the kitchen. *Bom bom.* She turns, irritated, only to hear the crash of ceramics cascading everywhere. *Bang.* The scream happens almost simultaneously, making her turn to see Gina limply floundering down the stairs. She has to look back at the couch. It's important but she isn't sure why. A car didn't backfire on the couch. She should be looking outside. Look. She can't. She has to. She turns. There's blood everywhere. At first, it seems like it's all of them—all three. They're all covered in blood. But then David lurches forward onto the floor, retching.

Abby is so still. Viv can't take a step forward. Abby isn't moving, but then, after an eternity, she does. Abby looks over at Fred and opens her mouth. What comes out of her doesn't make sense. It looks like a scream, but all Viv can hear is beautiful, lovesick singing. She wonders if she's the one who is dead. Then she realizes. It's Selena. The song is on repeat.

She can't find the speaker to stop it. She looks around slowly. The front door is wide open. It wasn't before. All she knows is that she wants the song to stop. She wanders outside and puts her hands over her ears. She can still hear it. Then, she's on the ground, and her head is between her knees, and all she can hear is the rushing of her own blood in her head.

ABBY

She's soaked. She wonders, for a second, if she has peed her pants. Fred would find that mortifying. Fred. Fred doesn't have the back of his head. There was a crash, and then a vaguely familiar man appeared, and he had something in his hands, but his hands were quaking. And now she's wet. And Fred doesn't have the back of his head. And the man. The man went out the front door. Abby looks slowly over to the door. Viv is there, ashen-faced. She steps outside.

It's then that Abby realizes she's already screaming. She has to stop screaming in order to call for Viv, to try and warn her. She can't stop screaming, though. There's another loud bang out front. Abby finds the strength to stop screaming, to get up. She's so wet. She has to stand. She somehow does, heads to the door, but the man on the stairs is much faster. He's already outside. Abby tries to fortify herself for the sight of Viv without the back of her head, too.

Instead, Viv comes reeling back in. She catches Abby by the shoulders, looks through her. "It's Andre. He shot himself."

Then David is there, and he's rounding them all up, and he's wet, too. He smells like vomit. Abby tries to back away, but he won't let her. The music is off now. He is saying that they have to figure out what to say to the police. The man from the stairs is nodding, holding tightly to the tall woman beside him. Viv stares at the ceiling. David shakes her, and she shoves him off.

"Too late. My equipment is everywhere. It's obvious what happened here, until Andre arrived. I can own up to what I know, because there's a lot that I had no damn part of. I don't want them thinking I have anything to do with that, David." Abby wonders how Viv can be so articulate right now. If she opens her mouth, she's afraid she'll start screaming again.

David is in Viv's face. Abby wants to push between them, but she can't move. Maybe it's how wet she is, it's weighing her down. He's raising his voice. He also seems capable of speaking in sentences. She doesn't know how. Abby can't open her mouth again. She'll scream.

"Who do you think he was here for, Viv? It wasn't the reporter. I saw Andre look me in the eyes, but his hand was so shaky. Shit, he was *so* shaky. I couldn't move. The reporter was trying to stand up, for some fucking reason. Andre jumped a little, pulled to the right. I don't know why. I saw it in his eyes. I don't know why he couldn't stop shaking. He didn't mean to shoot the reporter. He meant to shoot me."

None of this makes any sense to Abby. Didn't Andre lock eyes with Fred? Didn't he wait for his head to bend down, for him to try and stand? The memory is already shaky, already fading to black. Her brain refuses to let her dwell on it any longer. Is the room not spinning for anyone else?

Viv shouts right back at David, "And how does that change anything now? Do you want a gold medal because you think you should have been the one to die?"

The man from the stairs gets in between Viv and David and starts to speak in a calming voice. He seems scared that his family is going to get in trouble, that his children are going to be left without parents to raise them. Abby wonders if Fred had any kids. He never mentioned them, but then again, that would be a very Fred thing to do. It took a while to learn anything about him. She had only just started. His girlfriend's name was Cindy, and this time, he felt like she was the one. They drank six-packs of hazy IPAs and watched baseball together. She was "a man in a woman's body, but not in a gay way." Abby wishes she had Cindy's number. She wishes she had time to see past more of Fred's rough edges. He was a good journalist, a good mentor.

There are lights out front now, turning the walls a garish red and blue.

Abby tunes out the bickering between the others, who are reaching a new level of panic now. She can't bring herself to look over at the couch. At the top of the stairs, three faces peek down between the bars of the railing. She turns to ready herself to speak with the police. It's important that she get every detail right, for Fred.

A quick movement to her right catches her attention. Viv has separated herself from the others and is diving for her camera bag. She picks up the camera she was using and fiddles with it. A side compartment opens and she takes out the memory card. There, kneeling in the alternating fun house lights, Viv shoves the tiny rectangle in her mouth and forcefully swallows. There's a knock on the open door. Abby turns to see more guns pointed in her direction.

DAVID

David has always prided himself on the fact that he's never had a run-in with the cops, other than that one officer he slept with for a summer. That was a bad decision all around. He mitigates risks, knows how to keep himself out of trouble. Of course, it's never completely up to him, and any activity can be construed as illegal, if done while Black. But he had been lucky, in that respect. He's always figured that if he ever were to come in contact with the police, it would be for a routine traffic stop on the highway for his perpetual speeding. Not for his own attempted murder. No matter what Abby Katz says to the police, he's still convinced that Andre meant to shoot him.

After the basics of the situation are explained several times, the police finally lower their guns from his face, where the muzzles have been trained since the officers came in the door. For a short period of time, he's treated like the victim. Then, the cops realize that the stolen body of Gina Perez-Miller is lying haphazardly on the stairs, and everyone becomes a suspect again. This time, the cops leave the guns in their holsters. Most likely because Sandra Perez is a smooth talker, knows how to work a room, even with her dead daughter lying on the staircase.

Whether it was from shock or because of David's cautionary glares, everyone is mercifully quiet when they are arrested. David and Viv end up shoved in the back of the same squad car, where they ride in queasy wordlessness, punctuated only by David occasionally retching into the plastic bag given to him by the officer in the passenger seat. Andre looked so desperate, so angry in those moments before. It had to be because of David—because of jealousy or hatred or some other unintelligible something. Why would that anger, that desperation, have anything to do with Fred Johnson? Then again, there are so many answers he will never get. Can never get because the bastard took that chance from him.

The ride to the station goes by in a blip, and then he's waiting for what he's sure are days to speak to anyone. He feels drunk, or high, like time is expanding and contracting to his heartbeat. Maybe he's just dehydrated. The night is many nights long in his head, the questioning exhausting and confusing, and the police refuse to let him change out of his blood-and-vomit-soaked clothes. When they finally allow him to use the phone, he contemplates calling Jerry. Instead, he calls his lawyer. After several more hours of sitting in holding, peeling the dried blood off his arms in swathes, Leighton shows up and gets him released. She's an old friend who did better for herself than he did—Howard University School of Law. She owes him a favor, as most of his friends do.

She brings him a T-shirt and an old pair of basketball shorts that belong to her boyfriend, who's a good foot taller than David. Swimming in the clothes, he still feels grateful to be out of his slacks and button-down. He shoves these in the nearest trash can, wishing he could set fire to it. Leighton drives him home in silence, the only sound his legs shifting on the plastic bags she laid across the passenger seat for him to sit on. At least he's stopped retching. At his door, she tells him, "Keep the clothes. He's not going to want those back."

There's so much more to discuss, but tonight is not the time. She tries to stay, to make sure he's all right, but he needs to be alone. Part of him is scared to turn the key in the lock. If this was retaliation, if this was Jerry's way of telling him to back off, then he won't be satisfied with a dead reporter. He doesn't leave jobs unfinished. It doesn't feel like Jerry's work, though. He isn't afraid to resort to violence, but usually, it's the playboy bar fight sort of violence. He's barely even responsible for any broken bones—and those were from his wild days in the nineties, when he would reign over Sundance with mountains of cocaine on his kitchen table. He isn't a real mobster—he just loves to pretend he is, with his penchant for antediluvian weapons and his friendship with the captain of the LAPD.

Jerry is well-versed in humiliation, be it physical, sexual, or psychological. But David still doubts he has *this* in him. It's his gun, though. That's for sure. The antique pistol was unmistakable as it shook in Andre's hand. And he has a motive—if he found out that David's been giving evidence to the police about his blackmailing scheme. In their game of chess, David was sure he was one step ahead, screwing Jerry over before Jerry could do it first. But what if that wasn't the case? Maybe this transgression is worth more than a pair of kicked balls and a lecture on how he'll never work in Hollywood again—that is, unless he gets down on his knees. Maybe this transgression is worth blood. Maybe David's life is a Dashiell Hammett adaptation instead of a stand-up special.

David opens the door, steps over the threshold. No point in stalling. There is no assassin waiting inside for him. In fact, there's nothing inside. The whole apartment is completely empty. His hard drives, computer, printouts that he was going to bring to the cops as evidence of Jerry's illicit dealings. Not only that, his bed, his couch, his espresso maker. Nothing is left except the dust that lived under his couch for the last two years. David breathes a sigh of relief and sits down in the middle of his barren floor. This is Jerry's form of retaliation, surely. Not a pistol in the middle of the night.

David lies back on the hardwood floor and relishes his one true and precious life. From dust he came, and now all he has is a dusty one-bedroom in West Hollywood. Maybe that's poetic justice. He starts weeping for his material possessions, embarrassed that he can't just be happy to be alive. If he can't be satisfied right now with what he still has, maybe he'll never be satisfied. The thought upsets him at first, but maybe it's just something to accept. He tries to let go of judgment, lying there on the floor, feeling the hardwood through the oversized clothes hanging off his bones. He tries to relish the crick he feels in his hip. Finally, he opens his phone and starts writing a stand-up bit about the things you find underneath your couch after finally getting rid of it.

PRIVATE DISCORD SERVER

PABLO D. (HE/HIM) 10/23/2024 2:45 PM
Yo, this place has been dead for, like, ever, no pun
intended. Is there really nothing going on for us
to look into? I have a sinking feeling that y'all
are just doing your own thing without me.

CONNOR B. (HE/HIM) 10/23/2024 3:10 PM
I'm feeling the FOMO, too. After good old Teddy boy
got stood up by David Le Clerc, I feel like everyone
just gave up. Either that or they're not looping us
in. I'd like to remind you boys that my girlfriend
is the one who got us that lead. I'm an asset.

PABLO D. (HE/HIM) 10/23/2024 3:12 PM
You two are still together? Congrats, man. I didn't
think you had it in you.

TED H. (HE/HIM) 10/23/2024 4:01 PM
This chat has been silent because it exists for the express purpose of speaking to each other about potential death portraiture cases in Los Angeles. There have been none. David Le Clerc has refused to speak with me, as has the photographer, Viv Klein, who I am sure is involved in this. As long as I am being stonewalled, there is nothing for me to do but wait. I've said this before, but I find it very troublesome that our contact at the **LA Times** died so unexpectedly last year. I suspect foul play. Eventually, the truth will come out. Trust me.

PABLO D. (HE/HIM) 10/23/2024 4:45 PM
Whether it was foul play or not, I just feel like it's weird we haven't heard anything. You sure you aren't playing me, Ted? I have a girlfriend, too, now. Maybe she could do some research for us like Connor's girl.

ZACH W. (HE/HIM) 10/23/2024 5:09 PM
Nice way to casually drop that, Pablo. Very subtle.

CONNOR B. (HE/HIM) 10/23/2024 5:12 PM
What I'm hearing is that everyone is hella bored. Why don't we finally meet up in person and hang out? We can talk about other things, too, you know. Like other suss things we see around the city, our predictions for the coming year in national politics. Like, that could be fun? This isn't the only crazy thing happening in Los Angeles. We could have a meeting of the minds (and bodies) at my casa, if y'all want?

PABLO D. (HE/HIM) 10/23/2024 5:25 PM
No.

ZACH W. (HE/HIM) 10/23/2024 5:27 PM
No . . .

CALEB Z. (HE/HIM) 10/23/2024 5:32 PM
Nah. Bad idea, man.

TED H. (HE/HIM) 10/23/2024 5:34 PM
What part of the integral issue of anonymity do you
not understand?

CONNOR B. (HE/HIM) 10/23/2024 5:40 PM
Don't you want to know who you're actually talking
to behind these stupid screens? I could be your
archnemesis, David Le Clerc, or Viv Klein for all
you know.

TED H. (HE/HIM) 10/23/2024 5:41 PM
Highly doubtful.

CONNOR B. (HE/HIM) 10/23/2024 5:43 PM
Why?

TED H. (HE/HIM) 10/23/2024 5:44 PM
They have both exhibited intellect.

LOS ANGELES TIMES

UNDERGROUND DEATH PORTRAIT BUSINESS MAKES MAJOR MONEY, LEAVES MULTIPLE DEAD

By Abby Katz | Staff Writer
Additional Reporting by Fred H. Johnson
December 31, 2024

An underground macabre art form harkening back to the 1800s is quietly capturing the interest -- and wallets -- of Los Angeles elites. Death portraits, photographs of the posed bodies of deceased family members first popularized in the mid-19th century, have been making a resurgence amongst wealthier Angelenos, who are seemingly not dissuaded by the potential illegality of the enterprise or the high prices charged by the outfits working in the space. While taking a photo of a deceased person is not illegal, death portraiture can quickly step over the line of legality when the body is transported after death, or the death is oncealed from authorities. More alarming than these misdemeanors, there are multiple people dead in conjunction with the portraiture industry's resurrection.

The L.A. Times followed this story extensively in 2023, embedded in one such business shooting death portraiture around the greater Los Angeles area until it became too dangerous to continue. Veteran L.A. Times reporter Fred H. Johnson was shot and killed while reporting on death portraiture on Nov. 27, 2023. Gunman Andre Carl shot Johnson and then himself, both fatally, while Johnson was on location during a death portrait shoot, according to police. The motive behind the shooting is unknown.

Times Senior Editor Megan Roberts said Johnson was a "consummate investigative reporter who tragically lost his life by being in the wrong place at the wrong time," in a December 2023 article following his death. Johnson was observing a death portraiture session with the author f this article, fellow Times journalist Abby Katz, when he was fatally shot. Months before the deaths of Johnson and Carl, the Times began shadowing a photographer who was working for the only known death portraiture business at the time. The founder of the business, who asked to remain anonymous due to the discreet nature of his work, told the Times that there should be nothing illegal about his industry. "I basically started the death portrait game in LA. It was important to me to always make sure that everything was above-board and safe. We aren't about breaking the law, at all. Maybe we're in a gray space sometimes, but it isn't wrong," he said. "It's a service to help grieving families honor their loved ones. I've used it myself for my mother. What can show you more than that how firmly I stand behind this work? I want to take away the stigma surrounding what we do."

The source allowed the Times to shadow three of his business's death portrait sessions in 2023, on the condition that the identities of the participants remained concealed. In many ways, these death portrait shoots look similar to typical other portrait sessions, just with a higher price tag and iron-clad NDAs signed beforehand that ensure the photography is never seen by the public. Unlike most photo shoots, the intent is to create photographs for private use, not to be displayed, though some clients have opted to publish the photographs for public consumption, much to the chagrin of the Times's source. "Privacy is key, but I can't fault a client for doing what they will with their photos. I don't want to give too many details, as we've realized that we need an even greater level of privacy after the events of last year," he said "But I absolutely haven't stopped our shoots in the face of the recognition we are getting. In fact, we're doing more business than ever. And I'm not the only one anymore. There is quite a demand for this type of work, more than I could supply alone." Multiple attempts to contact other death portraiture businesses for comment were unsuccessful.

Overall, the death portrait shoots observed by the Times functioned rather similarly to a small-scale traditional photo shoot. A single photographer shows up to the space chosen by the client with a few lights and a camera, then works with the client to create an image that follows their specifications. The footprint is small, with the photographer bringing only what fits in their trunk. For the clients of the Times's source, the spaces chosen for the sessions tend to be domestic, places where the client has complete control of the environment. Oftentimes, they are where the deceased has chosen to spend their final hours. The level of how staged the photo sessions are is left up to the client, with many opting to recreate a favorite setting or hobby of the deceased. At the end of the session, the client is left with all copies of the work. Any editing work done to the pictures happens on-site, before the photographer leaves.

While the environment is rather somber, there is something remarkably mundane about the shoots. Once the clients settle into the unconventional situation, there tends to be an almost meditative quality to the silence and reverence with which the photographer works. The same photographer shot all of the sessions that the Times shadowed in 2023. She has asked to remain anonymous due to hostile public perception of her work. She was the exclusive photographer for the Times's source prior to the deaths of Johnson and Carl, when she left the business. She told the Times, "I still love the work I was able to do. I think there is incredible merit to the business overall. But the work environment has been proven to be unsafe. I want to make art, and sometimes that is at the expense of my own well-being, but I refuse to let it be at the expense of anyone else's. Not again."

The photographer is adamant that she doesn't see a real difference between death portraiture and other types of photography. "I wish it wasn't seen as illicit. I'm trying to capture beauty with whatever I am photographing. I'm eternalizing a moment, and there is something extremely touching about memorializing someone before they are completely out of your grasp," she said. "There is something about them still tangible in a death portrait. Honestly, many of these people even put the photos up in their homes. Where is the difference there, between this and other photography?"

Not all parties involved with the death portrait industry are as certain of its benefits. One anonymous client wrote to the Times to express his misgivings: "I wish I had never taken part in that photo shoot. I was grieving, but it is something I've regretted every day since. I don't think death should breed more death, and it seems like it does this way. Maybe it doesn't have to, but I want nothing to do with it. If anyone asked me, I would say skip the death portrait and spend that money trying to move on with your life."

At the same time, other anonymous clients reached out to the Times to share their loved one's photos and their stories of how the sessions helped them process their grief. One such client told the Times, "I get to wake up and see my husband on my nightstand every morning, as he was but also not at all how he was. He hadn't looked that good in years. It's a blessing."

While public opinion seems split on the ethicality of the death portrait industry, there is no question that its impacts have rippled through the L.A. community. One month before Johnson's murder, Cynthia Leith, former co-CEO of the Leith Foundation, killed herself immediately after participating in a death portrait shoot for her deceased husband, gallery founder Oliver Leith. Johnson broke the news of Cynthia Leith's death for the Times in an Oct. 23, 2023 article. The Leith death and suicide made national news after a photo of the two philanthropists mysteriously appeared in the Leith Gallery after their deaths, with no explanation. Current Leith CEO Carolyn Leith, daughter of Cynthia and Oliver, has since acknowledged that the picture was taken after Oliver's death and was placed in the gallery with her explicit permission.

Following Los Angeles Police Department investigations into the circumstances surrounding the deaths of both Leith and Johnson, no one was charged with any crimes relating to tampering with human remains. Both cases were dropped earlier this year. The LAPD has declined to comment on either case. District Attorney Kevin Holmes says it is clear that the portraits run afoul of laws protecting human remains from tampering, "It is obvious that remains have been tampered with in both the Leith case and that of the scene where Fred Johnson was killed. In both circumstances, bodies had been moved without legal permission after death. There is a precedent there for prosecution. Of course, the law never talks about it in terms of moving a dead body in order to light it properly for a photo, but the sentiment is firmly there. In many circumstances, bodies are being outfitted in different clothes, makeup is being applied. Anyone who says that isn't tampering is trying to get around the meaning of the law."

Despite Leith and Johnson's deaths and the legal cases that followed, it appears death portraiture is here to stay. The source the Times shadowed in 2023 is determined to remain in the industry. In his last communications with the Times, he reiterated his dedication to death portraiture. "I don't spend a single day without looking at the photo that I have of my mother. I want that for everyone else, as well. Yes, I want to make money and kick the competition out of the water, but it's about more than that. This means something," he said. The source refused to comment on the deaths of Cynthia Leith and Fred Johnson throughout his extended correspondence with the Times.

The last death portrait shoot observed by the Times took place on Nov. 27, 2023. Both Katz and Johnson were present to observe the shoot. About an hour and fifteen minutes after Johnson arrived at the scene, while the shoot was still underway, Carl broke into the premises. Carl had been working for the session's client, and had stolen the body that was to be photographed earlier in the night from Cedars Sinai Medical Center. It was thought he had left the premises after delivering the body. It has been suspected, but not confirmed, that Carl was aiming for another man when he shot Johnson. After fatally wounding the journalist, Carl left the premises, where he shot and killed himself immediately outside. Johnson is remembered for his extensive career at the L.A. Times over the past 20 years, in particular his writings critical of gun ownership and his investigations into the National Rifle Association lobby.

While no official reporting mentioned Johnson's presence at the death portrait shoot at the time of his death, Internet forums quickly put the pieces together. As research, Johnson was himself involved in several Internet forums obsessively dedicated to stopping death portraiture in Los Angeles. One such forum user, identified as Ted H., had been in contact with Johnson prior to his death. "He was interviewing me because of my research I had done into the subject of death portraiture. When he stopped replying, it was easy to deduce what had happened," Ted H. said.

"He was worried that the industry was a breeding ground for trouble. It turned out it was. There's too much money involved."

According to his personal records, the founder of the business the Times shadowed in 2023 grossed $250,000 on his death portraiture venture. This has not been corroborated by the Times. "This could be done on a smaller scale, for less money. But people don't want to pay less money when it is their loved one," he told the Times. "They want to go all out. This is a luxury good – and we want people to tell their friends they need to do this. Honestly, I think you would be hard-pressed to find someone who has seen this process up close and disagrees."

Police retrieved Johnson's notebook from his laptop bag. Scrawled in his nearly illegible print on the last page in red ballpoint pen, was the following:"What an incredibly bizarre practice. It's both repugnant and fascinating. I can't see this not continuing past what we're looking into here. There's a reason this is coming back into fashion — we have no idea how to handle death. We're a visual society in so many ways. Maybe this will help some people. It will probably hurt a lot, as well, in the end."

DAVID

The crowd is already drunk, but what do you expect—it's New Year's Eve. It's a miracle anyone came out to some dusty, cannabis-scented black box theater for a stand-up show to begin with. David isn't sure if such overwhelming inebriation will make the crowd easier to please or harder. He is still learning how to read an audience. It has been six months of solid stand up work, a different club almost every night. Sometimes the places are packed, sometimes there is just the poor bouncer leaning against the door while David performs for the void.

So far, he's learned crowds are fickle and he doesn't know how to consistently hit home with them. A joke might land one night and fall flat the next. Of course, that could be his delivery. Some days, it's hard to get his energy up. Other times, his mind races so fast his mouth can hardly keep up. He can never gauge the correct frequency for the audience until after the first punch line. Sometimes not even then.

Still, there's something special about tonight. His sister is somewhere in the crowd, as well as that guy he's been spending time with the last couple of months. David isn't used to inviting people in his life to his stand-up shows. He prefers the criticism of strangers to that of friends. But he's proud of this set; he's worked hard on it. It's the pièce de résistance of his reformation. The sign that it worked, that he's a different person now.

No longer a model, fully a comedian. Well, a comedian and a bartender and a rideshare driver on weekends. But first and foremost, a comedian. A schlubby, five-o'clock-shadowed, flabby-stomached comedian. Losing his six-pack was hard work—something he quickly learned not to complain about lest it sound like bragging. But he's made a complete transformation. His mother is still dismayed, but he relishes it. Sometimes, he likes to fantasize about passing former colleagues from his modeling days on the street. In his mind, they never recognize him.

He's still attractive—there's nothing he can do about that. But he's no longer the Greek God sex symbol that rich, older men want to acquire. He's normal-person attractive. Honestly, with the time he used to spend going to the gym, he can now work through a lot more material. His stand-up is flourishing. There seems to be a direct inverse correlation between the apex of his physicality and his comedy. Sometimes it also feels like there's a direct inverse correlation between his mental health and how funny he is. He doesn't want to look too hard into that. He feels better than he has in months, more clearheaded. He doesn't have the physical capital he had before, but he has some sense of self, of his own value outside of that. Part of the time.

In so many ways, he's doing better than ever. He spent all his savings putting his sister through the rest of her fancy high school. What duty he feels toward his family after that, he's been working through in therapy. Dr. Ben says, over and over, that he has to give his dreams a try or he'll resent his family forever. It feels so distinctly trite and American, but then again, he is trite and American. Besides, he's afraid it's too late for that, anyway. Resentment feels ingrained in his system.

He has to let it go for now. Focus on the present, on the audience. He's found a man who takes the good with the bad and still wants to be with him. He's out there tonight. David still can't call him his boyfriend, but he's working on it. For the first time in a while, there's hope. Focus on the hope. Focus on what is happening right now, right here.

Tonight, the energy backstage is sizzling, despite the drunken crowd. Everyone here is up-and-coming, truly funny. You can feel their drive in the air, their forward propulsion in their careers, as they bustle around the greenroom drinking sparkling water and running through their jokes under their breath. At least one of them will be somebody in a year or two.

The girl David is introducing after his set is someone he idolized back in the day at UCB. She doesn't remember him from their sketch class, but he remembers her. He always thought if he ever knew someone who would make it to *SNL*, it would be her. And here he is, essentially opening for her. Not only that, but people are waiting to hear his act. Not just his sister and that guy. Comedy friends. That's still a novel feeling.

He takes a pull off of his weed vape, as he does consistently nowadays any time his heart rate goes up. Still, even now, it's hard to parse through what is actually a fight or flight response and what is just normal anxiety. He has panic attacks when someone yells too loudly onstage. He has to fortify himself for the clapping at the end of a set. He smokes a lot of weed, but it's better than the alternative. He's alive and trying to deal with it.

One day, maybe, he'll talk about his more recent experiences in his stand-up. Maybe, one day, he will be all right enough to do so. Today isn't that day. Today, his set is about weird-shaped dicks and badly phrased advertisements for modeling calls. All of it is real to his life, just not *too* real.

While the first two performers go onstage, he sits in the greenroom, sipping Diet Coke and trying to not harp on what is to come. To distract himself, he opens his notes on his phone. He had an idea, a couple nights ago, to write about his experience with Jeremiah Fink. Not as stand-up, but in prose form. In his mind, it would be published in the *New Yorker*. It would be beautifully formatted, with topical cartoons alongside. It would be shipped to so many of his exes' houses, to sit on a table, unread, for years to come. Finally, they would open it one day and see his name and his story and wish they had called. The ultimate revenge.

He's titled his messy conglomeration of notes "The Uber Rich and the Modern-Day Death Portrait: How an Obsession with Beautifying Mortality Led to Tragic Death." The title and subtitle are the most thought-out part of the article, for now. Part of him wants to send his ideas to Viv, to see what she thinks of them. But they haven't spoken since that night. He hasn't spoken to anyone involved since that night. Apparently taking all of David's worldly possessions was enough for Jerry, because he's never contacted David again. David takes it for what it was. His almost-death wasn't some sort of morality play. He doesn't need to repent and act accordingly. He never got an answer as to why it happened. Life is full of chaos, and if anything, it just emphasized the need for the hustle while there is still time. That being said, it also emphasized the unreliability of said time. Money is great, but so is happiness. He doesn't have enough of either.

Maybe he never will. But for now, he's leaning into happiness over money. So far, it doesn't feel any better, but he plans to stick with it for the time being. He has a sinking feeling that there is no right answer; he just has to decide whether or not he wants to keep on trekking. For now, there are still jokes he wants to tell. He keeps jotting notes for his *New Yorker* submission. His sister is out there, somewhere, as is the guy who keeps hanging around and who wants to get to know him, despite everything. He takes another puff off of his vape. Some people are almost worth living for. So are some jokes.

The audience erupts into booming applause, and David shoots back in his chair. He rocks back and forth conspicuously, making a horrible, strangled noise. The other performers look over at him, annoyed. No one knows him or his circumstances. They probably think he's too high. He isn't. He can feel his anger rising, as it so often does when people look at him like he's crazy. He ignores them as the next set starts. He needs to focus, be present here in this dingy black box. That is hard to do. He returns to his notes. There's something therapeutic about writing down what happened. Dr. Ben isn't wrong about that; it's just beyond his ability to make it funny. Try as he might, it comes across as tragic. He hopes that time will change that. It's easier to palate the idea of a tragedy that can at least be marketable one day.

The next comic lands their final joke to a mixed reaction and exits stage left. One more until it's his turn. David straightens in his chair. As the next performer starts speaking, he finds himself shaking. God, not again. Nerves are inherent to stand-up, only exacerbated by his personal history. Multiple therapists before Dr. Ben told him it was a bad idea to keep performing so soon after everything that happened—that it would only trigger him. That's why those therapists were fired. Dr. Ben sees the value in what he does, how it helps him through what's going on. David doesn't see the point in a therapist who doesn't support his comedy career; he can barely fathom supporting it himself.

Dr. Ben says nothing's off-limits so long as he feels it can help him heal. Of course, that's easy to say as an outsider. Still, he tries to take that to heart. One day, he imagines Dr. Ben will be in the crowd, impressed by the nuance of David's comedy. He'll laugh at the intricate, elevated ways that David will discuss the issues he brought up so many times in sessions. He'll pat himself on the back for being the reason that David can speak so lucidly about his life. For now, David will take the laughter of the intoxicated crowd. At least he's connecting with someone. He's learning how to talk about his life, without it being so personal that it depletes him for days. He knows he has infinite material; he just has to learn how to use it.

The performer starts wrapping up their set, and David's heart beats wildly against his rib cage. This is okay. This is a normal reaction. He is okay. He simply needs to put one foot in front of the other, stand up, and make his way beyond the black curtain onto the stage. David takes a deep breath, takes a hit, and steps forward. With the harsh frontal lighting pointed directly at him, it's hard to make out individuals. Somewhere out there is his sister. The man he's been spending time with. The motley UCB crowd. He is okay.

David takes a deep breath and looks across the dark, blurry space. He brings the mic up close to his mouth and smiles. "Look, I have something to say to you all. It's something no one is willing to talk about, but we need to. All right? First of all, you have to know I used to be a male model. Don't look astonished—that's rude. I can see you, okay? I know it's shocking, but I've really gone downhill the last year or so, really let myself go. Yeah, you're laughing at that. That's tacit agreement—also rude. I want you all to pretend I still have my six-pack; it'll really help my ego."

"Anyway. I used to be a male model, and people like to talk a lot about penis envy. Like, women have penis envy, men have penis envy of other men—like, they think he's more of a man. Everyone is supposed to be doing everything because of how envious they are of these dicks. But I don't think that's it. Not for me. Not for anybody who already has a penis. I think we actually have a bigger issue than envy, all right? Call it dick dysmorphia, not penis envy. I have a penis. I'm not envious of him also having a penis. I'm envious of him having a *better* penis. Overall, I'm good in my body. I'm fine not being a skinny twink. I'm fine with my thick ass. Look at it." David turns to the audience and does a quick, sporadic twerk to a smattering of applause.

"It's just my dick. I don't have full body dysmorphia. I have dick dysmorphia, which is like the opposite, but on a smaller scale. I look at myself in the mirror, and I look way smaller than other people see me down there. What do you all think? Does my dick look small in these jeans? I feel like it does." David turns several ways in front of the audience, to mixed laughter. "People talk about looking in the mirror and seeing an elephant, right? They look at themselves and think they look like an elephant. I look at my dick and it looks like a mouse, all right. That's what's going on over here."

His eyes have adjusted to the bright stage lights. He searches the crowd. He can see his sister in the second-to-back row, along with the man he has been seeing. They are seated together, laughing, mouths wide open, heads tilted back. Other people look uncomfortable at his use of the term "dysmorphia," their arms crossed in their laps, mouths pulled down in frowns. A couple people just look blank, bored. Still, this is a success. He is here. His heart pounds. He'll need to take another hit as soon as he gets offstage.

ABBY

Fred's birthday was a week prior, but Abby couldn't bring herself to acknowledge it, other than as a passing feeling of sadness. She hadn't even known when his birthday was, until his birth and death date were printed in the paper. Still, it has been lingering in the back of her mind. She feels like she has to do something. So, here she is, back at Saint Martin of Tours for the first time since her run-in with the priest. For now, thankfully, she's the only one here, other than an older woman kneeling at the altar. She doesn't know what she'll say if she sees the priest again. She's still having dreams of her terrible and imminent death, but now she knows how terrible it can truly be.

She hasn't lit a votive candle in a Catholic church before, but it feels more suitable for Fred than a yahrzeit candle. She doesn't know for sure, but it seems like he was probably some vague kind of Christian. If he wasn't, she doubts he'll be offended from beyond the grave. Her abuela used to light votives from time to time, as well as the prayer candles she had at home with Jesus and the Virgin Mary on them. She's probably supposed to say a prayer or something. Instead, she crosses herself twice after lighting the candle and mutters, "Hail Mary, full of grace." She can't remember past that part. Hopefully that's enough. The events of the last year have only strengthened her belief that she doesn't want to know the inner workings of the universe. But more than ever, she doesn't mind hedging her bets, trying not to offend any powers that might be. She has enough trouble as it is.

She stares at the candle as it wavers in the draft. There are a couple of other lit candles, but she swears his burns brighter. She lifts her travel mug to the candle in a salute and takes a deep sip. Having a cup of coffee in his honor feels more spiritual than any prayer. Maybe it's depressing proof that she didn't know him that well, but coffee did seem like a large component of his personality. She watches the candle in silence, meaning to stay till it burns out. But after a few minutes, she realizes she has no clue how long votive candles burn. It could even be a full day, like a yahrzeit candle, for all she knows.

The woman at the altar gets to her feet and makes her way past Abby, out of the church. She is truly alone now. Abby watches the candle for a few more minutes, then turns to go. She stops at the door, impulsively. There are visitor cards to fill out, for those who want to be apprised of the goings-on at the church. She doesn't know why, but she grabs one and jots a note to Father Juan. *Father Juan, what I've learned from my dreams is that they aren't scarier than real life. In some ways, that's reassuring. In other ways, it's even more terrifying. I hope you're still having vodka with your father. I had a coffee with my mentor today, it was nice. —Abby, from the service last year.* She shoves the card into the wooden box next to the pens and exits St. Martin's into the sunlight.

It's a clear, crisp day in Brentwood. The feeling in the air is one of quiet anticipation. In a matter of hours, the city will come alive with parties and fireworks and drunk drivers, but for now, peace pervades the atmosphere. The last day of the year always holds a soft melancholy for Abby, only exacerbated this year by her thoughts of Fred. The end of the calendar will never come again without reminding her of him. November and December will never hold the same joy. Maybe one day they won't cause her so much torment, but for now, the veil is still thinner this time of year. The memories incapable of being pushed down. Abby's phone rings. It's Gwen. She's been calling all day, ever since the blasphemously early hour that the papers hit the sparse newsstands and those front porches that still receive the physical form of the news.

Abby ignores the call. She's supposed to see her in a couple of hours, for Gwen's annual New Year's Eve bash. If her mother wants to gush over the article, she can do it there, when Abby will already be drunk. The story being out in the ether has finally released something in Abby, but it's not the same effusive victory that Gwen feels. It came at too high a price. The piece was put on the back burner for so long due to red tape and investigations that Abby wonders if it even matters to the public anymore. It's the last day of 2024. This is going to be yet another blip in the news cycle, overshadowed by the constant, whirling shitstorm of international politics that always consumes the public discourse. He was one man. Not even a famous one.

Sure, there will be shock at the outrageous idea of death portraits in modern day Los Angeles. But she fears any public interest that could have been harnessed and focused after the death of a journalist is long gone. Fred's death was too tenuously connected to the whole enterprise for it even to serve as the kind of scathing indictment that Abby wishes she could unleash. He was killed by an outsider—not because of the death portraits. At least, that's what Jeremiah said. Because of Jeremiah Fink, no arrests were ever made in conjunction with any of the death portrait sessions. Not even for the verified assistance of the Perez-Miller family in Andre Carl's abduction of their daughter's body. Everyone got off completely free.

Abby doesn't want to see the Perez-Millers put through any more hardship. Their children already watched a man die while sitting on their staircase with their dead sister's body, but the utter invincibility of Jeremiah Fink leaves her irate. It was his gun that killed Fred. He claims he didn't even realize it was missing until the police told him. It's hard not to go down hypothetical routes. If Andre didn't have easy access to a weapon . . . if Jeremiah didn't tell him that David had refused to steal the body, so he had to do it . . . if Jeremiah only treated Andre better after his years of hard work . . . if Jeremiah hadn't lied about not having ammunition in the house . . . if Andre wasn't worried that David would tell Fred about Jeremiah's illicit activities . . . if Andre didn't care about the actions of David or Fred or Jeremiah or whoever . . . if, if, if.

She brought this story to Fred, and now he's gone because of it. That's what it boils down to and always will. She'll carry that with her for the rest of her life. And now, on what few newsstands remain, sits her life's biggest journalistic accomplishment to date, along with the reminder that it's her fault Fred is gone. In a fit of masochism, she starts to drive to the nearest convenience store that sells the *LA Times*. She hasn't seen the article yet in newsprint. Also, she could go for a slushie.

Ten minutes later, she's back in her car with a copy of today's *LA Times* and a cherry and cola slushie, which immediately gives her a sugar headache and she regrets spending two dollars on it. She expected to feel more, seeing her name and Fred's in print. She doesn't feel much at all. Her words are finally out in the world, and the world keeps on turning. She even told the cashier that she had an article in the paper. He nodded like he hears it every day. Maybe he does. Maybe disillusioned reporters frequent his store, buying newspapers and slushies and trying to figure out what comes next.

She pulls out her phone and idly opens her email. There are stories to be written on cultural events happening in the next several weeks, interviews to be scheduled. The death portrait article changed some things, but not everything. The truth is, she isn't an investigative reporter, like Fred. She's too influenced by every story, too prone to getting over-involved. Fred left work at work, went home to his girlfriend and his six-packs of beer and his garden and fully relished the idea of creating a separate life, a place cleaved from the *LA Times*. She wants to blame it on Gwen, for never setting an example of how to divorce work and life, for only really living when she was on a film. But the truth is that Isaac never feels the need to conflate the two, only her.

She wonders what he thinks of the article. She sent him a version, via email, but he hasn't responded. He's somewhere in Alaska with limited Internet, but at least he took the satellite phone she bought him. For the first time, she thinks about disappearing with him. She still doesn't understand him and maybe never will, but at least she's starting to see the appeal of the life he leads. It isn't an escape; it's the clarity of being with no one but yourself. She's never felt that clarity. Maybe it would be nice, or horrible. But it would be different, of that she's pretty sure.

She opens a new email. She doesn't really think through what she's doing, she just does it. It's the inevitable next step, in so many ways. There isn't much emotion left to spare on it.

#

Ms. Roberts,

This email is to give you a formal two weeks' notice of my leave from the LA
Times. *I am happy to jump on the phone with you in the new year to discuss
how I can assist in transferring my workload. I am committed to finishing
out the two articles I am currently working on to the best of my ability, and
I want to be as helpful as possible in this transition.*

*Anything I can do to assist any writers stepping into my position, please
let me know.*

My time at the LA Times *has been so beneficial to my growth as a writer
and as a human. I hope that you can understand, after the events of the last
year, my need to step away from this position.*

Happy 2025,
Abby Katz

#

She hits send and belly-laughs. She just resigned from her dream job in
a convenience store parking lot, sipping on an overly sugary slushie. Life
is truly absurd. She can feel her spirit lift, though. It's one of those circumstances where the answer is so obvious, it's impossible to doubt it.
She isn't meant to be at the *LA Times*. There's so much to do, so much
life to live—or not live. But either way, it isn't within the confines of the
LA Times. She wanted to be a reporter so badly, but maybe that dream
has been carried through to its logical conclusion. Maybe not. Maybe
she needs to go to Alaska to figure it out.

Either way, for now, without thinking, she heads to Pasadena. She
hasn't let herself consciously think about Viv Klein in quite some time.
Still, she saw the advertisements for the gallery opening. She checks up on
the photographer every now and then online, even though they haven't
spoken since the night Fred was killed. Viv has been constantly working,
shooting concerts and weddings and all sorts of banal events. At the same
time, she has apparently also been creating this show. Something within
Abby knows that if she dares to show up to the Leith gallery tonight, she
will be allowed in. Something in her also knows that if she shows up, she'll
be sucked back in. She can't allow it, but here she is. Driving to Pasadena.

She keeps the radio off, sitting with her thoughts as she drives. It's still early, the roads aren't crowded, and she makes good time. Too good. The light is just starting to shift, darken, as she finds a place to park. Her mother calls again. She sends it to voicemail. She's never been inside the Leith gallery before. She spoke with Carolyn several times over the last year, but always over the phone. It was Carolyn who first alerted her to the fact that other parties were starting their own death portraiture businesses. Still, Carolyn didn't alert her to Viv's gallery show. Abby wonders what work Viv will be showing and whether Jeremiah knows about it.

Abby waits in the car as the sky completes the transition to black. She almost expects to receive an email back from the *Times*, but she doesn't. It's New Year's Eve and time is in limbo. She closes her eyes. Her whole body feels heavy. She's dreading it and anticipating it—it's time to go inside. She walks the two blocks to the gallery in tense silence, hands shoved deep in the pockets of her chinos. She turns the corner to see the old-fashioned marquee out front lit up and a line waiting outside. Life in Retrospective, the sign reads in bold letters. Abby gets in line.

A man in a suit with a tablet stands at the door. He asks for Abby's name, sliding his finger down a long list. She's admitted after just a quick scan. It doesn't surprise her. Inside, the gallery is sleek—all concrete floors and twenty-foot ceilings. The opening night event is already crowded, to Abby's relief. It's easy to slip into the groups milling about, sneaking her way around the periphery of the lobby. She isn't ready to see Viv yet. She surveys the space, contemplates heading to the makeshift bar in the corner. Instead, she heads away from the throng in the entryway. The exhibit is on the smaller side for the Leith, but the empty spaces only draw the eye more completely to the works on the walls.

The first print Abby sees is the photo of Cynthia and Ollie Leith, all contrast and confetti and the two of them seemingly absorbed in each other. It's brightly lit, ostentatious even, as it inhabits the space it so famously appeared in a year ago. On the wall, a large description tag features in its entirety Fred's *LA Times* story about the appearance of the photo. There's also a tiny picture of the Keith Haring in the staff bathroom. It's audacious. Abby can't help but crack a smile.

From there, she works her way clockwise around the room. There are the familiar photos of Amy Lee and of Jeremiah Fink's mother. Both have plaques next to them with their obituaries. Viv has added her own editorializing to both. It's poetic, surreal, maybe sacrilegious. Maybe not. On the wall near the front door, huge block letters declare—

Permission has been given for the presentation of these photographs by some of the families of the subjects you will see in this room. Any offense taken by the audience as to the delicate topic of these photos is not intended by the photographer but is the prerogative of the audience. Each viewer is reserved their right to leave and write a scathing review for whatever audience they can. The photographer hopes viewers can see the respect and care with which these subjects have been treated. At the very least, she hopes this shows death doesn't have to be horrible but, in fact, can be quite beautiful. Sometimes it is both.

Amid the familiar photos are several prints Abby has never seen before. Pictures of detritus on Hollywood Boulevard, of discarded shoes hauntingly left on the side of a hiking path. Pictures of life uninhabited. She recognizes the photo of Cole Martin's hat, the photo published through the local Joshua Tree news after Viv saved the dehydrated hiker. The news story of his rescue is printed on the plaque next to the photo, along with Viv's editorializing scrawled to the side in third person: *The time she decided she was a good person because she did one good act.*

There are several portraits of the Perez-Miller family, both painfully staged on the stairs, and after they started singing. They are arranged in a large triptych, taking up one whole wall. In the middle, Sandra's eyes gleam in the candlelight as she sings into Gina's ear. Abby can't make herself look at the photos for longer than a second. She has to push through a huddle of people studying the photos in order to get away. She slows her breath and turns to the next wall.

There is Karen Elmes. The photo that started it all. The deep pool of water, the effortlessly floating figure, the neon lights even more striking on a larger scale. Abby can't help but understand Viv's need for the photo to be seen. It is spectacular in the truest sense of the word, and also sad, because we see so many spectacular photos that we become desensitized to them. At this moment, Abby doesn't feel desensitized. The plaque next to the photo is dedicated to the issue of domestic violence, as well as to telling the story of the woman whose life was cut short.

Abby wanders through the space, taking her time in front of each print. She lets one lead her to the next, not looking ahead until she gets there. It's because of this that she finds herself reeling as she glances up at the final wall. She's utterly unprepared for what she sees. She grabs the arm of the woman next to her, not even embarrassed. The woman pulls away, and Abby is left alone, staring at Fred.

She doesn't know when or how Viv took the photo, but it's Fred. It's Fred in macro, as it has to be, because otherwise it would be horrifying. The photo is close in on his right eye, which is fixed on something in the distance, his lips pursed determinedly. There's a slash of light on his face from the stairs, reflected in his eye, a bead of sweat on his nose. The blood isn't visible at all, but the circumstances in which the photo was taken are unmistakable. It captures him in some kind of romantic glory, in black-and-white—apt for the consummate reporter. He doesn't have one plaque, he has a slew of them, detailing his career, his life, things Abby didn't even know. Tears form in the corners of her eyes.

The wall is an ode to Fred, but there is another print on the far side—smaller, humbler in scale. It's of a fallen shape, hardly discernible in the moonlight, out of focus behind a bright-white pillar. Abby knows what it is without having to read the plaque. In every way that Fred's photo is idealistic, larger-than-life, dynamic, this is the opposite. It's small in size, desolate and empty in framing. Abby tears her eyes away from the print to look at the plaque. It doesn't mention what is depicted in the photo. Instead, it speaks about gun violence and mental health. It isn't malicious. If anything, there is a compassion in the print and plaque that Abby has yet to muster for the man who did all this.

Viv has again added her own editorializing in third person to the plaque: *She never had an answer. No one did. So, does that mean none of it had meaning? Or did she just have to make her own meaning in the circumstances? She decided to lean into existentialism and get out of bed.* Abby can feel the tears welling over her eyelids.

She blinks them away and turns, pushing her way through the crowd back toward the lobby. There are waiters now, passing hors d'oeuvres, who she has to dodge. The distant exit sign shines like a beacon above the crowd. If only she can make it there before she completely breaks down. The group in front of her parts, and there is Viv Klein, talking animatedly in the middle of a circle of avid listeners. She's shining, like there's a spotlight on her, which is ridiculous but also not implausible, because the lobby is full of dramatic swathes of light.

It's like she can feel Abby's eyes on her from the other side of the lobby.

She turns her head, making eye contact with Abby for the slightest of seconds, and then turns back. Abby doesn't even fully feel the sting of disappointment before Viv leaves her circle midsentence, her companions watching in confusion, left hanging on her words. Viv walks determinedly toward Abby, a small, sad smile on her lips. The exit sign is forgotten. Abby tries to gather herself.

Another group of patrons crosses in front of her slowly, laughing in a raucous way that makes her want to hit them. They continue on their way, but Viv and her group are long gone, replaced by another group that is oblivious to Abby's confused gaze. She's discombobulated, off-balance. She turns around. There is Viv.

VIV

Viv stops giving value judgments to her ideas long before it is time to write New Year's resolutions. She lives now in a time of simple existence. The gallery show just *is*. As is her decision to never shoot another death portrait after the night of Fred Johnson's murder. She is tired of analyzing the merits of any given decision. They just are. Just like it's impossible to reach out to David. Just like it's impossible to reach out to Abby. There are chasms that cannot be crossed, words that cannot be spoken. Things are what they are.

There are photos that can be taken, though, and that's her lifeline to humanity throughout 2024. She's learned to enjoy the uncomplicated pleasures of a wedding shoot in a way that she never did before. There's something unreachable, aspirational, about that much joy. She even went back to shooting with D, before he signed on to a bigger label and got it in his head that he could go viral if he had the right image. Now, he has another photographer, who shoots exclusively on Polaroid cameras for some godforsaken reason. She doesn't mind. It's easier to let things go now. Work will come, or it won't. She even started substitute teaching again.

One day, she showed up at the Leith unannounced, baselessly hoping that Carolyn would actually be there. She was. Viv expected Carolyn to turn her away at the door, run her out of the place. Instead, they talked for hours, and now she's opening her first real gallery showing at the Leith. It's bittersweet, if it can be said to be sweet at all. But it feels inevitable. She isn't going to keep this work in her closet for all eternity. That would be the real sacrilege. She would paste it on the side of a building before she let it gather dust in her studio apartment bathroom. She would let Jeremiah Fink drag her to hell for breaking his NDA before ever acquiescing to him.

Sometimes, she thinks of Emily Dickinson and how awful it was that she could never speak for herself, for her work. Discovered after death—what a nightmare. Even worse is the thought of all the Emily Dickinsons whose work was thrown in the recycling along with all their other earthly possessions and who were never recognized for what they were in the first place. All the geniuses and dolts and middling artists who will never be known. Many of them probably wouldn't even mind. God, it's a curse, wanting to be seen. If she could just be content with the art . . . but she can't. The art and her are so intertwined. She wants to be recognized. She wants the art to be recognized. She knows she's insufferable, forever harping on it, but it consumes her thoughts. She doesn't know how to be happy. She knew that before, but now she doesn't feel like she deserves to be. Not without paying homage to Fred, to Amy, to Cynthia and Ollie, and Elsie Fink. She lives a life populated by ghosts.

Carolyn Leith seems to understand that, at least in some sense. She's patient with Viv, even during the times that she goes off the grid for weeks at a time. It feels impossible now to be part of public life for any extended period. That part of her is irrevocably broken, it seems. The process for the gallery show was slow going and painful and came with more than one angry voicemail from Jeremiah Fink reminding her about her NDA. Still, she ground on with the patience of Sisyphus, or rather with no patience at all, but with a lot of complaining to Carolyn and comparing herself to Sisyphus.

Her favorite photos from the glacially paced months since that night at the Perez-Miller household are of flowers. That surprises her. She's always loved a human subject. But life moves at a different pace now, and the way time moves for flowers makes more sense to her. She finds herself traipsing through people's gardens in Los Feliz, getting shooed out of patches of lilies in Hancock Park for trespassing. In essence, she is still breaking the lawfor her work, still doesn't know how to stop that impetus to peer behind curtains where she isn't allowed. But the flowers are beautiful.

She shoots them in macro, with wide lenses, close up and far away, night and day. She can't get enough. Always with natural light. Never disturbing the way the plant lies normally. She has no interest in picked flowers, only those still growing. A lot of the work feels like basic exploration of colors and saturation, but she feels she's going somewhere with it. She fantasizes about tending a garden herself one day. It was so cold in Minnesota, growing up. There are so many temperate flowers she was never exposed to. There's so much to learn, so much still to explore with her camera and her hands in the dirt.

The flowers are one reason to stay in Los Angeles. The reason that makes sense. She also still feels tied to people she no longer speaks to, but that's another matter. Sometimes she thinks she sees David on the street, but it turns out to be another man. She doesn't let herself think about Abby. People are ephemeral. The real reason to stay is the flowers. The tangible reason. Without them, she tells herself she would have moved to Joshua Tree, or some new place she has never been. But Los Angeles has become more tolerable with the discovery of the flowers. There's quite a lot of flora and fauna around, if one has their eyes open to it.

The children she substitutes for like the pictures of the flowers more than they ever liked her street photography. Of course, she isn't supposed to be showing them any photography, but instead teaching them about the Korean War or Watergate or some such event in history. The children prefer the flowers. She tries to mix in a little of both, Nixon and chrysanthemums. If the school ever asks her to stop, she will, but so far, she hasn't gotten any complaints. Flowers are a lot more palatable to the masses than some of her other subjects.

Sometimes, she thinks about Mr. Smith back in Kimball and what he would think of her teaching. One day, she decides to look him up. He's older now, which make sense, but it still surprises her when she finds a grainy picture of him with gray hair online. He's moved to Florida, has a husband and questionable political views. She thinks about messaging him, but doesn't. She doesn't even know what she would say. Minnesota has only grown farther and farther away.

It feels like an indeterminable amount of time has passed since she first spoke with Carolyn about the gallery exhibit, but also like it went by faster than the aperture could really close and open again. Once the process got started, she wasn't in any hurry to get the exhibit opened. As the date draws nearer, though, she dreads the idea of speaking with people about the work. So much of it feels impossible to speak about. That's what the plaques are for. Attending feels pointless, but Carolyn insists that she be there.

Carolyn draws up the guest list for the opening night, in conjunction with her team—something she has because she's immensely busy, Viv has been told. Too busy to speak with a neurotic artist who's still thinking about pulling her show completely. Viv hasn't seen her in weeks. It's always the team that she talks to, the team that answers the phone. Carolyn's assistant emails, asking Viv if there are any personal friends she wants added to the guest list. She almost replies no, before impulsively adding David Le Clerc and Abby Katz to the list.

Viv finds out about Abby Katz's article midmorning on the day of the gallery opening, when she habitually opens up the *LA Times* to check the news while drinking her second cup of coffee. Part of her is hurt that Abby didn't warn her about the story, but then again, she hasn't warned Abby about the gallery opening. The *LA Times* did their due diligence— she was made aware of the circumstances, she knew her words could be used in anonymity. Now they are being used.

The fact that the article was published the morning of the gallery opening was an unfortunate coincidence. There will be no time in which the anonymity of Jeremiah Fink and Viv Klein will be kept, other than the hours before the show opens. Abby removed the names from the story for nothing. Everything detailed in the article is shown explicitly on the walls of her exhibit. It is a relief to finally have it all out there. It's also a torment.

Dressed in her only ill-fitting pantsuit, Viv spends the first hour of the opening wandering dejectedly from room to room, unable to look at the walls. Eventually, she realizes that no one is paying attention to her. No one knows what she looks like. This grants her immense relief. She can flit between groups of people, listen in on their thoughts about the exhibit. It's mostly positive. She hates that this buoys her mood.

Viv eventually settles down, finding a place in the corner of the lobby to observe. It's here that Jeremiah Fink finds her. He slides in next to her, watching the crowd in silence.

"You broke my NDA. I could take you for everything you're worth," he finally says.

"I'm not worth that much. And I've already thought it through; it's worth it to me. I think it's worth it for Elsie." Viv pushes off the wall, looks Jeremiah in the eye. He smiles back at her, tense and with too many teeth.

"I'd prefer you leave my mother out of it, but yes. I see the merit in what you've done here. You should think about coming back to work for me. This show is going to give you great publicity, you know. I've heard what people are saying. Plus, with Abby's article, there is going to be a lot of interest." Some things never change.

As soon as Viv can, she extricates herself from the conversation. Unfortunately, people have started to recognize her as the photographer, and she's stared at everywhere she goes. A group of eager Leith donors surrounds her, asking about the show and her visual ethos. She doesn't quite know what her visual ethos is anymore. It isn't something she can put into words, but she can talk about Fred, about Amy, about Cynthia. So she does. As she's speaking, she can feel eyes on her. There have been many eyes on her, but these feel different.

She turns her head. Abby Katz stands across the room.

Viv leaves off midsentence, making her way toward Abby. A group of people stumble toward the door, loudly. It seems they've made good use of the open bar. Part of her wonders whether Carolyn has gone over budget on this. Viv tries to veer around the rowdy group. A glint of metal outside catches her eye. Police cars are pulling up out front, three of them. She wonders vaguely if Jeremiah had a change of heart. Perhaps he's decided to punish her for refusing to work with him again.

She pushes forward. A man steps in front of her path, trying to get her attention. He's disheveled, sweaty. His meaty face is spread in a wide grin of victory. "Viv Klein. We finally meet. You've been ignoring my emails. You've stolen what's on these walls. Do you know that?" Confused, Viv pushes past him. Maybe he's one of the Internet trolls who wants her dead. She doesn't care anymore.

There is Abby, directly in front of her, facing the other direction, her back awash in red and blue. She turns around, seeming to sense Viv behind her. She doesn't appear to have seen the police cars yet. Her eyes are lively, full of things she wants to say. Over her right shoulder, Viv can see the officers pushing through the front door. She and Abby both open their mouths to speak at the same time.

Abby laughs. "You go first." Viv shakes her head. The police are headed straight toward her. There isn't much time before they will be interrupted. The exhibit will be shut down, or she'll be arrested, or some other unforeseeable misfortune will befall them. There's no way to know. Right now, it doesn't matter. She straightens, fixes her eyes on Abby.

"So, did you actually look at the photos this time?"

ACKNOWLEDGMENTS

I would not be the writer I am if I wasn't allowed to be a voracious reader. So, if you hate my writing, blame these people. Thank you to Mrs. McFadden at New Vistas Academy in Chandler, AZ for instilling in me a lifelong belief in my ability to read anything I want. I have never felt more special and like my creative voice was worth being heard than in the Desert Vista High School black box theatre with director Kenneth Fajman. A teacher's mark can be indelible, even more so when they are a mentor as well. I will never forget the support of Susan Salas at Pepperdine University. She was the first person who gave me money to write, via a scholarship to create my college web series, and she helped me develop a belief in my ability to be a storyteller. A life in the arts is one full of rejections, and I would not be able to continue on without dipping into the deep wells of affirmation that have been dug for me by the adults I looked up to before I was fully baked.

I am indebted to my first readers, who made the time to read *It Will Last Longer* when many of them didn't even know I was writing a book until I foisted it upon them. Liam Bell, Caitlin Garrett, Chelsey Maus—thank you for the encouragement and notes. Special thanks to Cassie Stephenson, consummate journalist and splendid human, for the newspaper know-how. I would be remiss in my thanks if I did not include the trifecta of cats, Woolf, Joan, and Reid, who gave me the necessary distractions, cuddles, and occasional bites to keep going.

Thank you to Jeff and Michelle Jenkins, my parents, for the support in getting this novel finished and into the world and for believing in the potential of my work. You have always believed in me as a writer, and I appreciate that immensely. To the entire Brooks and Yates families, I appreciate your encouragement and steadfast belief in me more than I can say. I am incredibly blessed to be surrounded by good people and I count myself lucky beyond belief to me a member of your family.

This novel would not have been possible without Constance Renfrow, my editor, who tolerated my constant switch from past to present tense and helped reign in my grammatical chaos. The beautiful cover design and formatting are courtesy of the immensely talented Barış Şehri.

Lastly, Emily Brooks, you are the love of my life and my

biggest inspiration. Thank you for taking this endeavor seriously, as it helped me give myself permission to as well. I do not know how birds end, but I know how my novel does— with my never-ending appreciation of you.

* * *